Black December

Scott Hunter was born in Romford, Essex in 1956. He was educated at Douai School in Woolhampton, Berkshire. His writing career was kick-started after he won first prize in the Sunday Express short story competition in 1996. Scott's fantasy novel for children, 'The Ley Lines of Lushbury', was long-listed for the Times/Chicken House Children's novel competition in 2010. His archaeological thriller, 'The Trespass', is a *Kindle* bestseller. Scott combines a career in IT with a parallel career as a semi-professional drummer. Where he fits the writing in is anyone's guess. Scott lives in Berkshire with his wife and two youngest children.

Scott can be contacted via his website at
www.scott-hunter.net

Black December

Scott Hunter

Black December

A Myrtle Villa Book

Originally published in Great Britain by Myrtle Villa Publishing

A CIP record for this book is available from the British Library

ISBN 978-0-9561510-3-2

For Claire, Tom and Emily, and
Peter Moore, a patient teacher of French

Acknowledgements

Cover Design:

Books Covered

'Indeed, history is nothing more than a tableau of crimes and misfortunes'
(Voltaire, 1694–1778)

Prologue

Charnford Abbey Boarding School, Berkshire, UK November 1967, 11.28pm

"Hurry *up*, will you?" Phillips called anxiously into the dark abyss of the monks' refectory. "Someone's going to catch us for sure–"

A boy with dark, unruly hair appeared in the doorframe. "You've got the jitters, Phillips. You're pathetic. Just keep a lookout and leave the rest to us, all right?" He pulled a face and disappeared into the shadows.

Phillips stayed put, agitating. If Leo found them there'd be hell to pay. Bad enough being caught coming back from the pub after lights out, but stealing food from the monks' ref . . . he bit his lip. Well, it would be a beatable offence, for sure. And Leo's beatings were legendary. He'd seen the marks on Docherty's bony arse – everyone had. They'd been visible for the rest of term; angry welts, stripes of pain. Docherty had paraded them in the showers like battle scars.

Phillips shifted uneasily from foot to foot. Why had he listened to Vernon in the first place? He could be tucked up in his cubicle, safe and secure, but here he was in full view of anyone coming down the monks' cloister. If he hadn't had that second beer he'd never have agreed . . .

Vernon reappeared with an armful of bread rolls. "Take these." He dumped his booty into Phillips' reluctant arms and called into the darkness. "Lowndes! Come on – that'll do."

Vernon grinned and tore off a chunk of bread as Lowndes came out, furtively scanning the cloister. He was clutching a box of cornflakes and a bowl of sugar.

"Look, you can't nick the crockery as well–"

"Calm down, Phillips," Lowndes hissed. "No one's going to notice one stupid sugar bowl." He barged Phillips out of the way, leaving a beery wind in his wake.

Phillips grabbed Lowndes' arm as a flicker of movement passed across his peripheral vision. "Wait! Someone's coming!" He pointed down the cloister to the swing doors.

"No they're not." Lowndes tucked the cereal box under his arm. "They're going into the chapel," he observed through a mouthful of cornflakes. "And it's not Leo either, so stop belly-aching."

Vernon's eyes narrowed. "It's that moron from the kitchens."

Phillips scanned the cloister. The moonlight filtering through the leaded windows was playing tricks with his eyesight. Taff Lowndes was right; it was only Fergus Dalton, the Irish kitchen porter. "So what? He's harmless. Let's just get back to the dorm–"

"But what's he doing in the chapel at this time of night?" Vernon's eyes shone. Here was a little mystery that needed investigating.

Phillips groaned. "Look–"

"Come on. *Chicken*." Lowndes grinned widely and flapped his arms, clucking.

"Shut *up*!" Phillips whispered hoarsely. Then, in a more moderate voice, "I'm not chicken. It's just that–"

But the other two were already creeping along the cloister, moving with exaggerated stealth, mocking him. Phillips gritted his teeth and followed in a half-crouching shuffle. At the double doors Vernon held up a commanding hand and peered through the window to where the Court of Arches lay silent but for the low hum of the hot drinks machine, a haven of comfort in the winter months when the only way to keep warm was to stand with your back to one of the wheezing radiators and suck on a polystyrene cup of hot chocolate. Phillips fancied one now, but it was too risky; the Court could be observed from the stairway leading up to the prefect's gallery and from the end of the senior wing. At either of these vantage points a housemaster or a prefect could be lurking, hoping to spot exactly the sort of illegal operation in which Phillips now found himself entangled.

"All clear," Vernon announced. "Let's take a look, eh?"

They broke cover, and keeping close to the wall they turned the corner by the locker room into the outer sanctum that led into the chapel.

"Might even see the White Lady," Lowndes grinned.

"Don't be stupid. That's just a story." Phillips shot a quick look behind all the same. "No such thing as ghosts."

"*Woooooh*!" Lowndes waved his arms above his head, spraying cornflakes in a ragged arc.

"Idiot!" Vernon punched Lowndes hard on the arm. "Follow me, and keep it down, all right?"

They crept into the chapel and Phillips immediately saw a pool of light spilling from one of the corner alcoves. Each alcove housed a mini-chapel: altar, candles, tabernacle, the lot. He remembered when he'd had to serve Mass at some ungodly hour of the morning, freezing his balls off while Father Augustine muttered incantations at the wall. Phillips had avoided further acolytic duties by bribing a willing fourth former to take his place – well worth the price of the odd chocolate bar or averted eye when he was on junior dorm supervision.

The chapel was cold and the scent of stale incense hung in the air. Despite his fear, Phillips' curiosity was aroused. What *was* Fergus Dalton doing in the chapel at this hour? The kitchen boy was harmless; a simple lad, recruited to help the Catholic Fathers in their work. It was employment – of a sort – although Phillips didn't suppose the money was much good. Just a roof over his head, hours of toil in the busy kitchen, and daily fun poked at him by the likes of Vernon. When it came down to it Phillips felt sorry for Fergus, but right now he was intrigued. He peered over Lowndes' shoulder.

The altar had been moved obliquely aside to reveal an open space and a set of roughly-hewn stone steps. A furtive, shuffling sound could be heard from the depths. This *was* strange – a secret room under the altar. Who'd have thought it? Phillips felt a warm thrill of excitement.

Vernon winked and disappeared into the gap. Lowndes followed with a grin of anticipation. As Phillips began his descent he heard Fergus give a yelp of alarm.

At the bottom of the steps Phillips found himself in a rectangular, low-ceilinged chamber. Vernon had Fergus in an armlock and Lowndes was sprinkling cornflakes on the Irish boy's head.

"I baptise thee Dimbo Thick-As-Shit," Lowndes chanted in a deep monotone.

"Get *off*!" Fergus struggled but Vernon's grip was firm.

"In the name of the cow dung, the sheep's bum–"

Dalton's eyes shone with hatred and panic. He shook the cereal from his hair, cheeks blazing, tendons in his neck straining as he tried to free himself from his tormentors.

Phillips looked around the chamber. There was a small altar set into the brickwork, and on top of it a heavy glass case. Two candles had been lit and a censer, suspended on a thick gold chain, wafted incense into the small space.

"Sure, begorrah, what'll youse be doing down here at this toime of noight?" Vernon asked the struggling boy. "All secretive, loike, eh? Let's be havin' the answers, young Fergie." Vernon twisted Dalton's arm and Lowndes grabbed a lock of ginger hair.

"Leave me alone!" Dalton tried again to pull away. "Father Leo will be here any minute!"

"Now don't be tellin' any fibs, young Fergus," Vernon said, tweaking Dalton's nose, "or you'll never go to heaven – hasn't the good Father told you that?"

Phillips was drawn to the altar and the glass case. He wondered what its significance could be. The case was buffed to a high sheen. By its side, a soft cloth and an open can of polish explained the nature of Dalton's interrupted duty.

Dalton yelped as Vernon probed his wiry body, searching for sensitive areas where pain could be invisibly inflicted. Phillips turned away, suddenly feeling nauseous. Dalton was paying the price for his carelessness, but that didn't mean he had to watch.

He turned his attention back to the case and its contents. Inside lay what looked like a strip of charcoaled wood, dark with age and discoloured, perhaps by some past exposure to fire. Closer inspection revealed faint markings, sweeping, curved letters that reminded him of something he'd seen before but which he couldn't place.

Phillips spun as he heard the sound of a fist connecting with flesh and a grunt of surprise and pain. Vernon was clutching his jaw. "You little bastard!"

Vernon advanced on Dalton, who had assumed a defensive crouch, the Irish boy's expression an odd mixture of triumph and fear.

"What a beauty!" Lowndes nodded appreciatively, munching his contraband. "Caught you a right smacker."

Phillips froze. He couldn't believe Dalton had retaliated. Vernon was a big shot, captain of the Under Sixteens and destined for the Firsts. *Nobody* got into a fight with John Vernon.

Vernon was breathing heavily. Drops of perspiration had appeared on his forehead, glinting in the candlelight like a halo. He was clenching and unclenching his hands, circling Dalton like a boxer. Phillips felt a sudden rush of dread as the scene seemed to switch into slow motion. He knew he had to intervene to prevent some terrible tragedy, but before he could convert thought to action Vernon had launched himself at Dalton with renewed ferocity.

Lowndes was knocked aside by Vernon's charge and fell, sprawling. The sugar bowl shattered, cornflakes flying across the flagstones like yellow confetti. Dalton raised his hands to defend himself but Vernon was heavy and muscular. The Irish boy was driven back by the impetus of Vernon's charge, twisting awkwardly to one side as he struggled to stay upright. For a moment he teetered and then fell heavily, striking his head on the altar's edge with an audible crack that made Phillips' bowels turn to water.

Vernon bent over the crumpled body, breathing hard. "Little bastard. Get up and fight."

Phillips' hands were shaking. A pool of blood had formed beneath the fallen boy's head. It was dark crimson, almost black. There was a lot of it.

Lowndes had stumbled to his feet. "Oh my *God*! You've *killed* him!"

Vernon took a step back, his face ashen in the candlelight. He jabbed a finger in Lowndes' chest. "Well don't just stand there. Clear it up."

Lowndes stared at Vernon, horrified. "Clear it–?"

"Use your shirt."

Lowndes pulled his rugby vest over his head, got down on his haunches and dabbed it gingerly in the spreading puddle. As he did so there was a light footfall on the steps and a shadow fell across the chamber. The voice, when it came, was measured and even, each word carefully articulated so that there could be no misinterpretation.

"What in the name of the Almighty are you boys doing in *this place*?"

Father Leo Horgan filled the chamber with his presence. Phillips cowered against the cold stonework. His bladder was in rebellion and it was only with a supreme effort that he was able to bring himself under control.

Horgan's eyes fell on Dalton's prone form and his face blanched. He quickly bent and held the boy's wrist. When he looked up his expression was neutral. The eyes beneath the thick, horn-rimmed glasses were steady and dry.

"You – Lowndes. Go to the trunk room. In the corner cupboard you will see a shovel. Bring it to me." Lowndes took the steps two at a time. Horgan turned his attention to Vernon. "And you. This is the key to my room. Above the wardrobe you will find a folded tent and a canvas sleeping bag. Bring the sleeping bag to me."

Phillips' heart was still imitating the school orchestra drum corps. He tried to make sense of Horgan's words. Surely he wasn't going to–

"And now *you*." Horgan's basilisk stare could not be avoided. Phillips emerged from the shadows, legs shaking.

"Mop, bucket. Janitor's closet by the kitchen door. Go." He presented his back and stooped over the body. Phillips was rooted to the spot, paralysed by the enormity of Horgan's rapid and unexpected solution to their problem. The monk hiked up his black cassock to prevent it trailing in the stream of blood pouring from Dalton's matted scalp.

"I said *go*!"

Phillips went. When he returned ten minutes later work was already underway. Two flagstones had been shifted and Vernon was labouring under Horgan's supervision. Lowndes was fumbling with the sleeping bag zipper, pulling it clumsily past a lock of ginger hair.

Two hours later Phillips lay numb in his cubicle, eyes fixed on the dormitory ceiling. He wished the partitions separating him from the other sleeping boys would melt away. He felt very alone.

Forty years later

DCI Brendan Moran wasn't expecting to die. Life expectancy obviously weighed a little heavier on his mind now he'd hit fifty, but then most folk gave mortality *some* consideration at the half-century milestone. Moran liked to work with averages. His father had lived to seventy-five, and his grandfather a more generous eighty-four. Aiming down the middle, that was a small improvement on the Biblical three score years and ten. Small, perhaps, but worth having – if he was *compos mentis,* of course.

Moran had spent a joyless and fruitless afternoon at the Thames Valley Police Strategy Seminar. The fact that it had been held in Basingstoke only compounded Moran's irritation. People thought Reading was a dump until they visited Basingstoke.

Moran steered the jeep round a gentle bend in the snaking country road. Bad reputation, these bends. What were they called? *The eight bends of death.* Nice. He relaxed his right foot. No point in taking chances, even if he was in a hurry. A lorry hurtled past, lashing spray. Moran tickled the brakes, rechecked his mirror. No chance of getting to the allotment tonight, not in this weather. He'd have to brave the elements for Archie's sake, but gardening was a non-starter. He dipped his headlights and squinted as a motorbike fizzed past, water rebounding from the rider's helmet like machine gun fire. *Another madman for the ICU . . .*

He flicked to main beam. *Focus, Brendan. Time for the daily review . . .* Moran's ordered mind began its routine perusal of the day's events, relayed via voicemail in Phelps' unmistakeable East End rasp: two robberies, one stabbing. No witnesses, of course. One missing child, one suspicious death in Coley – Phelps was handling that one – and a *partridge in a pear tree . . .* no, wrong season. No partridges ... just a hell of a lot of paperwork. Tomorrow. Mañana.

He eased off the accelerator and shifted in his seat, wincing – the old back injury was on form tonight, probing his spine like a knitting needle. Moran chuckled grimly. *You sure aren't getting any younger, Brendan. Two score years and ten . . .*

He extended his distance from the blurry brake lights ahead, easing off the pressure with his right foot. There was a petrol station somewhere nearby, he recalled. Bad position – on one of the bends. Not this one, though, Moran muttered as he took the corner. But then suddenly it *was* this corner and the car in front had stopped, indicator blinking. Moran slammed on the brakes, all too aware of the unfavourable physics of wet tyres and rain-slicked tarmac – oil too, probably, outside a petrol station . . .

Moran hung onto the wheel. It gave him the illusion of control, but in reality there was no control at all in the sick, skidding journey he was making towards the rear of the stationary Vauxhall Astra. He felt a flicker of responsibility for the passengers, but the dangerous combination of obscuring hedge, country highway and petrol station was not *his* fault . . . by God it was *someone's* fault, though . . . the tyres sang a rubber-perishing scream as the soaked wheels failed to grip. Moran did a quick calculation; he'd been doing around fifty, and the braking would slow him to maybe ... thirty-five, forty? Still fast enough to do a lot of damage. He glimpsed a face freeze-framed against the rear window of the Astra before the jeep slewed crazily to the right. Then it was all about the oncoming lorry. Headlights blazed, blinding him. Moran squeezed in one last calculation. *New closing speed: around eighty…* The last thing he heard was the blaring of the artic's klaxon.

Then came the impact, the gagging stench of diesel, crushing pain, a sensation of floating.

And then he died.

But he didn't stay dead. The doctors told him later that he'd been technically dead for thirty-six seconds – until they'd managed to get his heart going again. Moran was glad he'd been dead while they were doing that, because they'd broken four ribs while they were about it. This was the pain he remembered when he'd finally come round. Ribs first, head second; right foot (shattered) trailing in third position in the agony polls.

But the dreams that accompanied his convalescence were worse than any pain. He'd swap them for cracked ribs any day. Thing was, he could cope with the nightmares if they were restricted to the six hours of restless tossing and turning he endured every night.

But they weren't.

Because Moran's biggest problem these post-trauma days was staying awake the rest of the time . . .

Chapter 1

"Guv?"

Moran's eyes snapped open. "What?"

"There's a monk on the phone for you."

"A *what*?"

"A monk." Phelps grinned. "You know..." The sergeant steepled his hands and raised his eyes heavenwards in an attitude of mock reverence.

Moran ran a hand through his thinning hair. The smell of the crash was in his nostrils. The impact, the flames. He shook his head to disperse the images. His foot was aching with a familiar dull throb.

"Says it's urgent. Sounds upset."

"Well, put him on, Sergeant. And get me a coffee, would you?"

"Will do." Phelps made as if to leave, but then popped his head back around the doorframe.

"Well?"

"This monk – I was just hoping, sir. It's nothing."

"Hoping what?"

Phelps' face broke into what, on his battered features, passed for a grin. "Well, sir, I hope he doesn't make a habit of it, that's all."

"*Out*, Phelps."

Moran was still smiling when he picked up the phone, but a moment later the joke was forgotten. As he listened to the shocked, tumbling voice on the phone his eyes grew wider. Two minutes later he slammed the receiver down, grabbed his raincoat and made for the door.

Moran was dropped off outside the school entrance. The front door was an ornate, solid oak affair with two astroidal windows set into the deep grain. They returned Moran's scrutiny with the indifference of age. This was the old part of the abbey, the dormitory and classroom block, plus the headmaster's office where prospective parents and their nervous offspring would be welcomed.

A newly-painted sign showed Moran the way to the abbey. He waited as a group of boys crossed the road in front of him. One, a tall ginger lad, gave him a courteous wave. Well, that was to be expected. Boys were sent here to be turned into young gentlemen, future high achievers. He found the expansive car park adjacent to the abbey church, an impressive building featuring a space-age cupola stretching high into the winter air.

A black figure approached from the direction of the school. As he drew nearer Moran could see the anxiety etched into the monk's forehead. He was in his late thirties, with a gaunt face, a serious slant to his mouth and a closely-trimmed beard in which traces of grey were beginning to show. He was wearing a black full-length habit tied at the waist with a leather belt. A pale hand appeared and extended in greeting. The grip was unexpectedly firm.

"DCI Moran? So good of you to come promptly. Father Martin Oswald, prior of the abbey. Please – follow me."

"Who found the body?" Moran enquired as Oswald started back along the path at a brisk walk. "And when?"

Oswald's pace slowed a fraction. A bell rang in some distant cloister and the sound of young male voices filled the courtyard ahead.

"Break time." Oswald gave a brief smile. "Just fifteen minutes, and then we'll have peace and quiet until half past twelve." He paused and stroked his beard. "Father Horgan was found by one of the older monks – and a boy who was serving Mass at the time. The boy has been sent home – very distressed, obviously."

"What time, exactly?"

"Around five forty-five this morning. Many of us celebrate Mass before breakfast. There are four small chapels within the main chapel. I'll show you."

Oswald opened a door and ushered Moran inside the school. The kaleidoscope of smells took him back: floor polish, the institutional tang of boiling vegetables, paper, ink, and the unmistakeable odour of adolescent youth. Oswald was walking briskly now and Moran had to lengthen his stride to keep up. His leg still pained him and he walked with a noticeable limp, but he'd be damned if he'd let it slow him down.

They stopped at an iron-hasped oak door; Oswald produced a set of keys and slid one into the lock.

"These are the only keys. No one has been in since – except me and the abbot."

"And the body?"

Oswald swung the door open. "Is lying where it was found. And that's strange enough in itself."

Moran resisted the urge to genuflect as they crossed the nave to the chapel's east side, where an ambulatory cloister ran from north to south.

"Strange in what way?" Moran clocked the curiosity in Oswald's voice – the monk was bursting to share the discovery. Moran couldn't recall the last time anyone had showed such unbridled enthusiasm at the site of a suspicious death.

“Over here,” Oswald gestured. They were standing in front of one of the side chapels. The altar had been pushed aside, and beneath it a dark gap revealed a stone staircase.

Moran fished in his pocket and produced a pair of rubber gloves. “Anything been touched?”

“Not that I’m aware of,” Oswald replied, his eyes shining with anticipation.

Moran hesitated at the rail. He hadn’t set foot within the holy boundary of an altar since his earliest years in Ireland. It was out of bounds to the common people; only the priest and his acolytes were permitted to tread within its mysterious perimeter. He pulled the gloves on, irritated with himself, and followed Oswald. *What are you thinking, Moran? This is a murder, not High Mass . . .*

“This chamber,” Oswald murmured. “Quite something. I’ve said Mass here countless times. I had no idea that it existed. I–”

Moran grunted. “At least two people knew about it – namely Father Horgan and his murderer.” He paused by the altar and peered into the stairwell. Father Horgan’s body was lying face up, his arms outstretched in what appeared to be a shallow recess in the floor. A pool of blood had begun to congeal around the head, and smaller droplets dotted the stone by the dead monk’s outstretched hands.

Moran went down, minding his footing on the crumbling steps. Glass fragments crunched under his shoes as he bent automatically and felt for the pulse he knew would be absent. The monk had a yellowed bone clasped in his right hand, but what was in the other? It looked like a sliver of wood, upon which were carved a series of marks; curved, sweeping strokes made by some carpentry instrument. The markings had been partially obscured by a dark stain, and the ragged extremities of the object indicated that other fragments had, in all probability, been lost altogether, whether by deliberate damage or excessive handling it was impossible to say.

Moran could feel Oswald hovering. "May I–?" The monk made as if to step closer.

"No further, if you don't mind." Moran held up his hand. "Forensics will need to give it the once-over first." His mobile gave three short beeps. "Excuse me a moment." He fished out his phone. "Moran."

Sergeant Phelps' barrow boy growl filled his ear. "Taylor's on his way, sir. Should be with you soon."

"Have Forensics got their fingers out yet?"

"Hang on, guv."

Moran heard Phelps yelling across the office. He took the opportunity to study Father Oswald as the monk stood over the body of his fallen brother, wringing his hands like the leading player in a Shakespearian tragedy. Genuinely shocked, Moran concluded. And keen to do a little amateur sleuthing. He made a mental note to sow some seeds of discouragement. Amateurs were always bad news.

"On their way, sir. Be with you as soon as," Phelps blasted in his ear. Moran winced and signed off.

The silence of death, Moran reflected, is a unique kind of silence. He was standing in the chamber, conducting what he called his 'prelim'. This involved a careful perusal of each and every angle of the crime scene, taking account of any loose objects, anything that seemed to have been displaced from its normal position, anything out of the ordinary. In this case, however, *everything* fell into the latter category. The fact that the chamber was, in effect, some kind of closely-guarded secret, and the fact that the victim was a man of the cloth for starters . . .

Somewhere in the distance he could hear the school returning to morning classes – the sound of running feet, whistles, the collective din of recently-broken male voices. If he closed his eyes he could imagine himself at Blackrock during his own schooldays. Lunch at the communal table, rugby training until four o'clock. Lessons till seven. Free time, then bed at nine. Moran shook his head ruefully. *Those were the days, my friend.*

"Inspector?" Oswald's earnest voice floated from the stairwell where Moran had insisted he remain. "Anything I can do?"

"You can arrange a meeting with the abbot and the headmaster for starters," Moran called back. "I don't want anyone leaving the school grounds until they've checked with me." His voice sounded flat in the small enclosure. He gingerly probed under the body, taking care not to disturb Horgan's position, which was odd in the extreme. His fingers found what he expected: more bones. Horgan had died on someone else's grave. Moran straightened up and climbed back into the chapel.

Oswald's expression was a contortion of unasked questions.

"I know what you're going to ask." The monk raised his finger. A brief smile played about his lips until it was dismissed by the look on Moran's face.

"Well, go on then."

"I – I *know*, of course, about the relic."

"Relic?"

"The wood – the *Titulus*. That's what the chamber is for."

Understanding dawned. "Ah, I see." So Christian relics were not exclusive to the Middle Ages. The provenance and value of the scrap of wood might be an avenue worth exploring. Had Horgan been trying to protect it? It seemed he had succeeded – albeit at the cost of his own life. "Perhaps I can have a quick chat with the abbot while we're waiting for the quack and the SOCOs?"

"SOCOs?" Oswald looked puzzled.

"Scene of Crime Officers. And the death needs to be certified. I can't get cracking until that's done and dusted."

"Ah. Forensics and so on? I see. I'll find the abbot for you."

"And the headmaster, please."

"Of course. Perhaps I can ask you to wait in the Court of Arches."

"Fine. Anything else I need to know about the chapel?"

Oswald stroked his chin. "Well, there *is* something. But it's rather fanciful . . ."

"Anything that might be pertinent."

"Every abbey has its ghost story," Oswald said. "And we are no exception. The spirit of a dead girl is said to haunt the chapel. She is known as the White Lady."

"I see." Moran sighed. "I may not follow that particular line of enquiry, Father, if it's all the same to you. Now, if you'll excuse me I have to make a few phone calls."

Schoolboys were beginning to emerge from classrooms along the length of the main cloister, laughing and joking or talking in small groups of two or three as they made their way to further places of study. Harassed-looking teachers were dotted along the passage issuing a warning here, a word of greeting there as the swarm passed them by. These be-suited laymen were supplemented by several older boys wearing distinctive blue ties; prefects, Moran supposed. He noticed that the younger boys showed respect for the blue ties – evidently discipline was a working concept at Charnford, Moran noted approvingly.

"I'll leave you here for a few minutes, Chief Inspector, if that's all right." Oswald gave a brief smile. "There's a coffee machine in the corner, if you're in need of refreshment. I'm sure the abbot won't keep you long."

"I'll be fine, thanks."

He watched Oswald glide down the cloister. The hubbub of scholarly traffic died away and the Court of Arches fell silent. Moran went to the drinks machine and inserted a coin. He retrieved the plastic cup, sat down heavily on a bench beneath a leaded window and considered the corpse. Throat slashed, left for dead. Had the murderer been disturbed? No effort at concealment had been attempted.

Moran jotted a quick note. A shaft of sunlight stole into the cloister, motes of dust swirling in the beam like a miniature galaxy. The radiator next to him clanked as it cleared some hidden airlock. From behind closed doors came the muffled mutterings of academia. Moran closed his eyes.

"Excuse me. Are you okay?"

Moran was still dreaming. He knew that for sure, because Janice was dead. Long dead. And he'd recognise her voice anywhere; from behind the wall of sleep or from within the vaults of his memory, that sweet sound lived on. He didn't want to let go, even though he was aware that the dream had reached its nightmare stage: they kissed, parted, and he watched her walk across the car park, her red hair catching the sunlight, seeing the half turn, the wave. A moment frozen in time, the last time their eyes had met. Then a pause as she opened the car door, another second or two as she turned the key in the ignition. Then an orange blossom of flame, a hot wind that blew him off his feet, particles of glass and metal flying. Blood on his clothes, a pall of black smoke. The bomb that was meant for him. His car. Not hers.

"*Hello*?"

Moran woke up. And gawped.

"I just thought you might have been lost – I don't think I know you . . ."

The voice, the face, the hair. So like her. Moran heard himself clear his throat and mutter an apology. He stood up, the hairs on the back of his neck tingling.

"Holly Whitbread. English Lit. and RE." She smiled and offered her hand.

"Chief Inspector Brendan Moran. Pleased to meet you." He cleared his throat, tried to keep his voice steady.

"Are you sure you're okay? I didn't mean to startle you."

"Fine, thanks." Moran smoothed his hair. "I haven't been sleeping too well."

"Well, with your job I'm not surprised." She smiled again and Moran worked to control his emotions. It was as if Janice had come back to life, younger and more beautiful than ever.

"You've come about Father Horgan, I suppose." Her forehead creased. "Poor man. But he hadn't been keeping well. I imagine you're obliged to be present at the scene of a sudden death?"

"A sudden death?" Moran frowned. "Of course, absolutely." So that was the story. Why hadn't Oswald told him? "Did you know Father Horgan?"

"Oh, yes." Holly Whitbread wrinkled her nose. "We all knew him very well. He was quite the disciplinarian. Very old-school."

"I see."

"But likeable with it," Holly went on. "I can't believe he's gone – just like that." She snapped her manicured fingers.

"Is the news on general release?"

"I'm not sure. I think there's to be an announcement at lunch. The boys know something's up – because the chapel is locked," she added. "No morning prayers. My class are still celebrating."

Moran smiled. "You're not turning them into little monks, then?"

"Hardly." Holly made a face. "Little devils, the lot of them." She tossed her hair back and laughed. Moran tried to swallow but his mouth had dried up. She could be Janice's twin, even down to the mannerisms. He pulled himself together with an effort.

"Do I detect a Cork accent?"

Holly inclined her head in acknowledgement. "You do. And I might ask the same."

"Close," Moran conceded. "I was born in Ardmore, but I moved to London after . . . after . . ." He couldn't bring himself to say her name. "After my fiancée died."

"I'm so sorry." Her forehead creased and her eyes locked onto his. The sympathy was so evidently genuine that it took him aback.

He cleared his throat. "Thank you. It was a long time ago."

"Can I escort you anywhere, Chief Inspector?"

"Well, I have an audience with the abbot. Father Oswald is tracking him down."

Holly's expression switched to one of admiration. "He's an amazing man. You'll enjoy meeting him."

"I'm sure."

A bell rang at the far end of the cloister. "Ah." She tucked her folders under her arm with a decisive movement. "The bell tolls for me. Shakespeare beckons." She offered her hand. "Nice to meet you, Chief Inspector."

Moran watched her walk briskly along the cloister, high heels clicking softly on the cardinal red tiles. *And you too*, he thought. *And you too . . .*

Chapter 2

Moran was shown into a dimly-lit room which evoked an atmosphere of contemplative study; the smell of books, papers, and the hushed stillness of undisturbed concentration, mixed with a tang of – what? Incense. That was it. The residue of countless High Mass attendances clung to the fabric of the abbot's domain like sweet tobacco. The heavy curtains were drawn, shutting out the cloudy December afternoon. A standard lamp cast a pool of circular light onto the corner of a large pedestal desk, behind which was seated a still figure, clothed in a similar fashion to Father Oswald but with a chain of high office about his neck. His hood was raised, obscuring his face in shadow.

Moran heard Oswald close the door softly behind him as he made a discreet exit. For a moment there was silence, and then the abbot made a gesture of invitation.

"Take a seat, Chief Inspector."

Moran's eyes were becoming accustomed to the low lighting; the abbot's features were still indiscernible beneath the Benedictine hood, but Moran could make out an aquiline nose, above which glinted startlingly blue eyes. The monk's voice was deep and measured – a voice that was used to being obeyed.

"Forgive me my den of darkness, Chief Inspector. My eyes are weak, and I find this more restful. Now –" A long pause. "How may I be of assistance in this terrible matter?"

Moran sat on the edge of the chair and undid the buttons of his coat. It was uncomfortably warm. "You can tell me all you know about Father Horgan and his duties, particularly with regard to the last twenty-four hours. Then you can tell me all about the chamber in the chapel. Who knew about it and had access? Did Horgan have any enemies? Anyone bear a grudge?"

The abbot raised his arm and leaned forward into the pool of light. Moran had to grip the chair arms to stop himself recoiling. The abbot's face was a parchment of repaired burns, the skin crinkled and warped like discarded brown paper. His mouth was a twist of grafts, the original lips burned away by whatever catastrophic blaze had caused his injuries.

"It's quite all right, Chief Inspector. I am used to strong reactions upon new introductions. I'm not as fierce as I appear to be."

Moran loosened his grip on the chair. "Of course. I do apologise if–"

The abbot waved the apology aside. Moran noticed the fingers were clawed, fixed into a permanent half-fist. He tucked his hand back into the wide sleeve of his garment and fixed Moran with a steady, appraising look.

"Father Horgan was a pillar of this community. He served the abbey and school for many, many years. He was trustworthy and dependable. Sometimes he could be unpopular with the boys; his punishments were fair, but sometimes a little – unpleasant. But the boys knew where they were with him. He commanded respect."

"I see. And what was he doing in the chapel – in the chamber?"

"Ah. Here we have to tread with a little delicacy."

"I'm listening."

"The chamber's existence is indeed known only to a select few. Father Horgan had responsibility for – tending to the necessary within."

"There's no need to be coy. Father Oswald has already told me about the relic – the *Titulus*, was it?"

The abbot slid back his chair and emerged from behind the desk. Moran was struck by his height. The monk moved to the window and turned, arms folded beneath his scapular in typical Benedictine stance. "You've heard of Constantine the Great, Chief Inspector?"

Moran had. "Of course. The Roman Emperor credited with popularising Christianity."

"Quite right. Whether he was an astute politician or a true believer, we'll never know. Certainly the former, perhaps both. But his mother's faith is beyond question."

Moran was wondering where this was going. He was also wondering where the hell the SOCOs and the police surgeon had got to. The lack of security at the murder site was gnawing at him. Maybe he should have waited until–

"I can see you have other matters pressing, Chief Inspector," the abbot continued, "but this is pertinent to your question."

"Please." Moran shrugged. "Carry on."

"Constantine's mother was the Empress Helena. In 320AD she undertook a journey to Jerusalem, to the site of the burial place of Jesus. A pagan temple had been erected on the site, but Helena had it torn down. In part, her mission was to oversee the building of a fitting monument to the Resurrection, a new basilica, decorated with all the splendour an Empress had at her disposal. In this she succeeded. However, during the early stages of its construction she made a remarkable discovery.

Perhaps it had been her primary intention all along; she had heard rumours that the true cross of Jesus Christ still lay beneath the temple."

Moran raised his eyebrows. He could guess what was coming.

"And she found it." The abbot was warming to his subject. "Along with two others. It was broken up and the various pieces are long since scattered across the globe. But a fragment – a significant fragment – remained in her possession. She took it to Rome, and it can be seen today in the chapel at Santa Croce. It is a section of the *Titulus Crucis,* the notice pinned on the cross at the injunction of Pontius Pilate. The sign that read: 'This is Jesus of Nazareth, King of the Jews'."

"I see. And the rest of it? You said 'a section'."

The abbot smiled. He removed his hands from his sleeves and made an open-handed gesture, signifying the pointlessness of spelling it out. "You will already have drawn your conclusion, Inspector Moran. Another *Titulus* fragment remained initially in Jerusalem, but during the Crusades it was taken into safe custody by the Knights Templar. From Jerusalem it travelled in the utmost secrecy through Europe to a small monastery at Douai in France. And from there, in 1893, it came to us."

Moran's mobile bleeped. "Excuse me a moment. Well?" he barked into the phone.

Phelps' voice: "Sorry, guv. RTA on the Bath road. Bad one. We'll be with you as soon as."

"You'd better be." Moran signed off. "Forgive me. Please go on."

The abbot had returned to his chair. He moved a sheaf of papers aside with an impatient gesture. "That's all there is to tell, Inspector. The *Titulus* has been kept and guarded here at Charnford ever since. As to its provenance, there are a number of clear indications that it is indeed a fragment of the true *Titulus*, and not some mediaeval counterfeit. Suffice to say that we are completely satisfied as to its veracity."

"A motive for murder?"

"That is for you to establish, Chief Inspector."

"You must have some idea, surely?" Moran raised his eyebrows. "Who else knew of it? Who may have harboured some ambition to own it for themselves? I can appreciate its value to a devout believer. Priceless, I would have thought."

The abbot drew a deep breath. His lungs rattled in protest. "Yes, priceless. But we are a community, Inspector Moran. We share, we pull together. That is the Benedictine way. There is no room for selfish ambition or covetousness."

Moran leaned forward and tried – without success – to keep the cynicism out of his voice. "Be that as it may, Father Abbot, we're all human. We'd all like the Mona Lisa hanging in our own private gallery."

"I can see you have much to learn, Inspector. I like to think that, although we are *in* this world, we are not *of* it."

"Father Horgan is not *of* this world either. Not anymore. Someone slit his throat." Moran paused to let his deliberately harsh reminder sink in.

The abbot had opened his mouth to reply when the door burst open. Father Oswald's face was pale beneath his beard, his arms flapping in agitation. "Father Abbot! Chief Inspector – I am sorry to interrupt, but it's gone. It's been taken!"

Moran frowned. "What has?"

Oswald lowered his voice as if imparting some critical state secret. “The *Titulus*!” The monk produced a handkerchief and mopped his brow.

“But the chapel was locked, Father Oswald.” Moran was on his feet. “And you told me you had the only set of keys.”

“Calm yourself, Oswald.” The abbot’s voice was steady, in control. “Sit down, would you please, and tell us exactly what happened.”

Chapter 3

Montgomery waited until he judged the bank to be at its quietest. Morning pre-work rush over. Lull till lunchtime. That's what they'd figured. He glanced sideways at Mason. Were his hands shaking a little? His own heart was beating like a pair of castanets For a second he thought: *I could go back now. It's not too late. I can walk away, change the future.* But then he remembered what was at stake: the future of the school. *His* school. So, a no-brainer.

He felt the weight of the gun in his pocket. It felt strange to be carrying a real gun. It didn't seem so long ago that he'd played with his friend Patrick, shooting each other down the length of the garden, fumbling and refilling their weapons with a fresh roll of caps. Montgomery remembered the smell as the caps went off with a snap, a thrilling, exciting smell. It sounded so real. And that whiff of smoke . . . for a moment he could almost smell the memory.

But this was real, not playtime. They'd planned it all, starting from the moment Maria had said, "You could always rob a bank!" And they'd laughed. Until Mason's bit – Bernadette – had come back with, 'Well, why not? Sure, we're well connected, y'know', in that infuriatingly sexy Irish brogue that had attracted them to the school maids in the first place.

It had all started via the usual channels of lust: the odd comment here and there in the refectory or by the kitchen phone box. Harmless banter, until Maria had leaned in close, the smell of vegetables not quite masked by her musky perfume – strangely erotic in the post-supper emptiness of the ref – and whispered, 'Fancy coming over to the cottage tonight? Bring a friend if you like.' Then a wink as she moved away to clear the top table.

Had he imagined it? Heart hammering with excitement he had rushed off to break the news to Mason. Mason was horrified and charged up in equal measure. 'It's totally out of bounds ... if we're caught . . .' His friend hadn't needed to say anything further. If they were found in the maids' cottage it would be expulsion without question. But how could they resist an invitation like that?

And of course, they hadn't. At the first opportunity they had stolen along the path that ran beside the First Fifteen rugby pitch to where the cottage nestled invitingly behind a tall hedgerow. Romance had been restricted to inexperienced groping and stolen kisses on the sofa – for all their apparent flirtatiousness the girls were as Catholic as the Pope. But it was hugely exciting nevertheless, and there was always the chance they'd wear down the girls' defences over time.

That had been the ultimate goal, anyway – until the night Bernadette made her fateful suggestion. Then another, even more daring, goal had been discussed. Everyone knew that Charnford was short of money. It was the sort of rumour that couldn't be subdued, despite the governors' best efforts. The threat of closure hung over both pupils and staff like some ghastly Damoclean theatre prop. For Montgomery and Mason it meant an end to friendships, familiar surroundings, the illicit liaisons with Bernadette and Maria – and, worst of all, an interruption to their A level studies at the worst possible time. It was an intolerable prospect.

Now they had a chance to do something about it. It was crazy, but desperate times called for desperate measures. That's what old Rufus Bell had taught them about Alexander the Great. He hadn't fannied around, agonising over what to do. He'd gone for broke, like all the people in history who were 'somebodys' and had made their mark. Who was it who'd said: 'aim for the moon, you might hit a star' . . . ? Montgomery couldn't remember, but right now it didn't seem to matter.

His nerves were pitched like some high tensile wire, stretched to breaking point. It was one thing discussing bank robberies with a can of Bud in one hand and Maria's charms in the other, but quite another standing here on the pavement with a loaded gun in his pocket.

We're well connected, y'know . . .

"Come on." Mason nudged him, tight-lipped. "This is it. You first, like we said."

"Right." Montgomery pulled the helmet visor down. He made sure the manila folder he was carrying was half open so he could fumble with the papers, appear to be concentrating on whatever transaction he was about to make. Helmets were probably a little risky, but they'd worked out that the bank wouldn't be too jittery if it looked like he was a regular member of Joe Public, biker apparent or not.

Montgomery took a deep breath and walked confidently into the foyer, horribly conscious of the semi-automatic bumping against his thigh. There was no one in the queue. That was good. One cashier. Two staff members sitting at desks in the open plan section. Both female. Even better. Montgomery placed his folder beside the credit card terminal and opened it. The cashier looked up. She was pretty, his type; blonde, petite. Nice smile. Relaxed. He selected an A4 sheet from the folder and held it to the window. The following message was written in black felt tip:

I have a gun pointing at your head. I will use it if I need to. If you make ANY noise I will shoot. Keep CALM, find me as much money, in large notes, as you can. Not less than £700,000, please. I know that you can do this. If you don't I will start shooting. Do what I say and I will simply walk out with the money and you will all be unharmed. DO IT ***NOW***

The girl's smile faded as she scanned the message. Her face paled and her fingers grasped the edge of her desk until the knuckles whitened. Montgomery's heart slowed. That was the worst part over. She hadn't screamed, hadn't made him carry out his threat, thank God. He gave her a tight smile of encouragement and a brief nod to set her to her task. She moistened her lips and stood up. Without a backward glance she walked to the end of the counter and spoke to a middle-aged woman in a pale blue dress. Montgomery held his breath. The brief conversation over, the woman opened a safe and withdrew with a curt nod. The cashier bent and began to fish out bundles of notes.

As she piled them on the desk beside the safe Montgomery began to believe that they might get away with it. He glanced at Mason, who was nonchalantly leafing through mortgage brochures. At the first sign of trouble he would signal Maria, parked at the ready down the street. A bead of sweat trickled down Montgomery's forehead and entered his right eye. He blinked it away. The cashier completed her task and straightened. Montgomery noted the sleek turn of her calf as she smoothed her dress. She gathered the bundles onto a tray and began the return journey to his window. *That's it, gorgeous. Come on now, just a little further . . .*

She sat down and plonked the tray on the desk. Without looking at him she began to pass the bundles under the glass one by one. Montgomery had his man-bag open, the one his mother had bought him for Christmas, and consigned each bundle to its depths, feeling unreality wash over him like a warm shower. Sweat prickled under his arms. It was all right; no one was paying any attention. The open-plan staff were making phone calls or peering at their screens. The woman at the helpdesk was chatting to a nicotine-fingered old man in a brown pinstripe suit. Mason was chewing gum, arms folded. A phone rang somewhere and was picked up. Two people had joined the queue behind him: a woman with a small girl attached to her coat, pulling her arm and asking for chocolate, and a young man in a white T-shirt and jeans.

The cashier was biting her lip; a small drop of blood had formed on her lipgloss. The last bundle was pushed under the glass. For a moment Montgomery didn't know what to do. 'Thank you' seemed inappropriate, but the words were out before he could stop them. The cashier looked him in the eye and clasped her hands as if she could physically squeeze the danger away. Her eyes darted this way and that and she seemed about to say something, but then she changed her mind and lowered her gaze. Montgomery hefted the bag and strolled away as nonchalantly as he could. His back muscles twitched. Mason met him at the door and a second later they were out. Relief exploded through him like a shot of adrenaline.

Maria was at the kerb, engine idling. Then they were in the back of the car and hurtling away towards the ring road. Mason burst out laughing and Montgomery joined in. He opened the bag and pulled out a wad of notes, waving them in Mason's face. "Look at this!" he roared. "Just *look* at it!"

Maria ground the gears into fifth, turned and shrieked over the boys' laughter. "I told you, didn't I? I told youse to listen to Maria! Problem solved, right?"

"Yeah, right!" Montgomery felt another burst of elation. He twisted in his seat to look behind as Maria swung onto the A4. No flashing lights. No pursuit at all. *We did it*, he said to himself. *We really did it . . .*

"You still packin' your piece?" Mason leered playfully. He made a grab for Montgomery's pocket. Montgomery laughed and pulled away.

"Yeah, man. But you is too young for firearms! *Way* too young!" He scooped up a fistful of scattered £50 notes and thrust them in Mason's face. "It takes a *real* man to hold up a bank."

"Oh yeah?" Mason said. "What's that supposed to mean?"

Maria signalled and sped past a dawdling estate car. She struck up an Irish folk song, punctuating the lyrics with a whistled chorus.

"Nothing," Montgomery said.

"I could have done it just as well. We tossed for it, you won, simple as that."

"Okay, okay." Montgomery threw the notes in the air. "Keep your hair on."

"Let me see the gun."

Montgomery sighed. “All right.” He produced the semi-automatic from his pocket and flicked the safety off with a theatrical flourish. “Da daaaaa. Happy now?” He pointed the pistol at Mason. “So go on, punk, make my day.”

“Don’t point it at me, you idiot.” Mason grabbed Montgomery’s wrist.

“Get *off*.” Montgomery pulled away sharply, but his finger was curled round the trigger and the action of withdrawal applied just enough pressure to set the mechanism in motion. The semi-automatic duly delivered a round with a sharp – surprisingly loud – crack. The car swerved violently to the right and Montgomery was thrown onto Mason’s side, bashing his head against the other boy’s shoulder. Pain drove through his skull. He tried to sit up but the car appeared to be canting to the left now like a big dipper plucked from its rails.

“Hey! Maria! What–?” Then he saw the neat hole punched into the back of the driver’s seat and the splash of red on the windscreen. The car swerved again as Maria’s lifeless body flopped grotesquely over the steering wheel.

“Oh *Jesus*,” Montgomery whispered. The car left the carriageway and mounted the central reservation. Montgomery saw another vehicle hurtling towards them and the world exploded into searing heat and pummelling, rending noise. The horror lasted mere milliseconds; by the time the spinning wreckage came to a standstill Montgomery and Mason were as dead as Maria.

They were standing by the chapel entrance near the Court of Arches: Moran, the abbot and Oswald. A line of lockers on either side led up to the chapel door. Boys were hurriedly depositing their books and belongings into the metal boxes before rejoining their classmates in the queues forming up in the main cloister.

"Right, let's go over this again," Moran said. "Oh, excuse me–" he leaned against a battered locker to let a hurrying kitchen maid squeeze by. "Sorry Fathers," she muttered under her breath. Moran's ears pricked up at her accent. As Irish as get out, his mother would have said.

The area around the Court of Arches was a hive of activity as boys and staff prepared for lunch. A monk in less formal attire (a plum-coloured polo neck and dark trousers) was ushering boys into the refectory, form by form. He was a large, portly man, in appearance exactly as Moran would have imagined a Benedictine to be: balding pate, horn-rimmed glasses, and, Moran noticed, a short cane tucked underneath his arm. The boys followed his instructions without comment or complaint. The cloister was emptying fast and the noise of adolescent traffic was soon replaced by the distant clatter of plates and cutlery.

Father Oswald was fiddling with a set of keys, passing them from hand to hand as if this would somehow undo the uncomfortable fact that somebody had returned to the scene and removed what was probably *the* most significant object of the investigation – with the exception of the corpse itself. Worse still, it had happened after Moran had supposedly 'secured' the crime scene. The Chief Constable would doubtless make reference to this fact during debrief, thus adding more fuel to the 'retirement on medical grounds' funeral pyre Lawson had been busy constructing for Moran since the accident. *What happened, Moran? Taking forty winks, were you? Wouldn't be the first time, would it? I've arranged another appointment for you . . .*

Moran pushed the thought aside. He would figure out how to deal with Lawson later, after he'd located the missing item. Which he would. His professional pride was stinging; the only way to fight Lawson's fire was *with* fire. And Moran had plenty of fire left in his belly.

"I just don't understand it," Oswald was saying. He would have wrung his hands if he hadn't been clutching the keys. "There is *no way* anyone could have got in," he finished emphatically.

The abbot fixed Oswald with a withering look. "Just tell us why you decided to revisit the chapel, Father Oswald." His voice was soothing, but Moran's radar caught the steel at the question's core.

Yes, tell us, Father, especially after I explicitly told you not to. Moran felt in his pocket for a cigarette, and then remembered he'd given up. He took a deep breath instead, over-inflating his lungs to imitate the effect of a sudden rush of nicotine-filled, carcinogenic smoke. It was a poor substitute.

Father Oswald glanced at him nervously. "I wanted to – I mean, I thought I could have a quick look around, perhaps find something of use while you were–" Oswald finally let the keys fall to his side in a gesture of defeat. "I know I shouldn't have. I'm sorry, Father Abbot."

"Did you hear anything that would suggest somebody followed you into the chapel?" Moran asked. Out of the corner of his eye he saw Holly Whitbread walking briskly towards the refectory. She gave Moran a wave.

Oswald repeated his statement. "I said that I locked the door behind me, Inspector Moran. I can assure you of that."

"Right." Moran could still feel the eddy of Holly's passing, a breeze of some peach-scented perfume. He tore his gaze away with an effort. "In that case there must be another way in. Ah, here's my sergeant–"

A commotion at the far end of the cloister announced Phelps' arrival. The DS caught sight of Moran and raised a hand in greeting. Three white-suited SOCOs followed in the sergeant's wake. Bringing up the rear was the unmistakeable figure of Sandy Taylor, the police surgeon, a tall, quick-witted Scot. Moran approved of Taylor's dark sense of humour and no-nonsense approach. His comprehensive wine cellar was another plus point.

Phelps brought the party to a halt and nodded a greeting. "Sorry we're late. Three fatals at the RTA. Bloody mess – excuse me, Fathers–" Phelps acknowledged the two monks. "Saving your presence, and all that."

The abbot smiled, the mottled skin taut across his scarred cheeks. "No apology required, Sergeant. We are accustomed to the language of the world."

Moran had to hand it to Phelps; the DS hardly batted an eyelid at the abbot's ruined features. Or maybe he just wasn't paying attention. Phelps looked pale and agitated. Moran wasn't surprised. It was the natural effect of witnessing a bad RTA. Never failed to put things into perspective; here one moment, gone the next. As if echoing that thought, Moran's leg shot him a sudden spasm of pain. Not that he needed a reminder of how close he'd been to the brink himself; his very own RTA was repeated every night like a tape loop of some disaster movie in which he played the leading part.

Sandy Taylor came forward, the habitual twinkle in his eye. "How do, Moran? Time presses, old friend. Best not keep the dead waiting, eh?"

Moran watched as the team moved through the chamber, dusting, scraping, examining. Sandy Taylor was bent over Horgan's prone body, taking care to avoid the congealing bloodstains. Eventually he straightened up and clucked his tongue.

"Nasty. Throat slashed. Time of death, seven hours ago. Give or take a few minutes." Taylor snapped his bag shut. "Massive blood loss. Not that it would have bothered him. He was probably dead within thirty to forty seconds of the attack."

"Anything else?"

"Nope. No defence wounds. Probably surprised from behind."

"Murder weapon?"

Taylor clicked his tongue. "Your average-sized carving knife – or sheath knife, perhaps. Serrated. Very sharp. Jagged cuts."

Moran winced. "You make it sound like a butcher's master class."

"Indeed." Taylor raised an eyebrow and peered at Moran over half-moon spectacles. "That reminds me – I have to collect the dog's meat from the abattoir."

Moran made a face. "*Please*. What about this?" He indicated the long bone grasped in Horgan's stiffening hand.

"Human. And there's more beneath, by the looks of it. Poor chap chose the right place to die, anyway."

"Sorry?"

"Well," Taylor shrugged, "it's obviously a crypt of some sort. Father Horgan is clearly lying on an old burial plot."

"So he just grabbed the first thing that came to hand?"

"*In extremis*, Moran, we are hardly aware what our limbs are doing."

"I'd have thought his hands would have gone naturally to his throat – to the wound?"

Taylor made a non-committal gesture. "He was attacked, twisted round, lost his footing, fell heavily . . . he would have been seconds from death by the time he hit the floor."

"So the grasping was just a reflex?"

"More than likely." Taylor shrugged, adjusted his tie and surveyed the scene. "So, two for the price of one, eh, Moran? Other chap's been here a bit longer, I'd say. Should keep you busy for a while."

Moran grunted, got down on his haunches and fished a small metallic object from the shallow grave. A zipper; very rusty, but a zipper nevertheless.

"Looks like he was wrapped in some kind of body bag, guv," Phelps offered.

Moran handed Phelps the zipper. "A *sleeping* bag, Phelps. But this–" He carefully withdrew his hand and placed a bundle on the flagstones, "– isn't part of it."

Phelps frowned. "Looks like a vest."

"In a manner of speaking," Moran agreed. "It's a rugby vest." Taking the utmost care he laid the garment out. Its fragility was apparent, the dampness of the earth having reduced it to rotting strips of cloth. Moran probed with his rubber-gloved finger. "Ah." He exposed the area beneath the collar.

"A name?" Phelps leaned over Moran's shoulder.

"Not quite, but it may be as good as."

"F362?" Phelps muttered. "Lost me there, guv."

Moran straightened up. "It's a linen number, Phelps. All boys are required to ID their clothing. I'm betting this is a boy's allocated linen number."

"Right." Phelps nodded, impressed.

Taylor finished packing his accoutrements away and closed his case with a conclusive snap. "Well, it looks as though you've a reasonable starter for ten there, Moran. Anything else – you know where to find me."

"Guv?" Phelps was examining the remains of the case. "Looks like something's missing." He shrugged. "Whatever was in the case, I mean."

"Something missing here too." Moran delicately moved the skeleton's rib cage with the tip of his shoe. "Our bony friend has lost his head."

Phelps tutted. "Very careless." The sergeant peered into the shallow grave as Moran bent down and prised open Horgan's fingers. Several splinters were embedded in the pale flesh.

"But you're right, Phelps," Moran agreed. There *was* something else."

Phelps produced a notebook and pencil. "Any chance of a clue, guv – so's I know where to start looking?"

Moran smoothed back his thinning hair, peeled off his gloves and pocketed them. "A clue, Phelps? Okay, the Empress Helena would be my first choice, but I think she'll be hard to track down. I'd start with the abbot. Let's see what you make of him."

Chapter 4

"Eight o'clock tomorrow, guv?"

"Eight o'clock." Moran hauled himself out of the car with an effort. "See you then." He waved Phelps off and made a run for his porch. The rain was coming down in rods. As he fumbled for his keys a shadow detached itself from the hedge and came unsteadily towards him. Moran's heart flipped and then steadied, his fright replaced by a hot anger.

"Ah, Brendan, it's yourself. I thought you'd never come home."

Moran ignored the outstretched hand. "What do you want, Patrick?"

"Nothing a brother couldn't manage." Patrick Moran's face broke into a drunken smile. "Just something to tide me over, you know, until payday."

"You've a job? Is that what you're telling me?"

Patrick waved an unsteady finger. "In a manner of speaking. It's in the bag. I promise you. Weekly pay and all."

"Pull the other one." Moran turned to insert his key in the lock. Inside he could hear Archie scuffling on the bare boards. He'd be hungry, and he'd need a walk.

Patrick placed his hand on Moran's shoulder. "Now, be reasonable, Brendan, I know we don't see eye to eye, but we're family, isn't that God's truth?"

Moran spun on his heel and shook his brother off. "And what would you know about *God's truth*, Patrick?

Your only spirit-filled moments occur when one of my PCs hauls you out of the gutter.."

They stood facing each other in a familiar stand-off. Moran did a rapid assessment of Patrick's alcohol intake. Not as bad as usual; money obviously ran out before closing time.

Moran took a deep breath. He was dog-tired, and the last thing he needed was Patrick. Not tonight. The elder brother who had shown so much promise. Medical school, exam results to die for, enviable placement as registrar to the top orthopaedic surgeon at the Middlesex. Then – bang. One complaint – misconduct. A tribunal. Struck off – 'an example needs to be made,' the chairman had emphasised. No quarter given. A career down the pan before it had started.

Then, the comfort of the bottle. And on, and on, and on. At first Moran had been as devastated as Patrick. It was a shocking, unexpected turn of events. But then, after the drinking had begun in earnest, he had lost patience. And with the loss of patience came the guilt.

"Please, Brendan. I've nowhere to stay."

"Evicted again?" Moran felt sick. "For God's sake, Patrick."

"I'm begging you. Just one or two nights."

Moran felt his defences crumble. "You'd better come in."

Archie greeted them with his pneumatic tail and half a torn shirt. "Give it to me, Archie." Moran made a grab and failed. The spaniel pulled away, delighted with the game. Moran gave up. He'd told the daily not to leave the washing where the pup could get at it.

Patrick crumpled onto the sofa, eyes closed. As Moran wrestled the remains of his shirt from Archie's vice-like grip his brother began to snore, an even pattern signalling contented oblivion. Moran went into the kitchen and threw the remains of his shirt in the bin. There was a note on the kitchen table. The notepaper was headed: *'Happydogz, daily dog walking adventures'*. Seven walks: £77. Who had told him to get a dog? Mary, his housekeeper. *It'll keep you company, Chief Inspector . . .* Moran snorted. She didn't have to pay for it, did she?

Moran found a blanket and covered his brother's thin body as best he could. Then he poured himself a glass of Pinot and thought about the abbey. What did he have? A secret chamber, two bodies. A missing relic. An over-helpful monk. A strong leader in the abbot – that would come in handy, because the community might not like some of the restrictions he had placed on them. Father Boniface would ensure they toed the line. *Boniface.* Moran thought of the abbot's scarred face and wondered if he'd chosen the name deliberately. He hadn't felt brave enough to ask.

Archie nuzzled his hand, tail wagging nineteen to the dozen.

"All right, boy. It's round the block for you and me."

Moran downed his wine and clipped on Archie's lead. Patrick hadn't moved, nor was he likely to. Moran knew he'd have trouble rousing him in the morning, but rouse him he would. Mornings were the only times his brother was sober enough to listen. Moran headed for the front door and stepped out into the rain.

A sacristy was a strange venue for an incident room, but it suited Moran's purposes. With the chapel secured there would be little intrusion from the school, which would function as normal during the investigation. He had agreed that with the headmaster, Father Aloysius – a choleric little monk with chipmunk cheeks and, Moran suspected, a quick mind – and with the permission of Abbot Boniface. The boys had been told to stay within the boundaries of the school grounds, and had also been kept in the dark concerning Father Horgan's cause of death. So far, so good.

Moran moved a brass candle holder aside and set his laptop down on the small table. Forensic officers were still crawling over every square inch of the chapel chamber – he could hear the banter floating up into the main chapel as they worked. A good clean result was what Moran wanted. Something efficient and tangible, to prove to Lawson – and maybe to himself – that his accident was history and that Brendan Moran was firing on all cylinders. Phelps had begun the interviews, starting with the monk who had found the body. The recuperating altar boy he would leave at home for the last few days of term. He was better there than spreading the truth around the school.

Moran turned his thoughts to the big question: motive. Horgan had no enemies, according to the headmaster and the abbot. Apart from the natural enmity between a strict school official and his charges, the boys had been, according to Aloysius, in awe of Horgan. Moran also thought it unlikely that a Charnford boy could be capable of killing in cold blood. Nevertheless, he had arranged a meeting with Aloysius and the house captains to assess Horgan's status. Perhaps a recent punishment had stirred something more than a standard adolescent reaction.

There was someone else Moran was keen to speak to, a visiting dignitary from the Vatican – one Cardinal Vagnoli. He had arrived on the day of the murder and the abbot was cagey about the purpose of his visit. Phelps had supplied some interesting facts on that one; Horgan's private line had made and received several telephone calls to and from Rome over the last month. That was worth a little digging. And talking of digging – what about the buried bones? It was no official grave; that much was clear. And that was why Moran had asked Forensics to send the bones for analysis. To complicate the conundrum, it seemed that the bones had only recently been disturbed. But by whom? Was that Horgan's mission? If so, why had he dug them up? How did they come to be buried there in the first place? And lastly, where was the skull? Why was it missing?

A slant of rain blew against the sacristy window and Moran shivered. Father Oswald had promised a heater but he hadn't seen the monk today. The door opened and Phelps' large frame blocked out the light.

"All right, guv? Gordon Bennett, it's parky in here."

Moran grunted. "Better this than Lawson on my case every five minutes."

Phelps blew into his hands, the sausage-like fingers curled like a New Orleans blues harp player. "He'll be even more on your case now, guv; we've got another body."

"I do not want that Roman meddler to know *anything*, Sergeant Phelps. Is that clear?"

Phelps kept his eyes locked on the abbot's. "I'm afraid that may not be possible – Father," he added. It didn't feel right calling this bloke 'Father'; Phelps hadn't known his real father. He tried to keep his temper on an even keel. The guv'nor had said to keep the abbot sweet. That was going to be difficult if he wouldn't co-operate.

The abbot spoke again. "And why not? Cardinal Vagnoli has no business here. His visit is wasted. I have told him as much."

"But we know that he was invited, don't we, Father Abbot? By Father Horgan." Phelps was sure of his ground here. He'd checked the landline record himself. Either Vagnoli had invited himself – which seemed unlikely – or he had been given an incentive to come.

"Horgan was acting on his own initiative. He did not consult me."

Phelps pressed on. "But you know *why* he was invited, don't you? It was to do with the relic. Horgan told him about it, didn't he?" This was an unproved connection, but Moran had told him to take a punt.

Abbot Boniface sighed and folded his arms. Phelps tried not to stare at the parchment-like skin. Whatever else the abbot was, he was a brave man. Phelps doubted whether he himself would be comfortable exposing such horrific damage to close scrutiny. The abbot wagged his finger, pointing at Phelps' chest.

"You're speculating, Sergeant Phelps."

"Maybe. But I'm right, aren't I?"

Boniface sat back in his chair and steepled his fingers. "The school has been in some . . . financial difficulty. Father Horgan is – was – very attached to his role and to the pastoral care of the boys. He saw them as his protégés."

"Go on."

"The presence of the *Titulus* is a closely guarded secret, Sergeant Phelps. We are proud of and humbled by our role as its guardians. It is our responsibility to ensure its safekeeping. It is neither appropriate nor desirable for it to be sold off like some common mediaeval artefact."

"But Horgan didn't see it that way?"

Boniface sighed. "His love of the school prompted him to take matters into his own hands. He saw an opportunity to secure the school's future and perhaps curry favour with the Vatican. All done, as I said, without my knowledge or endorsement."

"Did you speak to him about it?"

"Of course." Boniface made an open-handed gesture. "I was angry."

"Angry enough to kill him?" Phelps jutted his chin. This was the bit he enjoyed – pushing for the advantage, getting a suspect on the ropes. He hadn't suspected the abbot up to now, but why not? Anger was always a potential for murder.

"Now you're being ridiculous, Sergeant Phelps."

"Can you verify your whereabouts between midnight and seven o'clock yesterday morning?"

"Yes," Boniface replied evenly, "I believe I can."

Phelps nodded and tried to maintain an impassive expression – a challenging ask for an ex-boxer. He waited patiently as the abbot prepared to deliver his alibi.

"I was visiting Worth Abbey, and I only returned at ten o'clock yesterday morning." Boniface paused and sat back in his chair. "Father Oswald will confirm that he met me at the main entrance with the news of Father Horgan's death."

Phelps chewed his lip. He'd have to tell Moran that he'd given Boniface a hard prod. The guv'nor would be all right about it, though – he wasn't one to stand on ceremony. *Never be afraid to tackle the top man, Phelps*, he'd said once. *Just make sure you smooth out any wrinkles before you leave . . .*

“Thank you, Father Abbot. I hope you didn’t mind me asking. You understand that we have to be thorough.”

Boniface inclined his head. “It’s what I would expect, Sergeant.” The abbot leaned forward so that his face caught the desk lamp’s low light, and Phelps repressed a shudder.

“I want this man caught as much as you do, Sergeant Phelps. I want the *Titulus* found, but I want you to exercise the maximum discretion in your dealings with my monks and the school. Is that understood?”

Phelps produced his winning smile. “Absolutely. Glad we understand each other, Father Abbot.”

Phelps took his leave. He was glad to be out in the daylight.

Chapter 5

Moran was tired. Whenever he sat down he couldn't be sure of remaining conscious. In the overheated surgery waiting room he didn't reckon on lasting more than a couple of minutes at most. He tried to keep his mind busy; God knows, there was plenty of thinking material now the body count had gone up. And this time it was a celebrity – just the ticket to gain maximum exposure. John Vernon, the entrepreneur – friend of politicians, pop stars, writers. Vernon's face was all over the papers on a regular basis. And it would be tomorrow as well, but for all the wrong reasons: he'd been found in his hotel suite with a knife wound in the throat. On Moran's patch. The publicity would be lavish, the progress of the case closely scrutinised. Which was all well and good if Moran cracked it, but if he failed . . .

His eyelids were drooping when his name was called.

"How are you getting on?" Dr Purewal asked in her businesslike way. She was a strikingly pretty Asian woman in her early thirties. Moran liked her direct approach a good deal better than Dr Forsyth's; the practice head was an old-school medic who insisted on skating around his diagnosis like a reluctant *Dancing On Ice* contestant. At least you knew where you were with Purewal.

"Badly," Moran said. "I can't keep awake. Can you prescribe me something stronger than caffeine?"

She was on him like a predator, torch flashing in his eyes, fingers probing his damaged skull. Her perfume had a musky, primal scent. Moran found himself aroused by it, and shifted his weight self-consciously.

"You had a very serious head injury. It'll take time." She clicked the torch off and returned to her chair.

"It's been months. The headaches have stopped, but at least I knew where I was with them. This – well, it makes my job even more difficult."

She looked up from the screen and tapped a painted fingernail on the desk. "I imagine it does." She pursed her lips and made a clicking sound with her palate to accompany her drumming finger.

"What? Is there something else wrong with me?"

Dr Purewal sighed and crossed one slim leg over the other. "You may have a condition called narcolepsy. It's not that common, but it can occur after a serious head trauma."

"Terrific. Will it get better?"

"Only time will tell, I'm afraid."

She began to tap the keyboard, transferring the consultation to cyberspace. "Alcohol?"

"No." *Not much, anyway . . .*

"Good." Dr Purewal gave him a hard look. "Now then, Chief Inspector, I can give you something to help, but the best thing you can do is listen to your body. The brain is a very sensitive organ, the least understood of all. If it needs time out to repair itself, you'd do well to listen to what it's telling you." She returned to the keyboard, her articulate fingers dancing on the plastic keys.

"But I can't just carry on randomly drifting off to sleep. And I'm in no position to take 'time out'. It's damned inconvenient."

Dr Purewal stopped typing. "More inconvenient to be dead, I'd have thought, which you nearly were." She showed her perfect teeth in a sympathetic smile.

Moran sighed. He couldn't argue with that. And talking of death, he had two murders to solve. He thanked Dr Purewal, took the prescription and the smile with him, and left.

"Drop me off here, Constable, please."

"Are you sure, sir? It's a good mile's walk up to the abbey from here." The pretty WPC wrinkled her nose.

"I'm quite sure, Constable. The country air will do me a power of good." *And it might keep me awake for a few hours.*

"Well, if you're *really* sure."

"Sure." Moran got out, waved her off and buttoned his overcoat. It was turning colder, and the forecasters had promised snow before Christmas. Moran didn't put too much store in that prediction, but right now the Berkshire wind cut like a knife. He should have knocked off and had an early night, but truth be told, he didn't have the energy to deal with his brother. He needed time to think. A thought occurred to him – he didn't have to face Patrick tonight; he could spend the night at the Abbey, doss down in the sacristy. Why not? All the thinking time he needed and he could recommence his planned interviews first thing. Moran stamped his feet, threw his scarf around his neck and made for the foot of Charnford Hill.

"Inspector?"

The voice stopped him short. He turned. Holly Whitbread was standing in the car park of 'The Angel'. She waved her arm in half-greeting, half-invitation.

Moran returned the wave. He hesitated for a second and then found himself walking towards her. He had questions for Ms Whitbread, too.

"Hello, Inspector. Can I give you a lift to the abbey?"

"No. No, thanks. I'd decided to walk anyway." He felt tongue-tied, like some sixteen-year-old on a first date.

"Well then, a drink first, perhaps, to fortify you?" Her eyes twinkled mischievously.

"I'm on duty, strictly speaking."

"At this time of day?" She clicked her tongue. "I suppose a policeman is always on duty."

"Especially when there's been a murder." Moran watched carefully, looking for her reaction.

Holly bit her lip. "Yes, I heard. It's just – unbelievable."

"Murders usually are." Old news, then. So much for the school's spin doctors and their 'sudden death' tack . . .

"Just the one? I'd appreciate the company." Holly shivered. "They have a real fire in the lounge."

Moran felt his resistance collapse like a pack of cards. "Just the one, then."

Holly gave a little smile of triumph. "My round, Inspector."

She took his arm and Moran felt a thrill of pleasure. *Strictly professional? Who am I trying to kid?*

The lounge was warm and empty. Moran ordered an apple juice and a glass of Chardonnay. As the bored barmaid went about her business Moran watched Holly remove her coat and scarf and sit down by the log fire. The flames highlighted the redness of her hair as she settled to await her press-ganged policeman. So strongly did she evoke the spirit of Janice that Moran felt momentarily paralyzed and only got a grip when the barmaid returned with his order.

"So," Moran smiled as he set the drinks down. "What brings you here?"

"I was just popping in for some cigarettes, actually." She wrinkled her nose again. "Bad habit, I know. Can't seem to shake it off, whatever quack remedy I try."

"I sympathise," Moran said. "It took me months. Actually I'm still in the throes of withdrawal." He took a sip of his drink and grimaced at the sweetness. Scotch would have hit the spot right now. "What I actually meant was, what brought you to England, to Charnford?"

"Oh. I see." Holly laughed. "I'm sorry. Well, it's very mundane, really. I lost my job in Cork. I was working as a counsellor – with young adults, mainly – but I have a teaching qualification, and my cousin knew someone at the abbey. I got to hear about the vacancy and thought it would be a good chance to live here for a while and see how a modern monastery functions."

"Two birds, then," Moran smiled.

"Yes, I suppose so." She sipped her wine. "I'm a bit of an anorak when it comes to things like that."

"I'm sorry?"

"Well, you know. Unusual institutions, modern monasticism, how the monks apply their learning and their faith. I'm fascinated by it all."

"I'm sure there's a great deal to discover," Moran said. *Including how they go about protecting their secrets, murdering their colleagues, and . . .*

"But I'm very dull," Holly laughed. "I'm sure a policeman's life is much more exciting."

"It can be." Moran hesitated. "Sometimes 'dull' sounds very attractive." He smiled. "It's pretty routine most of the time, to be honest."

"I can't imagine solving a murder is particularly dull," Holly said, lowering her eyes. "I'm probably not supposed to ask this, but how are you getting on with your investigation?"

Moran wanted to tell her everything. About his permanent exhaustion, his drunken brother, the chief constable. The way Archie was eating him out of clothing. The fact that he couldn't get a straight answer out of anybody at Charnford Abbey.. Instead he said, "Well, these things take time." And hated himself for the blandness of the statement.

"Yes. Yes, I'm sure they do." She looked up. "I don't suppose there's any – danger, is there? I mean, you don't think the killer will strike again?" Holly grinned and flushed with embarrassment. "Will you listen to me – that sounds so dramatic, doesn't it? Like some awful TV drama."

Moran gave a short laugh. "Well, it's hard to say. Until we've established a motive, anything is possible."

"Oh. God. That's scary." Holly ran her thumb down the side of her glass. "But you're around, aren't you? So that makes me feel safer."

Moran wanted to reach over and embrace her. The pale skin on her forehead was covered in light freckles. It made her seem vulnerable, like a child. He cleared his throat. "Yes, we've set up an incident room in the chapel sacristy. It means I can keep an eye on things. But I have to tell you–" he leaned back in his chair and shook his head. "It's not the most comfortable room I've used – not by a long chalk."

"A woman's touch – that's what's lacking." Holly smiled broadly. Her teeth were white and even, and there was the finest layer of down on her upper lip. He noticed that her nose had the slightest upturn at its tip. Moran felt a huge wave of desire and gripped his thigh beneath the table.

"Monks are charitable enough," Holly went on, "but when it comes to home comforts . . . "

Moran grinned ruefully and took a final swig of his drink. "Yes, sadly lacking."

"Can I tempt you to another?" Holly produced a leather purse and inserted two slim fingers into its folds. "Go on." She flourished a ten pound note.

Moran held up a hand in protest. "No, thanks. I'd love to, but–"

"Duty calls, right?"

He laughed. "Right."

"Well, till next time, then." Holly raised her glass.

"Until then."

The air outside was cold. Moran drew his coat around him. If he'd been a betting man he'd have put money on the fact that it was more than a job offer and the chance to indulge in a little monk-spotting that had brought Holly Whitbread to Charnford. Whatever the reason, he was struggling to reconcile competing feelings of elation and foreboding.

As he began the slow slog up Charnford Hill he could see the lights of the monastery twinkling in the blackness, like the eyes of a wolf pack waiting to pounce on their prey.

Chapter 6

"How'd it go yesterday?" Moran rubbed his cheeks with both hands, feeling the stubble scratch against his flesh. "Did you get to the Cardinal?"

Phelps rolled his shoulders inside his ill-fitting suit. He looked as if he were about to burst out of the straining seams like some kind of Battersea Incredible Hulk. Moran wondered why his sergeant didn't shop at High and Mighty; financial constraints, maybe? A sergeant's pay was manageable for a single man, but had to be a stretch for a family. Moran hoped Phelps' kids didn't take after their dad as far as stature was concerned – he'd be bankrupt by the time they hit their teens.

The sergeant pulled up a chair and eased his large frame onto the slatted seat. "Not yet, guv. Every time I try and pin one of 'em down they're off to some ceremony or another. Matins, is it?"

Moran raised an eyebrow.

"Well, something like that, anyhow," Phelps went on. "They all troop off to the big church, and that's it for hours on end. You can hear 'em singing. Gives me the willies." Phelps shivered. "All that chanting and the like."

"*Plainchant*, Phelps. It's called plainchant." Moran had heard enough of that at Blackrock. Mixed memories of comradeship and the cane. Strange days . . .

"Plain or fancy, guv, it still gives me the creeps with a capital C."

Moran smiled. "I know what you mean. You should try spending the night here."

"That reminds me, guv. The big man's after you. Wants you to give him a bell. He's keen to get an update, especially about Vernon."

"I'm sure he is. He'll have to wait for the autopsy. And Forensics." And that was not all Lawson would be after, Moran thought. He'd be waiting on Moran's doctor's report. More bullets for the retirement gun. Well, he could damn well wait.

"He wondered why you've set up the IR onsite." Phelps gingerly fingered a spot on his neck that, in his hurry to get an early start, he had inadvertently drawn his razor across.

"Did he?" Moran stood up and pulled on his jacket. "Well, our beloved chief will just have to wonder." Moran felt shaky with fatigue. His dreams had been filled with bizarre scenes in which his brother, Holly Whitbread and the abbot vied for starring roles. He had woken in a cold sweat at five, convinced that someone had been in the sacristy while he tossed and turned. But the door was locked, the hair seal he had placed across the door frame intact.

Ridiculously, Oswald's ghost story had played on his mind, and alone in the sacristy his imagination had taken over. Eventually he had fallen into a fitful sleep, and when he awoke something was on the table that hadn't been there the hour before. Sitting on top of his pile of papers was the relic. Thoroughly spooked, Moran had locked it in the drawer to give himself time to decide how to respond; the *Titulus* had been clandestinely returned, but by whom – or what – he had no idea.

Clearly someone was trying to tell him something. Or perhaps ask him something? Had it been passed to him for safekeeping? Or for some other purpose? Whatever the reason, here was an opportunity to establish exactly what he was dealing with; a quick call and it was sorted. If anyone could declare the artefact fake or genuine it would be Reading University's Professor of Archaeology, Charles Sturrock. Moran also trusted Charles' discretion, and he needed plenty of that right now. After some thought he had elected not to share his acquisition with Phelps; for all he knew, that knowledge might be a dangerous thing.

Moran tried to stretch the stiffness out of his aching back and groaned. He glanced in the full-length mirror and wished he hadn't. He looked as bad as he felt.

"I need a coffee, Phelps. Then we'll see how Forensics is getting on – I hear the dulcet tones of TVP's finest diggers and scrapers."

"Anything of interest?" Moran bowed his head to avoid a sharp projection of stone above the vault entrance.

"Possibly," a white-suited female officer replied in a tone that suggested a reluctance to suffer interruptions, even from a senior officer.

"Prints?"

"Afraid not. The surfaces in here don't lend themselves to prints. Wood, rough stone. No good."

Moran heard a muffled curse as Phelps' crown made contact with the low ceiling. The Forensics officer straightened from her bent posture. "But we have found something." She jerked a thumb. "In the chapel. More bloodstains."

Moran raised his eyebrows. "Did you, though? Show me."

They followed the Forensics officer to the rear of the chapel where a small window had evidently been forced. The stone sill bore traces of dark brown stains.

"Have you got a lab report on it yet?"

"Any time now, sir," the brunette replied. "They said by three."

Phelps was examining the window frame. "Horgan's blood – or the killer's?"

"As soon as I hear, I'll come and find you," she said, a note of impatience creeping into her voice.

They left Forensics to finish up their work in the chamber. Phelps cocked his head as he lumbered along the cloister, his heavy forehead knitted into a frown of anxiety. "An outsider, d'you think, guv?"

"I don't know what to think at the moment, Phelps. What was the murderer looking for? Nothing's been stolen, according to our friend Oswald. At least, not at the time of the murder," he said, thinking of the *Titulus*. His mobile buzzed. "Moran."

"Hello, Mr Moran, it's Kelly."

Moran groped into his mental contact list and drew a blank.

"Kelly, from Happydogz," the voice prompted.

Moran stopped walking and Phelps leaned back on a convenient radiator with a grunt of satisfaction.

"Of course – sorry. What can I do for you?"

"Well, it's just that we were expecting to walk Archie today, but he's not there. We wondered if we'd got the wrong day."

Moran frowned. Not there? Then – he groaned as he put two and two together. *Patrick.*

"Is everything all right, Mr Moran?"

"Fine, Kelly – I apologise. My brother is staying over – he's probably taken Archie out. I should have let you know."

"No problem – we'll come on Monday as usual, shall we?"

"That'd be great. Thanks." He hung up.

"Problem, guv?" Phelps blew on his hands and rubbed them along the radiator's corrugated surface. "I can't believe how flamin' cold this place is."

Moran pocketed his phone. "My brother. He's taken the dog out."

"Bad news?"

"Very."

"I won't ask." Phelps reluctantly disengaged from his new-found source of warmth and fell into step with Moran. "Where next?"

"The linen room, then the headmaster. Oh, and the Cardinal. One each and one up for grabs. Shall we toss for it?"

"I fancy the Cardinal, guv, if that's all right?"

Moran shrugged. "Who am I to question your carnal tastes, Phelps? Be my guest."

The linen room was tucked behind the back entrance to the school, nestling between the tuck shop and the infirmary. Moran went to the counter and, finding no bell, knocked twice on the worn wood. A slight figure in a light blue dress appeared from within.

"Can I help you?"

"I hope so." Moran smiled. "You are–?"

The woman smoothed her dress. "Miss Coleman. I'm in charge of the linen room."

Moran showed her his ID. "I'd like to have a chat about linen numbers, if I may."

Miss Coleman chewed her lip and looked puzzled. "I don't see–"

"I'll explain everything," Moran said in his most reassuring voice.

"Very well." Miss Coleman raised the counter flap and Moran went through.

"Come into my office," Miss Coleman bustled past ironing boards, racks of jackets, piles of sports clothes. "Here we are." The room was small, just a table, two chairs and a cupboard. Miss Coleman invited Moran to sit.

"Thank you."

"What can I do for you, Chief Inspector?"

Moran studied the linen matron. She was fifty-something, maybe older. Her features were spare and angular; a long nose led to a small mouth framed by thin lips. The face was pale, her makeup heavily applied.

"How long have you worked at Charnford?"

"Since 1975. The seventeenth of November."

"I see. And if I gave you a linen number, would you have a record of who it belonged to?"

"Of course."

"You have archive records?"

"Indeed we do."

Moran put his hand in his pocket and produced a piece of paper. He squinted at his note. "F362."

"Oh, that's the old version. We don't use the house prefix any more."

"No? When was the change made?"

Miss Coleman pursed her lips. "That would be when the new house came in. There were three, you see, but they introduced another, Fortescue House, in 1970 I think it was."

"Do records go back before then?"

Miss Coleman raised a long finger. "They do. We'll have a look." She went to the cupboard and withdrew a fat volume. "Here we are. Well before my time, but it's all here." She placed the book on the table, moistened her finger and flicked through the yellowed pages. "This takes us up to the changeover." She looked up enquiringly. "Was there a particular year?"

"The boys go through the school in, what, five years?"

"That's correct."

"What have you got for 60-65?"

Miss Coleman turned the pages. And frowned.

"Problem?"

"The records only go up to F350 during this period. The number was unallocated."

"65-70?"

Miss Coleman bent to her task. And frowned again. "That's odd. Someone's torn the pages out." She placed her palms face down, as if to deny the anomaly. "I'm very sorry, Chief Inspector. I don't know why anyone would have done this."

Moran wasn't surprised. "That's all right, Mrs Coleman. Thanks for your help."

As he made his way to the head's office, Moran consoled himself with the thought that, at the very least, they now had a rough timeframe to work with.

Father Aloysius Strickland was a choleric little man with cheeks like an overfed hamster. His eyes were bright buttons, pinpricks of intelligence in the overripe plumpness of his vein-infused face.

"The restrictions will be lifted very soon, I trust?" Father Aloysius shifted papers around his desk nervously. "Jolly hard to keep a lid on this sort of thing – normal life must be resumed as soon as possible you understand, Inspector Morane."

"Moran."

"Of course." The little man bobbed his head. "We have parents to show around – an intake of new boys next term – only a few, you understand, but nevertheless if the parents get wind of, of –"

"I do understand, Father." Moran felt some sympathy for the headmaster. Times were hard, and a murder wasn't an ideal addition to the school prospectus. "My sergeant tells me that the school has been struggling financially."

"Struggling, yes, quite so." Aloysius articulated the word with distaste. "But we soldier on. Our reputation is second to none, you see. Second to none. Well, apart from Ampleforth, Downside and so on – but they are much larger schools, Inspector, much larger."

"They could ride out a scandal, you mean."

"Well. Yes, I suppose so."

Moran leaned over the desk. "But this is more than a scandal, Father. A man has been killed. And so far there appears to be more concern over the future of the school than with the abruptly terminated life of Father Horgan." Moran sat back to let his words take effect. "Now, why is that, I wonder?"

Aloysius adopted an attitude of studied concentration while the beginnings of a frown bisected his bushy brows. "Father Horgan," he murmured, as if to prompt himself to accurate recollections of the dead monk's character. "Not an easy man at all, I'm afraid."

"Unpopular?"

"Yes, in many ways, I believe so. Very capable – don't misunderstand me – he was a housemaster in his heyday, you know. Harder job than mine ... and latterly he excelled as the school librarian and archivist. But those boys–" the monk shook his head, clearly agitated. "The boys are members of his old house. Odd, all very odd."

"Boys? What boys?"

"They're missing, you see." Father Aloysius rubbed his forehead distractedly. "Two roll calls. That's too many," he added, half to himself. "Far too many to–"

"What?" Moran was dumbfounded. He sat forward in the leather-upholstered chair he had been ushered into a few minutes earlier. "Are you telling me that you have missing boys? How many? How long?" Moran felt his temperature rising. "Why haven't I been informed?"

"I wasn't sure – if it was pertinent to your investigation – a distraction, perhaps, might have been unhelpful, that sort of thing–" Aloysius trailed off.

Moran had left his chair and was standing by the window overlooking the monks' garden. A naked apple tree held court over the carefully tended lawn, bare branches swaying as a gust of wind chased dead leaves around the walled perimeter. Keeping his voice even with a huge effort, he turned to face the headmaster.

"I want names, ages, details. When they were last seen. Who with. Friends, enemies. Likes, dislikes. *Everything*. As soon as possible." He spun on his heel and grabbed the door handle. "What sort of a place is this, headmaster? I've heard of closed ranks, but Charnford really takes the biscuit. This is a murder investigation, not a temporary inconvenience. What about the parents? Have you informed them?"

"Just about to when you knocked." Aloysius gave the telephone a covert glance. "Quite right, about time I did." He reached for the instrument, but Moran had already departed in a paroxysm of repressed anger, having narrowly resisted the temptation to slam the door behind him.

Phelps strode purposefully down the path that ran alongside the monks' cloister leading to the abbey church and the playing fields beyond. He could see his target in the distance, walking slowly with hands clasped behind his back in an attitude of relaxed and leisurely exploration of the monastery and school grounds. Right, Phelps thought. Got you at last, Señor Vagnoli, or whatever your name is. The guv'nor was checking out John Vernon's hotel room – good job he'd had a reason to get away from Charnford for a bit. Phelps shook his head ruefully as he walked. The guv would have gone up in smoke otherwise. He'd never seen Moran so angry.

There was something about this place that made the investigation almost impossible. *Like wading through treacle*, Moran had spat in irritation after his interview with the head. Two missing kids, and not a peep until now. Unbelievable. Phelps was getting the distinct impression that the monks considered themselves above *all* earthly things, including co-operation with the police, the exercise of common sense; the ability to take a murder seriously . . . it was exasperating, to say the least.

Moran had told him to take a hard line – gloves off. Phelps lengthened his stride and thrust his hands further into his coat pocket. His breath formed clouds in the chill air as he narrowed the distance between himself and Vagnoli. When had it last been this cold in December? He vaguely remembered the winter of 1963, when his uncle had cleared the snow from their drive with two broken pieces of fencing. The snow had lain for weeks. Phelps stole a glance at the overcast sky and shivered. He wondered what sort of accommodation the monks had; he'd read somewhere that they slept in cells. Phelps snorted. If he had his way, he'd chuck the lot of them in the TVP cells until they started to sing a new song, never mind all that plainchant stuff.

A group of boys in rugby gear appeared on the path, tossing the ball to each other in easy comradeship. Their knees were raw with impacted grass and mud, but their spirits seemed high.

"Hello, sir," the tallest boy smiled as he passed. He stopped and held up his hand. The others came to a halt and waited a few paces away. "You don't by any chance have a light, do you?"

"A light?" Phelps was taken aback. "I'm not sure you're supposed . . . anyway, how do you know I smoke?" He drew himself up to his full height, but the boys seemed unfazed. They were respectful, but confident.

"Well, sir," the boy grinned, "it's the cigarette behind your ear that gives it away."

"Behind my–" Phelps' hand shot to his ear. His face broke into a grin. "Right, yes, so there is." He fumbled in his pocket and produced a box of matches. "Here you are. I never gave you these, all right?"

"Thank you, sir." The boy grinned widely and accepted the box. Then his expression changed. "May I ask you something, sir? I mean, you are a policeman, aren't you?"

"Is it that obvious?" Phelps smiled. Of course it was. He'd been at this game too long to look like anything else.

"Well, it's just that we've heard rumours about what's going on, you know? About Horgan – in the chapel – and Montgomery, and Mason. They've gone missing, haven't they?"

The other boys had moved in closer, their eyes echoing their spokesman's question. "Was it the ghost, sir?" one of them asked. He sounded serious, but the question drew shouts of derision from his friends.

Phelps cleared his throat. "No, it wasn't a ghost. But Father Horgan died under unusual circumstances and we're trying to find out what happened. My boss is going to speak to you all at your assembly tomorrow morning. As for your friends, I'm afraid I can't say any more about that at the moment. I'm sure the headmaster will make an appropriate announcement in due course." Phelps doubted that, but what else could he say?

"Oh, they're not our friends. Montgomery's a bit of a tosser, actually. Mason's all right I suppose. Anyway, they're in the year above, and we don't have a lot to do with them, really."

Phelps raised his eyebrows.

"Mason owes me 50p," one of the other boys offered. "Bet I don't see that again."

"Thanks, sir," the spokesman said, giving Phelps a jaunty salute. "Good luck." They continued their journey along the path, passing the ball between them.

I'll need it, Phelps thought as he watched them go. He turned and took one step in Vagnoli's direction, only to stop short with a curse. The cardinal had disappeared. He quickened his pace, but the only signs of life were a couple of straggling rugby players returning to the changing rooms. Not a monk or cardinal in sight.

Phelps' mobile bleeped. He pulled it out and answered testily. "*Yes*? Oh, hello guv. No, not yet. He's done the old disappearing act again." He listened intently. Moran sounded calmer, but there was something in his voice that set Phelps' antennae twitching. "A match?" He moved to one side to allow two trotting boys by – late for afternoon lessons, judging by their expressions. Moran was speaking clearly and slowly – always a sign that something heavy had gone down. "What's that, guv? *Horgan's* blood?"

"For God's sake, stop repeating everything I'm saying, Phelps. Yes, Vernon was stabbed, but traces of Horgan's blood have been found on his body," Moran's voice said. "And it was Vernon's blood on the chapel window – the tests have just come back."

Phelps scratched his head. "So Vernon's our killer?"

"Not necessarily. Whoever killed Vernon could have killed Horgan as well."

"But what was Vernon doing in the Charnford chapel?" Phelps acknowledged a passing monk with a half-wave. The rise and fall of a plaintive organ melody piping from the abbey church hurried the monk on his way.

"That's what you're going to work on, Phelps. What I'd like you to do is get onto BT and Vernon's mobile service provider. I want to know if Vernon and Horgan had a chat recently, because guess what?"

"What?" Phelps groped in his pocket for a cigarette.

"Because Vernon's an old Charnfordian, that's what."

Phelps lit the cigarette with his free hand. “Right. That makes sense. So I’m betting he wasn’t paying a social visit to his old alma mater.”

“Exactly,” Moran agreed. “Blackmail is my guess.”

“Maybe he was trying to hide something.”

“Or steal something – the relic, maybe? Anyway, I’ve got to get on, Phelps. Once you’ve chased up the telecoms people I want you to track down Cardinal Vagnoli. All this kicked off the day he arrived. It probably isn’t a coincidence.”

“Will do.” Phelps drew on his cigarette “You coming back up here tonight, guv?”

“I doubt it,” Moran’s voice said bleakly. “Once I’m finished here I need to check in at home.”

“Got it,” Phelps remembered. “You need to see a man about a dog.”

So, Phelps mused as he re-entered the school through a side door into what he’d heard Moran refer to as the Court of Arches. *Three* bodies. No motive apparent, interviews either inconclusive or elusive. Not a great start to any murder investigation. He found a coffee machine in a corner and fumbled in his pocket for coins.

Sipping his drink, he watched the school ready itself for afternoon study. A bell went off shrilly, causing a final frantic scurrying along the length of the cloister as suited pupils and black-gowned masters closed in on their allotted classrooms. Phelps noticed that a few of the teachers were monks themselves. One studious-looking Benedictine passed him with an air of lofty indifference, a clutch of coloured folders pressed to his habit. Doors closed. Seconds later the cloister was deserted.

How nice, Phelps thought, to have your life ordered by the ringing of a bell. Be here, be there, and be on time. Presto, the day is gone. One last bell for lights out, and nine hours of oblivion before the whole regime starts again at seven thirty. Wonderful. Phelps wished his life was as simple, as structured, but he'd killed off that possibility when he'd joined the force.

Phelps took another sip of coffee. He'd finish his drink, and then, come hell or high water, he'd find that damned Cardinal and give him the grilling of his life. Phelps reached for a cigarette and thought better of it. Later. He wanted to nail this for Moran. The guv had been through a hell of a lot in the past twelve months. It was a miracle he was still alive. Phelps swigged back his coffee with a grimace as he remembered visiting Moran in the ICU. He hadn't given any odds on his survival, but Moran was a tough bastard. Tougher even than Phelps had imagined. He'd pulled through against odds that had been so firmly and hopelessly stacked against him that when eventually he came off the ventilator and gulped his first wheezing, bloody-minded breaths, even the neurology consultant had been spotted shaking his head in amazement.

Phelps scrunched the cup and fired it into a nearby bin. He also knew that Moran's recovery was not complete – not by a long chalk. He could see that, and unfortunately for the guv, so could the Chief. Lawson had been on his case for weeks, asking this, asking that. Did Phelps consider Moran's judgment to be impaired by his injuries? Would he, professionally speaking, be able to trust Moran as before? And what about the dozing off? The lethargy? Surely that was proving a problem?

No, Phelps had declared emphatically. The guv is fine. Just like before the accident. Well, would Phelps be prepared to 'keep an eye' on things? Just to 'keep us all in the loop', so to speak? *No he damn well wouldn't*, had been Phelps' reaction, but he'd just given a quick 'Sir' and departed pronto. The guv deserved better than to be shafted by the likes of Lawson. Especially with Moran's top record. Jobs for the nerdy fast-trackers; that was Lawson' agenda. New policing– 'policing with brains.' My arse, Phelps thought as he strode down the cloister with Vagnoli firmly back on his agenda. The guv was going to crack this one wide open, and Phelps would bend over backwards to make sure it happened. Moran was the best he had worked with. They didn't call him 'The Ferret' for nothing. The guv'd get to the bottom of this, with Phelps' support. *Come on down, Cardinal, it's your lucky day . . .* Phelps whistled as he walked, drawing curious glances from behind classroom windows as he passed by.

Moran thanked the pretty constable for her minicab duties and opened his front gate. A black, bounding shape launched itself at him, paws flailing. He got down on his haunches, chuckling to himself.

"All right, Archie. I'm here now, calm down. Good dog, you're a *good* dog. You found your way home, didn't you? *Good boy*." He fumbled for his keys as Archie excitedly returned to the front porch where he had clearly been waiting for some time. Probably, Moran guessed, since the pubs had opened in the late morning.

No lights on. He went into the kitchen, fed Archie and poured himself a glass of Shiraz. As the lights flickered he caught a movement in the garden, beyond the French windows. He strode to the back door, hit the patio lights and stepped outside. "Patrick?"

He made a swift reconnaissance and drew a blank. Neighbour's cat? Or a fox, maybe. He closed the back door and retrieved his glass. So, what would the story be this time? 'I got to talking to this guy about a job, and you know how it is … we ended up going back to his place, had a few more, you know, Brendan …' and so on, and so on. Moran felt his muscles tense despite the calming effects of the wine. There'd be no reasoning with Patrick when he returned – if he returned.

All Moran's carefully prepared suggestions for Patrick's future inevitably fell on deaf ears – *drunken* ears – so there seemed to be little point in regurgitating the chiropractic idea, the holistic medicine idea, the sports therapist idea . . . any of which his brother was more than intellectually capable of handling. The guy had brains in spades; he just couldn't get his head out of a bottle.

Moran took another sip. Perhaps he was doing the wrong thing, having alcohol in the house. But it was *his* house, dammit, and if he wanted to have a glass of wine he'd have one. Or was that just the Moran family trait of general bloody-mindedness rearing its ugly head?

Moran sighed and patted Archie's head as the dog nudged his leg with a mouth clamped firmly around a ragged tennis ball. Should he wait for the inevitable call? Either the local station or Patrick himself, stoned out of his brains, wandering the streets in search of Moran's house. Or should he just leave him to it, switch off his mobile and turn in? God knows, he was tired enough. But he knew he wouldn't sleep. Oh, he could drift off during the day, no probs, but at night, little prospect. Not with the abbey to worry about; and the murdered celebrity, John Vernon. The fact that both bodies bore similar wounds, as well as the blood matches, meant that the link between the abbey and Vernon was clearly established. That was some small comfort, Moran thought as he reached for Archie's lead and drained his glass. A link in the chain of obfuscation which seemed to be Charnford's specialist subject.

And then there was Holly; he'd come close to making a complete fool of himself in the pub. Had he detected a reciprocal stirring of emotions? Or was it just his memory playing tricks?

Moran groaned himself to his feet. "Come on, boy." He whistled. Archie needed no further encouragement. Tail whipping with excitement, the small dog hindered Moran as he tried to clip the lead to his collar. "Sit *still*, will you?" Seconds passed as Archie eluded his tethering.

"Look," Moran said in exasperation, "this is for *your* benefit, not mine." Finally he trapped Archie's head between his knees and applied lead to collar. As they stepped into the cold air Moran reflected that nothing in his life was easy, not even taking the dog for a walk.

He passed the Six Bells on the corner, dark and silent. No tell-tale sounds of lock-in activity. Archie pulled violently as he spotted a cat idling across the road. Moran held on grimly; for a small dog the spaniel had shoulders like a canine bodybuilder. They turned the corner and Archie's pull became more insistent; he'd spotted the square where Moran would habitually walk him off the lead. It was an old Victorian square, well-tended by the council, delimited by laurels and attractive borders and punctuated with mature trees and shrubs. Around the square were sited several benches, resplendent in recent coats of green paint.

Moran bent and released Archie into the darkness. He found the path, intending to sit for a while as the spaniel burned off his repressed energy. But the first bench was occupied. As he approached, Moran recognised the familiar contours of Patrick's thin and undernourished body. It was bitterly cold, but Patrick was wearing only a T-shirt and jeans. Moran quickened his pace and, heart racing, felt his brother's cold wrist. There was a pulse, faint but discernable. Patrick stirred and groaned.

"Patrick!" He prodded the prone figure. "Wake up, will you, for God's sake? It's below freezing and you're dossing in the square?" Moran heard the harshness in his voice and took a breath to calm himself. "Patrick!" He shook the inert body, once, twice. On the third shake, Patrick leaned over the arm of the bench and was violently sick. Moran stepped back from the spray. Archie appeared, sniffing the warm mess before licking it tentatively. "No, Archie, *no*!" Moran reached down and clipped the lead to the dog's collar, attaching it to the bench leg by Patrick's feet.

"Brendan? S'at you?" Patrick half sat up.

"It is," Moran replied, tight-lipped. "Luckily for you, Pat, you complete *eejit*."

"There's no need–"

"No need?" Moran hissed. "I leave you in charge of my house and dog, and you go on the razz and lose him? No need? He could have been killed or stolen for all you knew. What were you thinking?"

Patrick sat up, swayed, and grabbed Moran's arm for support. "It was just a quick one, Brendan. I left the dog outside – he was fine, sitting outside the door. I kept an eye on him through the window, honest to God. But, there was this fella–"

Moran sighed. "There always is." It was true; there always was.

"No, really, he's a great lad. From Romania, of all places. Had a bit of bad luck right enough, but a real good sort. We got to chatting, and you know, one thing led to another."

"Did it."

"Serious though, you'd like him." Patrick wrapped his arms around his torso and shivered. "I'm not feeling too great, Brendan, if I'm honest."

"No, I don't expect you are. Come on, I'll get you home."

Patrick rose stiffly to his feet and held fast to Moran's arm. There was a wet patch across the front of his jeans. He stank, the nostril-flaring reek of a liver abused for way too long. Moran felt himself recoil and was instantly ashamed. Patrick was his brother, whatever condition he might be in. With Archie tugging one arm and Patrick on the other they made their way slowly out of the square.

"Patrick," Moran asked quietly, "do you still have the key I gave you?"

Patrick turned his head sluggishly to face Moran. "That's what I was going to tell you, Brendan. It's all right with you, is it?"

The words were slurred, but a cold hand had seized Moran's heart. "*What* is all right with me, Patrick?"

They staggered into Moran's road. The street lights lit up Patrick's face in yellow and blue. A siren ululated somewhere in the distance, faded and was gone. Moran halted their progress.

"I said it would be okay for Mihail to stay a wee while." Patrick's face widened in a drunken grin. "You'll love him, Brendan – by God he'll cheer you up, man. He's a real crack."

Moran's blood froze. "Please tell me you didn't give him your key."

"It's only a wee key." Patrick made the shape of a tiny object with his fingers and guffawed with laughter.

Moran could have hit him. "You mad bastard." He dragged Patrick the length of the street and stopped outside the house. Archie began to bark loudly, recognising his home yet aware that something had changed. Moran gawped in horror at the two burly men watching them from the bay window. The curtains were open and a party was clearly in progress. He could hear the sound of bottles clinking and music blaring from his CD player. One of the men in the window raised a bottle and said something to his friend, who threw back his head and laughed, pointing at Moran as if his return was some kind of huge joke.

Patrick raised his finger and pointed unsteadily. "That's Mihail, right there, sure enough."

Moran's brain was racing. What should he do? He knew about squatters, knew how they operated. But it was usually vacant premises that were targeted. They must have thought it was their lucky day when Patrick turned up. They hadn't had to break and enter; they'd been *invited*, for God's sake. Where did that leave him legally?

Moran reached for his warrant card. He left Patrick leaning on the stone pillar of the gate and slid his key into the lock. It had been immobilised from inside. He rapped sharply on the door. A moment later it swung open and the two men from the bay window barred his entry. He flashed his card.

"I'm a police officer. You'd better clear out right now unless you want a night in the cells."

The door closed in his face. Moran cursed. There was no point in trying to reclaim his property single-handed. He needed help, the right sort of help. He needed to know the small print, and only one person fitted the bill – Kay Kempster, a police lawyer he trusted implicitly. She could quote him chapter and verse on squatters' rights. He didn't want to call her, but he had no choice. The fact that they had some history would have to be dealt with as and when. First, though, he had to sort Patrick out. He punched a number into his mobile. "Taxi please, thirty-one Lorne Street."

Patrick bent double and vomited retchingly into the gutter. Archie circled, sniffing cautiously. Moran dialled again. "Hello? Kay? It's Brendan. Listen, I'm sorry to call so late but I have a wee problem."

Chapter 7

"Ah, DS Phelps. Come in," Lawson beamed. "Take a seat."

Phelps did as he was bidden, wondering in his usual suspicious way what could have prompted such a cheery disposition in the notoriously moody chief constable at this hour of the morning.

"Coffee?" Lawson indicated the tray and percolator positioned invitingly on Phelps' side of the desk. A plate of chocolate digestives lay untouched beside the carefully laid out cups, saucers and spoons. Meticulous in every detail, the chief. Even the sodding biscuits were standing to attention. The coffee would be of unquestionable quality, the temperature spot on. But Phelps wasn't in the mood for elevenses just yet. He knew when he was being buttered up, so he signalled a polite refusal and waited while Lawson helped himself, took an appreciative sip, sat down in his leather chair and replaced the cup carefully in its matching saucer, taking care that no errant drips spoiled the gleaming whiteness of the china.

"Well then, Sergeant." Lawson smiled. "Bad business at the abbey, by all accounts."

"Yes sir. A murdered monk, an unmarked grave, two missing boys and now a murdered old boy."

Lawson nodded, a professional frown playing about his temples. "And in your view, how is the investigation proceeding, Sergeant Phelps? I understand there's a clear connection with the Vernon murder?"

"The guv – I mean DCI Moran – is on the case, sir. Vernon's an old Charnfordian – he was in touch with Father Horgan a few days ago. We've just got to establish why, so we're in the process of interviewing the teachers and monks associated with Father Horgan–"

"Associated? I should have thought they were all 'associated', living in the monastery and school as they do?"

Phelps shrugged. "Well, sir, not all the monks are involved in the running of the school. Three are housemasters, and others who teach across the board – 'scuse the pun – during the school week. We're starting with those who would have been in close contact with Father Horgan during a normal school day."

"I see. And is DCI Moran happy with progress so far? I've been trying to get hold of him, but to no avail – you did give him the message, didn't you?"

"Yes, sir. Thing is, the guv is having a spot of bother with–"

"What about these boys? Has he been able to establish their last movements at the school?"

Phelps cleared his throat. So much for empathy. He could feel something inevitable brewing, for which this conversation was just a preliminary formality. He didn't think Lawson was particularly interested in their progress – no more than he ought to be. Rather, he was continuing his ploughing of the Moran fitness furrow, looking for weaknesses that could be exploited. Lawson wanted the guv off the case – off the force, if possible. Was it a natural dislike of the steady Irishman that motivated Lawson's campaign? Or a preference for new blood, a response to pressure from on high?

"I'm interviewing the sixth formers closest to the missing lads tomorrow morning, sir. We'll soon flush out any secrets. It's probably some stupid runaway thing, I imagine. I very much doubt if it's linked to Horgan. If it is, I'm sure the guv will nail it before the weekend."

Lawson nodded, lips pursed, as if weighing the likelihood of a Moran success. "Yes, yes, I'm sure. Now then, Sergeant Phelps, I know you're very attached to DCI Moran, so you mustn't take this the wrong way." Lawson took another sip of coffee, smacked his lips and brushed an imaginary mote of dust from his razor-creased trousers. As if on cue there came a confident knock at the door. Phelps frowned. Now what? A sinking feeling flushed down from his throat to his bowels. *Gordon Bennett – he's taken the guv off the case . . . he's really done it . . .*

"Ah, splendid." Lawson bounced to his feet and strode across the room to welcome the newcomer. "Sergeant Phelps, this is DS Gregory Neads. He'll be needing a briefing from your good self before lunchtime."

"Pleased to make your acquaintance." Neads offered a wiry handshake. He was tall and very thin, with closely-cropped ginger-blond hair and a suit that hung on him like a poorly erected tent.

"A briefing, sir?" Phelps resisted the urge to wring Neads' hand until he screamed. He was angry enough, but he contented himself with a challenging stare. *It's not the guv – it's me. Dumped. And this fancy boy is my replacement . . .* Phelps took a deep breath. Well, at least the guv was still on the case. For now. That would be Lawson's next move, and he suspected that Neads had entered stage right to play a leading role.

"It's nothing personal, Sergeant Phelps. You are a good, solid detective. And I don't just mean your build–"

Neads smirked at the feeble attempt at humour. Phelps could have hit him. "If I may, sir, I know how DCI Moran works. We have an understanding; we get along well, and we have a track record that speaks for itself. I think it would be a big mistake to–"

"Just so, just so." Lawson nodded in a horribly patronising gesture. "But you have to understand, Sergeant, that I am under considerable pressure regarding John Vernon. The man was chairman of my club, for heaven's sake. All eyes are upon me, you see. DS Neads here has a number of – *finer* skills to bring to the table, and as it happens I have one or two things you could help me with, Sergeant, items of an urgent nature. A little tedious, but they need to be picked up. I'm sure you'll do a grand job for me."

Off the case, *and* straight into Lawson's admin backlog. Phelps could have howled with indignation. Instead he gave Lawson a stiff smile and said, "Very good, sir. If that will be all?"

"Yes, yes indeed. Make sure you catch up with DS Neads later this morning. In the meantime–" he smiled ingratiatingly at Neads, "the sergeant and I have several – pressing – matters to discuss."

I'll bet, Phelps seethed. "I'll leave you to it, then, sir." He about-turned and gave Neads a parting glare. He was reaching for his mobile as the door closed behind him. The guv needed to know what was heading his way. Sharpish.

"Kay, I can't tell you how grateful I am." Moran drained his tea and frowned as Archie's fevered barking filtered through from the back garden of Kay Kempster's well-maintained semi.

"Rubbish. If we can't help each other, what good are we?" Kay smiled the easy smile he knew so well. She was still attractive, only the faintest trace of laughter lines creasing the corners of her intelligent, grey-blue eyes.

Moran chuckled. "Okay, but I promise I won't make a habit of turning up at midnight with a drunken brother and a hyperactive dog in tow."

"I *know* you won't." Kay laughed. "But you are *in extremis*, so you did the right thing. And you can stay as long as you need to."

In extremis. Moran shivered as he remembered Sandy Taylor's dry observation in the chapel chamber. There were degrees of *extremis*, he mused, and however inconvenient his current situation, he had to admit that Father Horgan's had been considerably greater.

"Are you all right, Brendan?"

"Fine. Look, Kay, you're an absolute star, but I can't impose on you. I feel bad enough as it is."

"See? There you go again."

"It's Patrick. He's – well, unpredictable. A real handful."

"Is that so?" Kay finished her drink and hooked a long finger through the handle of his mug, whisking the empty crockery away to the draining board. "Well, I'm unpredictable as well, so we should get along just fine."

Moran exhaled deeply. "Kay, seriously, I can't burden you with–"

"You have quite enough to be getting on with, Brendan Moran, without worrying about offending my sensibilities. Now, grab the phone and sort out that eviction order like I told you. Leave Patrick and Archie to me. I'm off till next Tuesday, and I have absolutely no plans except maybe a little late Christmas shopping. When you get those – *undesirables* – out of your house you can invite me over for a drink."

He reached out and gave her shoulder a squeeze. "Thanks, Kay. I don't deserve you, really I don't."

"No, you jolly well don't." She mock-scowled and reached for her coat. "If you can hang on for ten minutes, I'll pop to the corner shop and get something nourishing for your brother."

"He'll be as nice as pie when he wakes up," Moran offered. "He won't remember a thing."

"Whatever. I'll sort him out, don't worry," Kay called over her shoulder as she closed the back door with a firm click. Moran heard her footsteps recede and imagined the swinging arms, upturned chin and bouncing hair as Kay attuned her energy to the needs of her new charges. He shook his head. She *was* too good for him. There had been a time in their chequered relationship when he'd almost got to the point of a proposal. Well, perhaps not a proposal, but certainly a statement of commitment of some kind. And then – what? He wasn't sure. Something had not been right. *Yes*, his subconscious whispered, *she wasn't Janice, that's what wasn't right . . .*

His mobile beeped, saving him from the discomfort of further analysis.

"Ah. Phelps. Any joy with the telecoms?"

Moran's face clouded as he listened to Phelps' update. "You have *got* to be kidding."

"Wish I was, guv," Phelps' voice replied morosely. "Murder investigation to paper chase in five minutes. That's how it was. I thought he was laying *you* off at first, but this Neads bloke – just watch him, guv. I don't like the look and feel."

"Right. Listen, Phelps, I'll see what I can do. This is just plain ridiculous. I can't have my senior DS laid off at the drop of a hat." Moran glanced at the clock. He had to get a move on. He had to be at John Vernon's autopsy in forty-five minutes. Damn – he'd have to divert his lift as well. No one knew he was here.

"What's that, guv?" Phelps' voice scraped across the wire.

"Nothing. Just thinking aloud. Listen, I have to get to the autopsy. Sit tight, don't do anything stupid, and I'll come back to you as soon as, all right?"

"Got it, guv. Take care now."

Stoical as ever, Moran thought. But the loss of his sergeant was a serious setback. Lawson was applying the big guns. Well, to hell with him; the CC had better be prepared for a return of fire. Moran called for a car and shrugged himself into his coat.

Kay breezed into the room and dumped a bag on the table. "Everything in order?" she asked brightly, "oh, I got Archie some breakfast as well." She pointed to two tins on the drainer.

"Kay–"

"I know, I know. Now, get going."

"I'm already gone. See you later." He bent forward and gave her a kiss on the cheek. She responded with a tight little smile that made him feel awful. She still carried a torch, then, however low it had burned. No time to think about that now. He looked in on Patrick, sound asleep in the spare room with his mouth open. *All right for some, eh, Pat?*

Moran wrinkled his nose as Dr Moninder Bagri selected a wicked-looking length of steel and surveyed his audience. The path lab was chilly, colder still than the biting December wind that had cut through Moran like one of Dr Bagri's surgical instruments on his way into the building. But this shiver of anticipation, he knew, was a normal reaction to the imminent exposure of a human being's internal workings. How many autopsies had he attended? A hundred? Two hundred? It made no difference. He still experienced a conflicting mixture of emotions as another violently curtailed life was laid bare before him.

"All ready? Good. Off we go then," Dr Bagri announced cheerily to the assembly. He was a small man who reminded Moran of a more robust version of Mahatma Gandhi. Bald pate, round glasses, a ready smile and a clear passion for his job – which he was damn good at. Many times he had surprised Moran with the close attention to detail that he regarded as an essential part of his work. If anyone could provide the clue he was looking for, it was Moninder Bagri. Moran tried to relax and pay attention. Next to him a student pathologist was shuffling her feet, wetting her lips in preparation. Moran knew what was going on in her head. *Don't faint. Don't show yourself up. Concentrate. It's only a dead body.*

On Moran's left, DS Gregory Neads hovered impatiently, a faint smile doing little to offset an expression that was bordering on arrogance. Moran had taken an instant dislike to the tall, elasticated twenty-something when he'd introduced himself earlier in the day. Phelps had been right on target with this one; he had 'Chief Constable's man' written all over him.

"Fine figure of a fellow." Dr Bagri appraised the corpse. "A bit of an athlete in his time, wouldn't you say, Chief Inspector?"

"Yes, he was," Moran agreed. "First Fifteen captain, First Eleven captain, captain of cricket, triple jump county record holder. I could go on."

"You see, my friends?" Dr Bagri waved his cutter in an expansive gesture. "First point of observation: stand away and note the obvious. When we get into all the details you may forget to look for what is clearly before your very eyes."

The student gave Dr Bagri a weak smile. Moran wondered when she would fall. It was only a matter of time. He shifted his weight slightly, ready to catch her.

"A common end for all the rich and famous, just as we, the poor, will also go the same way." Dr Bagri bowed his head for a moment. "Mr Vernon is well known to us, with his picture in the papers and all that. We may have formed opinions about him, but these we leave aside now, as all human life is sacred, is it not? And so it must be accorded the greatest respect."

Moran was used to this little ritual. He found it rather comforting, not to say appropriate. He hoped that he would be given similar treatment by whatever pathologist got to slice him open when the time came. DS Neads, however, was apparently not of the same view. He cleared his throat theatrically and sighed whilst simultaneously contriving to shuffle his feet.

Dr Bagri looked up and met Neads' insolent expression with a steely one of his own. "Just a moment, my young friend, that's all; *then* we make a start, isn't it?"

Moran repressed a smile. Bagri was used to dealing with younger grades in his own, and other, professions. He was glad not to have been on the receiving end of such a withering look. But the doctor was now scrutinising the gaping neck wound, gently probing the ragged flesh for signs of foreign matter that Forensics may have missed. A faint, cloying smell arose from the table as the little man worked, inspecting every centimetre of John Vernon's neck and shoulders with his usual pedantic diligence.

"Serrated implement, like a carving knife, we can determine," Bagri announced. "Most likely the cause of death. Until we open up we won't be one hundred percent sure, though, isn't it?"

There was a general murmur of assent. This was the moment. Moran took a breath.

"So, an incision just at the top of the shoulder, and moving down towards the sternum." Dr Bagri worked quickly, his small brown hands moving skilfully across the corpse's white flesh. "And so, down past the belly button, excuse me sir, and there–" The doctor stood back to admire his work. "Good. You observe there is very little bleeding. No cardiac forces at work, isn't it?. Next, the removal of the rib cage."

Moran's mouth was dry, but he'd seen this too many times to be affected physically. He watched with interest as Bagri sawed away the chest plate and lifted it clear to expose Vernon's internal organs. "And there. All in the open. Oh–"

Moran stepped rapidly aside as the student bent double and emptied the contents of her stomach over the sterile floor.

"A cup of tea and a sit down for five minutes. You'll be right in the rain afterwards," Dr Bagri told the retching girl. "Off you go."

"I'm sorry," she muttered as she staggered, hand over mouth, towards the exit. Moran glanced at Neads whose colour was pale, his lips a thin line.

"Nothing odd so far, Dr Bagri?" Moran asked, more to push the investigation onwards than anything else.

"No, Chief Inspector. All normal and ship-shape, apart from the neck, of course."

Thirty minutes later each of Vernon's internal organs had been given a careful assessment and declared to bear no unusual signs of trauma.

"So we're back with the knife wound," Neads said, in a voice that suggested that the last forty-five minutes had been a complete waste of his time.

Dr Bagri stepped away from the table "Five senses we have, young man." He held up his hand. "Most of these we need to make an assessment. Today, I have used four, though perhaps you will not have seen me do so. And I have found nothing untoward, as you say, apart from the trauma on the neck. He was a fit man, no problems with his fine body." A smile broke across Bagri's features. "But you know, I have a very acute sense of smell. It is my best gift to my profession." The pathologist moved in closer and sniffed the corpse's neck, as if savouring some lingering perfume. Neads wrinkled his nose in distaste.

Moran's excitement was mounting. The show was almost at an end, but Bagri would not be denied his finale.

"Come. Come." The little man gestured.

Moran obliged, gingerly moving his head so that the tip of his nose was centimetres away from Vernon's ruined throat.

"Good Now, tell me. What do you smell?"

Moran tried to concentrate, to sift out the conflicting odours of the pathology lab. He shrugged. "I give up."

"We will take a sample, hm? Then we shall see if I am right."

"Spill the beans, Dr Bagri, please."

Bagri beamed. "The beans will be all over the floor in a short moment! Now, the assailant was a fastidious person, for sure. He has cleaned his weapon very well before use. Too well, perhaps, for his own good."

Moran grunted. A clue, at last. "Knife polish? Is that it?"

"Just so." Bagri gave a slight bow. "We will find out the brand, and you can look for the person who uses this polish. It has a distinctive nose."

"And so do you, Dr Bagri." Moran extended his hand. "Once again, my thanks."

"Like a connoisseur of fine wine, isn't it?" Bagri chuckled and pumped his hand vigorously.

"But I noticed you used the word 'assailant', Dr Bagri," Moran smiled, reclaiming his hand. "And I know you are a man who chooses his words with extreme care. Would you be so kind as to explain why you used the word 'assailant' and not 'murderer'?"

Bagri chortled and wagged his finger. "You know me too well, Chief Inspector!"

Neads raised his eyes to heaven. Bagri's *modus operandi* was evidently trying his patience to the limit.

"Observe." Bagri bent and raised the flap of Vernon's neck like a piece of choice fillet. "A serrated wound here." He indicated the ragged strips of flesh. "But here, a little further along, a smooth cut, like a dissection, you see?"

"You're saying there were two weapons involved?"

"Without a doubt. One, the serrated cut, probably life threatening but not fatal. The other, the smooth cut, has severed the windpipe. Let us see if anything is within, shall we?"

"Within?" Moran peered over Bagri's shoulder.

"Just a small moment, just here – ah." In a few seconds Bagri had winkled out a tiny shard of metal and held it up triumphantly in his forceps.

"You are a *marvel*, Dr Bagri." Moran was elated. "Neads, down to the lab with this, first priority."

"Sir." Neads was paying full attention now, the look of contempt replaced by one of grudging respect.

Bagri wasn't finished. "And look here–" Bagri stretched out Vernon's arm, opening the fingers. The palm was cut and ragged. "The serrated edge has caused these. Same on the other. Defence wounds, I am thinking. So, the clean cut to the neck was a surprise for Mr Vernon, I would propose. Not so the other."

Moran nodded. "So, DS Neads; two assailants it is."

"But only one murderer, isn't it?" Bagri beamed.

"We're obliged, Dr Bagri, as ever." Moran inclined his head respectfully. "I'd be most grateful if you would bear Mr Vernon's injuries in mind when you tackle our other victim. I expect there will be similarities. And Father Horgan's brethren are anxious to conduct the funeral service, so . . ."

Bagri inclined his bald head and removed his gloves with a practised snap. "It will be my pleasure, Chief Inspector Moran. All will be attended to most quickly.

The holy man is next on my list. And of course, you will be the first to know my findings."

Moran turned to Neads, who was trying to conceal a cynical expression and failing. "Come on then, Sergeant. You can show me the proper way to conduct an investigation – I can see you're dying on your feet. Better leave before Dr Bagri gets his hands on you, eh?"

As they left the lab the echo of Moninder Bagri's rich chuckle followed them all the way to the car park.

"Any thoughts, DS Neads?" Moran asked as they made their way across the rammed parking lot. If someone could invent a way of stacking cars on top of one another they'd make a mint – and make life less stressful for patients and relatives too, Moran thought irritably.

Neads swung his key ring as he walked, a habit Moran found particularly irksome. "Actually, yes. A few – sir."

"I'm listening."

"Okay – well, we know that Vernon was injured in the chapel, and the wounds on his hands suggest that the damage was done by the serrated knife."

"Good. Go on."

They reached the car and Neads fumbled under the dash for a scraper. He set to work on the frosted windscreen. "He was able to drive back to his hotel, so he probably wasn't fatally injured at that stage."

Moran blew into his hands. "Agreed. But someone was waiting for him. Someone who discovered that his intended victim had already been conveniently injured."

"You don't think the chapel attacker followed him to finish the job?"

"I doubt it – the whole set-up in the chapel has an interrupted feel about it. I think that Vernon disturbed somebody – someone working to an agenda, so our Mr X wouldn't have hared off in pursuit of an injured man."

"Or Miss X, or Mrs X," Neads offered. "Or Father X."

"Yes. All right, Neads. Thank you. What I'm thinking is that if the killer wanted to finish Vernon off, then why change weapons?" Moran shook his head. "No, I think we're dealing with two separate incidents here." Moran got in, shut the door, and scrunched his hands into his pockets. His breath fogged the windscreen. He watched Neads' hand move back and forth across the windscreen, flakes of ice flying from the scraper head.

Neads slammed the door, turned the blower on full and gunned the engine. "So, perhaps Father Benedict came closer to confronting the perpetrator than he realised when he arrived to say Mass – luckily for Vernon. In the meantime, Vernon got out as soon as, leaving his attacker just enough time to make himself scarce." Neads navigated skilfully through the rows of parked vehicles. "We need to check the hotel's CCTV footage, sir."

"We do. Put that on your list, Sergeant. But for now, the lab, then back to Charnford. And while we're there, you can nip into the kitchens and find out what knife polish they use." Moran settled back and shut his eyes. "In the meantime, there's just one thing bugging me."

"Sir?"

"What in God's name was John Vernon doing in Charnford chapel at five o'clock in the morning?"

Chapter 8

Snow was beginning to float from the overcast sky above Charnford Abbey as Neads swung the car into the car park. Moran dispatched his new sergeant to the school kitchens while he made a swift call to Kay. He frowned as he listened to her cultured voice dispensing the news he didn't want to hear.

"The problem is, Brendan, the squatters have to actually force entry for us to serve an eviction order. But in this case they didn't."

"I know, but they weren't exactly invited, either. Doesn't that count for anything?" Moran said in exasperation.

Kay paused. "Well, they were and they weren't. It just makes things a little more complicated." Moran could hear the clink of cutlery in the background. Patrick, presumably, making a good breakfast. That was something to be grateful for, he supposed.

"Your best bet, in my view, is to go and talk to them. Try and persuade them to leave."

"They're not going to respond to persuasion, Kay. Take it from me."

Kay sighed. "No, probably not, from what you've told me. Or you could maybe offer to help them with alternative accommodation – lend them a deposit?"

"I'm not offering them *anything*."

"That's what I thought you'd say."

"Can you blame me?"

"No, of course not. I'd feel the same. Oh, hang on a mo–"

Moran heard Patrick commenting in the background. No doubt he was the epitome of charm today. Until the pubs opened.

Kay's voice returned. "Patrick is offering to speak to them. He said he got on with one of them very well."

Moran gritted his teeth. "Absolutely not. Put him on."

"I'll do no such thing while you're in that mood, Brendan," Kay said sweetly. "I'll pass the message on, okay?"

Moran harrumphed. "Is he giving you any trouble?"

"Not a bit. We're getting along fine."

"Right. Well, that's great."

"Don't be such a stick in the mud. He's very charming," Kay cajoled.

"Of course he is," Moran said. "When he wants to be."

"Just leave him to me, Brendan, all right? Now, I'm going to try and obtain an IPO for you–"

"A what?"

"An interim possession order. But it may be difficult due to the squatters' means of entry."

"I know you'll do your best, Kay. I'm very grateful. I just haven't got time for this."

"I know. Once I've got it sorted I'll call you, okay?"

"Thanks again, Kay. See you later."

Moran checked his watch. Time for assembly. He went into main reception and along the monks' cloister, joining the press of boys as they made their way to the study hall.

Hayward Hall was a lofty-ceilinged, high-windowed room presided over by two enormous plaster statues of the martyr Hugh Faringdon and the Virgin Mary. Double desks were set out facing these stern adjudicators, while in the centre of the hall a tall wooden dais gave a lofty, bird's eye view of any misdemeanours taking place during study periods. Moran took a self-conscious seat on this scaffold-like platform beside the headmaster. The hubbub was worse than some of the press conferences Moran had been obliged to chair over his long career. And, in contrast to these encounters with his least favourite profession, where he habitually relished the opportunity to clash swords with representatives from national or local rags, on this occasion he had to admit to feeling unusually nervous.

Father Aloysius began with an ineffective plea for silence and attention, which was roundly ignored by the school until reinforcements arrived in the person of Father Oswald, wielding a quarter-length cane, which he rapped sharply on the dais leg in support of the head's request.

"Good – thank you Oswald. Now then–" Aloysius began, his plea still making little impression over the barely subdued corporate murmur.

"*Silence*!" Oswald yelled in a voice that would have done a Covent Garden market trader proud. The cane swished and hit the dais again with a sharp crack that made Moran's behind smart at the memory of his own Blackrock beatings. He wondered if the national prohibition on corporal punishment didn't apply within Charnford's walls, or whether the cane was just a useful prop. Either way, the effect was dramatic. A hush fell as though someone had thrown a switch.

Aloysius seized the moment. "As you are all doubtless aware, we have experienced a sad loss. I have with me

Chief Inspector Moran of the Thames Valley Police who will be speaking to you in a moment. I must add that I expect you to give the Inspector and his colleagues your fullest co-operation and support."

A few hands were up. Aloysius waved them away as though swatting a clutch of irritating flies. "You'll have an opportunity to ask questions later. Now then, let us bow our heads in prayer and remember Father Horgan."

During the devotions Moran allowed his eyes to rove around the assembled school, checking out the faces, the winks and nudges. Oswald, he noticed, kept an equally vigilant eye on the proceedings as Aloysius offered up his prayers.

"And now, boys, please give Inspector – *Chief* Inspector Moran your closest attention."

Moran got to his feet and surveyed the upturned faces. "Morning, gentlemen. My name is Chief Inspector Moran. You've probably seen me snooping around over the last few days. First of all, I want to quash any rumours by being absolutely straight with you. Father Horgan was found in the chapel in the early hours of Wednesday morning by Father Benedict and one of your peers. And yes, he died in what we would term suspicious circumstances."

A ripple of interest swept through the hall. Oswald raised the cane and silence fell. Moran moistened his lips. "Now, there is absolutely no reason for you to be fearful for your own safety. We are following a number of leads, but I am satisfied that the perpetrator means no harm to any of you or your peers. It is likely that Father Horgan's death was precipitated by some personal disagreement." Moran cleared his throat. "It may even have been a terrible accident. At this stage I have to be honest with you and say that I can't be certain. However, I can assure you that school life will continue as usual for the last few days of term. Father Aloysius and I would be most appreciative if you would attend to your work, duties and relaxation in the normal way until then."

Moran paused to allow the school to digest his words. As he mentally prepared his next point he looked beyond the open hall doors and the scrum of jostling boys crowding the entrance. A still, observant figure was standing by the notice board of the main cloister. His blood-red habit gave away his identity; Cardinal Vagnoli was evidently intending to keep abreast of developments. Father Aloysius coughed and Oswald looked up at the dais enquiringly. Moran took a breath and plunged on.

"Now, you probably have a thousand questions, and I will endeavour to address these in the time we have available. Anyone want to start us off?" Moran surveyed the anxious faces beneath him. A hand was up at the back. "Yes?"

"Has this got anything to do with Montgomery and Mason, sir? Do you know where they are? Are they in trouble?"

Moran waved his arm to silence the catcalls and name calling – the boy was clearly used to acting as spokesman, and Moran recalled that Charnford was proud of its thriving debating society. It had produced outstanding orators in its time – John Vernon for one. Moran tried to inject a note of optimism into his reply. "We're not certain. At the moment they are still classed as missing."

Another hand, a younger boy this time. "Sir, are we going to miss Christmas?"

More catcalls, this time interspersed with genuine expressions of support for the fourth former, were quashed once again by Oswald's swishing baton. When the noise had died down Moran said, "I sincerely hope not, son. I may well be asking some of you to spend a little time with my sergeant or myself to give us a clearer picture of the life of the school over the last few weeks, but I doubt whether I'll need to keep you here after the end of term. Christmas is safe, all right?"

There was a loud cheer in response. Moran felt a sudden rush of empathy as he watched the raised arms and relieved expressions. With this came a fresh determination to cut through the thinly-disguised veneer of apparent yet ineffective co-operation that had plagued him since the start of the investigation.

As the boys dispersed for their morning lessons he reflected that, in all his years investigating unexpected deaths, this had to be the strangest case by far. The parameters were of a different order. Was he dealing with a crime of passion? Unlikely; the monks were dead to any worldly passion. Greed, then? No. Each had taken a vow of poverty. Pride, perhaps? Doubtful; the Benedictine's pride was, if anywhere, in his compassion to his fellow man. *But they still have sinful hearts, Moran. Don't forget that. You can wear a habit and profess to reject worldly things, but does the soul comply with that request? Or is it still subject to the desires of the flesh?*

Moran watched the snowflakes settle on the windscreen. He could hear plainsong echoing around the vault of the abbey church, carried on the wind to the surrounding playing fields. He levered himself out of the car before sleep caught him unawares and followed the path to the church door. Where better to ambush the good monks of Charnford than on their way out of Benediction?

The church interior was a vast, lofty space brightened by the lightness of the stone from which it had been built. It felt airy and welcoming, quite unlike the sombre, wood-panelled Anglican churches Moran had visited for sundry weddings and funerals over the years. The monks' voices rose and fell with a hypnotic quality, filling the void with an insistent and seductive charm.

The monks were seated at the far end of the nave, facing each other in carved chorister stalls. A scattering of laity sat at respectful distances from each other on the simple wooden seating. The nearest of these attentive souls was Holly Whitbread, her hair gathered into a neat bun at the base of her shapely neck. Moran deliberated for a moment, and then slid into the seat at the end of her row. She acknowledged him with a smile and a downward tilt of her eyelids and he felt his heartbeat quicken. *Come on, Moran, concentrate on the job . . .*

It took a few minutes to identify the gathered community. The abbot was instantly recognisable, even from this distance, and the headmaster equally so. Who else did he need to talk to? The bursar, that was it. Moran wanted updates on the finances; he also wanted to probe deeper into the headmaster's reluctance to act concerning the missing boys. Moran tucked his notebook away. It was going to be a busy afternoon.

The ritual concluded twenty minutes later and the monks fell silent. No one moved. Holly glanced over and motioned that she wanted to join him on the adjacent seat. Moran concurred, trying not to feel absurdly pleased that she had granted even this small intimacy. He grudgingly admitted to himself that the prime subject matter demanding his attention was neither the late Father Horgan nor John Vernon, nor the posse of migrants who had stolen his home, nor even Patrick's rehabilitation, but a teacher of English Literature named Holly Whitbread.

"Hi," she whispered. "I hope you don't think me rude for not joining you earlier. I didn't want to break the spell." She smiled, her clear eyes alert for his response.

"I know what you mean," Moran agreed. "There's something captivating about plainchant. Hypnotic."

"Isn't it?" Holly agreed. "Takes you out of yourself."

"That wouldn't be a bad thing in my case," Moran conceded.

"Oh dear. That doesn't sound good." She inclined her head to one side and Moran caught some subtle fragrance in the small movement of air. He wanted to touch her, to take her hand and lead her away into some idyllic future where murders and monasteries were things of the past, but as the monks began to file towards the cloister that led to the school buildings he made himself stand up. "Please excuse me." He nodded towards the black figures. "I have to catch one or two of the community."

"Oh, well, don't let me hold you up," Holly said. "If you fancy a break later, I'll be doing some marking in the cottage. You could drop in for a coffee?"

"I'd like that very much." Moran tried not to let his exultation show. "See you later, then."

He walked briskly up the aisle and reached the cloister just before the abbot. The procession stopped in its tracks.

"Inspector. Was it myself you were after, or one of the brethren?"

Moran returned a businesslike smile. A thought had occurred to him, an appealing thought which meant an end to the cat-and-mouse games of the last few days. "I'd like to speak to all of you actually, Father Abbot. Each in turn, in the chapel sacristy, starting at four o'clock, at fifteen minute intervals. I'd be obliged if you would draw up a timetable for the brothers. Save a lot of time and bother. We'll start with you, if you have no objection?"

The abbot hesitated. The eyes of the community were upon him. His parchment-like skin gave away no emotion. "Very well, Inspector. I look forward to speaking with you at four."

Moran stepped aside to let them pass.

The abbot closed his study door and stepped into familiar, comforting shadows. He freed his head from its enclosing black cowl and swept a gnarled hand over what remained of his chalk-grey hair. Who had disturbed Fergus? And why? It was an outrage. There'd be trouble for sure, a great deal of trouble.

Boniface moved slowly across the room and sank into his padded leather chair. His back pained him; the choir stalls were not designed for comfort. But comfort had been an elusive companion for a long time. His skin itched and irritated with every movement of clothing; his starched bedclothes rubbed and chafed whichever position he assumed. One got used to it, of course, in a way, but there were days when he longed for the sensation of silk against cool flesh, nights when he dreamed he had sloughed off his seared skin like a snake. And yet he endured – indeed, it was fitting that he did so. The community must be led by example. The Bible decreed that sin must be ruthlessly expunged, and his ruined body was a living example of the mortification of the flesh; that's how he had always dealt with his failings

– even before he had taken the cloth. He was grateful that God had shown him the need to burn away the chaff so that atonement could be made, because his sins had been many. One in particular – a sin of *o*mission, not *co*mmission – a time when he should have acted, should have *done* something. And yet he had not. How different life might have been if during that instant he had *acted.*

Boniface poured a glass of water and sipped it thoughtfully. He had to take care, great care. The contents of the blessed chamber must be restored and the *Titulus* reconsecrated to the community when all this was over. He licked his scarred lips. Yes, that was the right approach. The secret was out, so a little damage control was going to be necessary. But perhaps the knowledge of the presence of the *Titulus* would act as a spiritual incentive to the lives of the brothers.

A problem remained, however: who had removed the *Titulus*? He had an inkling, the ghost of a notion, and if he were to be proved correct it wouldn't be too much trouble to retrieve it – after due punishment had been inflicted, naturally. No, the *Titulus* hadn't gone far, he was sure, so that was one little worry to put aside.

The main issue was poor Fergus. How often he had tended him, quietly, lovingly, sharing fellowship in the quietness of the chamber – like father and son. The abbot smiled, savouring the memories. Such communion over so many years, and not even that interfering so-and-so Horgan had suspected.

Boniface ground his fist into the polished wood of his desk. That dictator had paid for his presumption, although the fruit of that presumption had yet to be ejected from the orchard like the rotten apple it was. Yes, Vagnoli was another priority, that meddler from Rome, hovering in the cloisters like some disease waiting to spread poison amongst the brotherhood. How dare he contemplate the idea of returning to the Holy See with Charnford's most precious relic under his arm? No, it was not going to happen. The sacred *Titulus* would find its way back to its rightful home. He would make sure of that.

The abbot folded his arms in his lap, rocking back and forth to the rhythmic creak of his chair. And Fergus, the dear boy – what monster had disturbed his rest? It had to be put right. The boy would be feeling disoriented, perhaps even angry . . . Boniface quickly downed his water, this last panicky thought spurring him into action. *It's all right, Fergus, I'm coming. I'm coming to find you . . .*

Moran consulted his watch. Seven minutes past four. He hadn't expected the abbot to be late. Should he call Kay while he was waiting? No point; she'd be in touch as soon as she had something. And where the hell was Neads? He hadn't reappeared from his kitchen mission. How hard was it to interview a few kitchen maids? Moran blew out his cheeks and rubbed his hands to get his circulation going. The sacristy was like a fridge. Phelps had been right: there was something about Charnford that seemed to hold the temperature down, as if the abbey were under some kind of Narnian spell. Moran rapped his knuckles on the desk. *Give it a rest, Moran. You'll be seeing ghosts next . . .*

A sharp tap on the door made him jump. "Come in!" His voice thundered in the enclosed space.

The abbot appeared, a quizzical expression stretched across his puckered features. "There's no need to bellow,

Chief Inspector. I apologise for my lateness – I had something urgent to attend to."

"Please, have a seat," Moran gestured.

Boniface inspected the skeletal chair Moran had provided for his interviewees with distaste. That was fine; Moran wanted to meet Boniface on *his* terms this time, out of the comfort zone of his curtained office. It might unsettle the man enough for him to slip up – provided he was withholding information, of course. But Moran was sure of his ground here. He knew when someone was holding back.

The abbot settled himself and folded his arms. "What would you like to know, Chief Inspector?"

Moran studied Boniface before replying. Was he imagining it, or did the abbot seem a little agitated? Whatever he'd been up to had obviously been stressful in some way. "Are you all right, Father Abbot? You look a little flustered." An opening exploratory shot across the bows, just to see what came back.

The briefest look of alarm appeared on the abbot's face before his customary mask of composure descended like an altar curtain. "I am quite all right, Inspector Moran. My duties are onerous and sometimes unpleasant. Forgive me; I had not expected to keep you waiting, but I could not abandon the task in hand to a later hour. All is well now, and you have my full attention."

Moran nodded. "Good. Are you aware that there are two boys missing?"

"I am." Boniface bowed his head. "I have been praying for their safe return."

"I'm sure you have." Moran smiled a smile of understanding. "Not your jurisdiction though, really, is it? More the head's responsibility?"

"Quite so. My role is one of pastoral leadership for the community. There is some crossover with school affairs, but matters of this nature are, as you quite correctly state, the remit of Father Aloysius and other members of the school staff."

"Any connection with Father Horgan's death, d'you think?"

Boniface ran a long finger down the bridge of his nose in a gesture Moran remembered from their first meeting. Was it significant? People gave away so much with their body language; the position of their limbs, the movement of their eyes . . .

"I very much doubt it, Inspector. I can't imagine what sort of connection there might be."

"Let me help you, then. These two boys, let's say, were punished by Horgan for some error of conduct, and they cooked up a plan to get their own back. Only the plan went a bit too far and they killed him. Then, knowing what was likely to happen, they did a runner. How's that for starters?"

The abbot laughed, a scraping, injured sound that set Moran's teeth on edge. "Wildly imaginative, Inspector. No Charnford boy would behave in such a manner. It's not the sort of attitude we encourage." He laughed again, until he was interrupted by a fit of dry, unproductive coughing.

Moran pushed the water decanter towards him and waited while Boniface poured and sipped. "I don't know," he told the abbot as the coughing subsided. "I was a Blackrock schoolboy, and some of the things that went on there would chill the bones of the dead."

Boniface knocked the glass aside with a jerk of his hand. Water flooded the desk and covered Moran's notebook. He pushed himself backwards to escape the deluge.

"Ah! I do apologise, Inspector. Sometimes I experience involuntary muscle contractions. The doctors tell me it will never improve. Perhaps I should have warned you. I hope I haven't spoiled your records?"

Moran was mopping the desk with his handkerchief. Involuntary contraction it might have been – or had he touched another kind of nerve? As he was wringing his handkerchief into the bin Neads burst into the room in a state of excitement.

"Guv, a word please?" Neads hovered, breathing heavily.

So, Moran thought, irritation wasn't the only emotion Neads was capable of expressing. He turned to Boniface. "Excuse me a moment, Father Abbot."

"Of course." The composure was back, the mask firmly in place.

Moran closed the sacristy door and turned on his DS. "What is it, Neads? It had better be urgent."

"It is – *sir*," Neads added as an exaggerated afterthought. "Those missing kids. They're not missing anymore."

"Well, that's something," Moran said, before he caught something in Neads' expression. There was more to come. He folded his arms and waited for the punchline, which Neads was obviously savouring before delivery.

"They're not missing anymore – because they're dead."

"A kitchen maid, you say?" Moran strode along the monks' cloister on his way to the kitchens, Neads buffeting along in his wake.

“That’s right.” Neads managed to sound laconic even at the brisk pace Moran was setting. “Bernadette McBride. She’s in a right state. Says her mate – Maria – was driving a car for some kind of bank job. They never came back, and she passed a burned-out vehicle on her way into Reading the next day. Reckons it belonged to this Maria. Feels guilty as hell because she didn’t talk her out of it.”

“Bank job? Are you kidding? Kitchen maids don’t raid banks, Neads. Are you sure you’ve got it straight?”

“Hard to say, really. Woman’s hysterical. That’s the gist of it, though. And the interesting bit is that the perpetrators were two Charnford boys – lower sixth formers, one James Montgomery and his buddy Stephen Mason. I checked it out with uniform. Three John Does, fried to a crisp. One female, two male. It fits.”

“She was the getaway driver?” Moran halted and stared at Neads incredulously.

“Apparently.” Neads shrugged.

Moran shook his head in disbelief. What a waste. He glanced at Neads for some empathetic reaction, but Neads obviously didn’t share the same view; the DS had sidled over to examine a canvas of some previous prior or abbot.

“For God’s sake, Neads, we’re not on an art gallery excursion.” Irritated, Moran walked on, nostrils flaring as the smell of overcooked vegetables wafted down the cloister. The smell became overpowering as they drew closer to an arched slatted door. “In here?”

Neads nodded, and Moran found himself in a large kitchen where a few white-overalled figures scurried here and there at the command of a squat personage in Benedictine garb. Moran followed the sounds of sobbing which rose above the clatter of pans and plates, and came to a hunched figure in a corner by a chipped enamel sink. He looked around for some indication that the girl was being seen to. Casting a withering eye at Neads, he gently touched the heaving shoulders.

"I'm sorry to bother you – DCI Moran, Thames Valley Police." Moran fluttered his ID, but he might as well have produced a handkerchief and waved that for all the attention the girl was paying. Her head was between her knees and every few seconds her body shook with a fresh spasm of weeping.

Moran got down on his haunches. "Listen – Bernadette – I have to ask you some questions. I'll make it brief for now." He cast his eye around the busy kitchen in frustration. "For God's sake," he shouted above the clamour, "can someone please attend to this woman? Neads – sort her out a cup of tea, would you?"

Neads raised his eyebrows a fraction, did the opposite with the corners of his mouth, and ambled off.

Five minutes later Moran had Bernadette sitting at one end of the top table in the school refectory sipping from a steaming mug that Neads had conjured from the depths of the kitchen. The DS was draped across one of the refectory's long benches, his expression leaving Moran in little doubt that he considered the duties of a tea boy well beneath him. Moran didn't care; his interviewee was stabilising.

Bernadette took another sip of the hot liquid and shivered. "I can't believe it, sir, I just can't."

"Tell us what happened, Bernadette. In your own time." Moran knew from experience that patience was the key. No point in going in with all guns blazing; besides, a relaxed interviewee was more easily caught off-guard.

The girl pursed her thin lips and ran a hand through her short, peroxide bob. She was pretty in a straightforward sort of way, but her reddened complexion told a tale of too many hours slaving over steaming pans. As she spoke she toyed restlessly with the gold ring encircling the index finger of her right hand. Her fingers were stubby and functional, the chipped nails bitten down to the quick.

"It was Maria's idea, really," she began. "She's always been a bit of a dreamer, y'know. Makin' things up, talkin' big about what she's going to do. I suppose we used to encourage her – y'know, just for fun." Bernadette smiled weakly. "Ozzy was always teasin' her, eggin' her on. But I'm to blame too," Bernadette went on quietly. "I should have spoken up when I realised what they were thinking. It was mad. Just mad." She shook her head and pursed her lips, her eyes blurring with fresh tears.

"Ozzy meaning Father Oswald, I take it?" Moran inquired.

"Yeah, that's right. Sorry." Bernadette flashed an apologetic smile, like a thin blade drawn across Plasticine. "We all call him Ozzy."

Moran pressed on. "Tell me about the idea. And the boys."

Bernadette sighed, her fingers busily intertwining with each other and the mug handle as she struggled to control her emotions. "James was the one. Maria always fancied him. She likes the cheeky ones." A sad smile flickered across her face. "And his friend, Stephen, he was quieter but well fit. I liked him from the off. They shouldn't have come to the lodge, but they did. Maria encouraged them. There'd have been all kinds of shit if they'd been caught."

"To the maids' quarters, you mean?" Neads spoke up. "Out of bounds, I suppose."

"Yes. We're all told when we start here. Any carrying on with the boys is instant expulsion for them and dismissal for the likes of us."

"But they still risked it," Moran prompted. Not surprising really – three hundred young males incarcerated with a handful of Irish girls. Bound to happen sooner or later.

"Yeah, but Ozzy thought there was somethin' going on. He moved us out of the lodge to the garret." Bernadette sniffed loudly and flicked away a stray tear with an angry gesture. Moran offered his handkerchief. "Thanks a million." She took it and dabbed at her cheeks. "I'll be all right in a sec."

Neads gave a loud sigh and tapped a staccato rhythm on the table top. He shifted his weight on the bench, leaned back on the table and crossed one leg over the other. Moran half-expected him to start twiddling his thumbs.

"But before that," Moran returned his attention to Bernadette. "James and Stephen came to see you? And you talked, amongst other things, and then Maria just came up with the idea?"

"Not exactly." Bernadette looked up. "James told us that he'd heard a rumour about the way the school was being run. There wasn't enough money to keep it going."

"I see." So, job threats for the maids, nooky threats for the lads. And the answer? A *bank robbery*? The solution certainly cut to the chase, Moran conceded, but what were they planning to do with the proceeds? Leave a sack of money outside the head's office? Pay it anonymously into the Charnford account? He voiced his thoughts. "And what was the plan? How were they going to do it?"

"Maria and I have some contacts, back home," Bernadette said, lowering her eyes. "I said I could probably get hold of a gun if they needed one."

"A *gun.*" Moran let out his breath in a weary sigh. He glanced at Neads. "Any sign of a gun at that RTA?"

Neads frowned. "Not sure – guv."

"Well, get onto it now, and be damn sure when you come back." Moran stared hard into Neads' look of surprise.

The DS got the message. "Oh. Right." He slid off the bench and loped away towards the massive refectory doors, beyond which the sound of impatiently queuing boys could be heard like a low roll of distant thunder.

Moran watched Neads slip out and close the doors behind him. They clunked into place with a resonant *boom* that called to Moran's mind a controlled explosion he had once witnessed in Derry. On that occasion the disposal squad had found the device before it was too late. On other occasions they hadn't been so lucky . . .

"Shall I go on, Inspector?"

Moran started. He realised he had drifted into a half-awake, half-slumbering state. The narcolepsy Dr Purewal had diagnosed was back with a vengeance. He rubbed his eyes. "I'm sorry, Bernadette. Please – do go on."

"I knew someone, you see . . ." she hesitated. "Maybe I shouldn't be sayin'–"

"It's all right, Bernadette. Ireland is well outside my jurisdiction these days." And gladly so, Moran thought. In fact, the past couldn't be far enough away for his liking.

"Oh, well, it's my uncle. He has contacts. You know, with people who know about these things."

"Terrorists, you mean." Moran frowned.

Bernadette looked at her shoes. "I suppose." She looked up suddenly and met Moran's steadfast grey eyes. "But he's a good man really – really he is, Inspector Moran. He doesn't get involved in all that stuff these days."

These days. Moran considered the statement. Disarmament was to be applauded, but you couldn't disarm a mindset. Had anything changed? Moran doubted it. He had first-hand experience of the depths to which human minds could sink; it had often been bad over here, sure, but the atrocities he had witnessed during the Irish troubles were of a different order altogether.

"You won't go after him, then? My uncle?" Bernadette clasped and unclasped her hands. There was fear there, real fear. A moment later Moran knew why.

"And his name, this uncle of yours?" he prompted gently.

A moment's hesitation, then: "It's Dalton. Rory Dalton."

Moran felt as though an icy probe had entered his bloodstream, searching out every corner of his body, freezing the marrow of his bones in paralyzing shock. Dalton. *Rory Dalton.* Wanted terrorist. Never caught. Never brought to trial. No case ever proven against him.

Rory Dalton.

Janice's murderer.

Chapter 9

Moran leaned on the red-bricked wall of the chapel, sucking in draughts of cold air. He bent double, hands on thighs, in an effort to quash the reaction sweeping through his body. *Rory Dalton.* The name rang mockingly in his head. Of all names, why his? And yet there was something inside him that – in contrast to his physical reaction – exulted at the unexpected opportunity to draw a fresh bead on the Irishman's head. This time there would be no evasion, no cover. Moran straightened and exhaled slowly, watching his breath dissipate in the evening chill. Just like Dalton's previous conviction: in the bag one minute, then gone like a puff of smoke.

But not this time . . .

Three insistent beeps from his mobile. He remembered a previous unanswered call. The display read 901. Moran hit the call button, taking steadier steps along the path that ran parallel with the kitchens, his shoes squeaking in the fresh snow. Kay's voice: *Hello Brendan. Look, nothing to worry about, okay, but Patrick's had a spot of bother over at your place. He was adamant that he could talk this chap round. But* – a slight hesitation in her voice – *well, he got roughed up a little. But he's all right, Brendan – nothing I can't sort out. So – don't worry. We'll see you a bit later, okay? Or I guess that you may be staying up at the abbey tonight? Let me know what your plans are when you can, no probs – everything's all right, really. Bye.*

Moran groaned. The auto-operator pressed on: *Next message, message left at . . .* "Get on with it," Moran growled into the handset.

Guv? Phelps here. Moran felt a smile lift the corners of his mouth despite himself. Did Phelps really think he needed to introduce that voice?

. . . bumped into that looker from Forensics half an hour ago . . . Liar. Moran smiled to himself again. 'Off the case' was not a phrase Phelps understood too well. Moran mentally substituted 'made sure I was in the right place at the right time' for 'bumped into…'

. . . She's going to write it all up but I thought, better early than later, right? So anyhow, the deal is, those bone fragments in the chapel chamber? They reckon around forty years deceased. Male. And they found something else – well, weird or what?

Moran could almost see Phelps' worn features creasing in bemusement.

. . . It's a cornflake, guv. You know, breakfast cereal. Shrivelled, but definitely a cornflake. I said, 'what, not a Frostie then?' and she gave me one of them looks, you know. Phelps adopted a cultured accent. '*We measure the sugar content, Sergeant, and I can assure you that the reading is considerably lower than if the fragment had been a Frostie'.* Phelps snorted at this point in his message. *So there you are, guv – thought you'd like to know – bones and breakfast cereal.. Make of that what you will. Oh – one more thing: I checked the missing persons files for that period – no one showing up. So I'm guessing that our bones ain't going to belong to a Charnford boy – the parents would have played hell, right? Would at least have made the local press. But there's zilch. Oh – one last thing – lab report on the*

shard of metal from Vernon's neck. Lab says hunting knife, custom job. They're trying to get a fix on its origins. Uh oh – gotta go, guv – the CC is making a beeline. Cheers for now . . .

From within the school walls floated the sound of feeding and raucous conversation as Moran considered Phelps' report. A missing person who was not missed? What sort of person would fall into that category? A visitor to the abbey, perhaps? A gentleman of the road? Benedictines were renowned for their hospitality, especially to down-and-outs.

And then there was Rory Dalton, the name dredging up a period of Moran's life that he had never been able to bury. Dalton and a gun. And what else? A knife? A *hunting* knife? Moran's head hurt. He longed for an oasis of calm to gather his thoughts. Then he remembered Holly Whitbread's invitation. With this new, appealing, purpose in mind he retraced his steps and made his way through the silent cloisters to the main school gate. Holly's cottage lights twinkled an irresistible welcome. Moran crossed the road and knocked on the door.

"Well, hi!" Holly Whitbread's face lit up with pleasure. Genuine pleasure, Moran noted. That alone made him feel a lot better.

"Well? Are you coming in, or practising for first-footing? You look frozen stiff!" Holly held the door open as a flurry of snow whipped into the cottage. "Quick!"

Moran ducked his head under a low beam and entered a surprisingly large but snug lounge, furnished with a two-seater settee and matching armchair, a low coffee table straddling a butter-brown rug, and neat, cream-patterned curtains shuttering the two leaded windows. It was tastefully but sparsely decorated, the only item of incongruity being a large wooden crucifix, suspended prominently between two exposed beams on the far wall.

Holly followed his gaze. "Comes with the cottage." She smiled apologetically. "Bit gruesome, isn't it?"

It was. The agonised figure of Christ looked down at them beseechingly. Above the head was a representation of the *Titulus Crucis*, the text shortened to *INRI*: IESUS NAZARENUS REX IUDAEORUM – *Jesus the Nazarene, king of the Jews*.

Moran studied the effigy. Was the missing relic the genuine article? He doubted it – forgeries were *de rigueur* in the Middle Ages. The likelihood of something as extraordinary as the *Titulus* surviving into the twenty-first century was remote. Or was it? The abbot had spoken of a similar fragment on display in Santa Croce, a church near Rome. Moran wondered if it had been subject to forensic examination, carbon dating . . . A line of scripture fell into Moran's head unbidden. *Forgive them, Father, for they know not what they do . . .*

He noted that the plaster figure had been designed with something of the reality of Christ's sufferings in mind: here and there across the body's painful topography bones gleamed whitely beneath the tinted skin, facsimiles of the pre-crucifixion scourging Jesus had endured. A picture of Horgan's body came into Moran's head, a bone grasped in one hand, the *Titulus* fragment in the other . . .

"Tea? Coffee? Something stronger?"

Moran tore his eyes away from the crucifix, his mind grasping at something but failing to connect. A drink? He supposed he was off duty in a sense – until he returned to the school premises. The thought of a night in the sacristy made his mind up for him. “Okay, perhaps a small glass of wine, just to warm my stomach?”

Holly smiled broadly. She was wearing a figure-hugging woollen dress, belted at the waist and stopping a good distance short of her knees. Moran found himself drawn to the gap between the hem and the point at which her legs disappeared into a pair of soft leather boots.

“Red or white?”

“Red – if you have it.”

“Shiraz or Cabernet?”

“Shiraz. Please.” Moran inclined his head in appreciation.

Holly disappeared into the kitchen. “Sit yourself down, Chief Inspector,” she called back, her voice accompanied by the clink of wine glasses.

“We’ll have to dispense with the formalities, you know,” Moran replied. “Brendan will be fine.”

“All right – Brendan.” Holly appeared in the doorway with a glass in each hand. The use of his Christian name caused a not unpleasant constriction in his throat. He accepted the glass and resisted the temptation to down it in one.

Holly sat down on the two-seater. She patted the empty seat. “Come on, Brendan, for goodness sake. I won’t eat you.”

“Right. Thanks.” He manoeuvred himself onto the sofa whilst trying to maintain a discreet distance. It wasn’t easy; the sofa hadn’t been constructed with discretion in mind.

Holly crossed one long leg over the other, revealing a generous portion of thigh. She gave him an appraising look. “So, Brendan, what’s shaken you up?”

Moran was taken aback at her directness. "Excuse me?"

"You look awful. What's happened?" Holly playfully cocked her head to one side, waiting for his response.

Moran sighed and aligned his glass carefully on the coaster Holly had placed on the adjacent nest of tables. "What *hasn't* happened may be quicker to answer." And that was the truth of it, he thought wryly.

"Either will do," Holly said brightly. "I'm in no hurry." She flicked a lock of hair from her cheek and settled back on the cushions.

Moran laughed. "All right . . . well, for starters, my house has been commandeered by a bunch of immigrants and my brother's been beaten up trying to sort it out."

"No way!" Holly's hand went to her mouth. "That's awful. Is he okay?"

"As far as I know. It was his damn fault in the first place."

Holly sipped her wine and retained the glass, running her finger along the rim. Her nails were finely manicured, painted a deep red. "Can't you just get your buddies along and chuck them out?"

Moran shook his head. Admittedly, that had been his first inclination, but as Kay had pointed out, Patrick's mates had been *invited* onto the property, which would make things awkward if they lodged a complaint against the police. "Not that easy, I'm afraid. Still, at least I have the sacristy as an alternative for the time being." He raised his eyes to heaven and grimaced. He was making a play act out of it, he knew, but he had no desire to examine his apprehensions more fully; he knew he was scared, and Brendan Moran took a lot of scaring.

"But you need to take legal advice, surely?" Holly's face was the epitome of attentive consternation.

"I do – and, well, I have, in a way." Moran hesitated as he wondered why he was finding it hard to reveal Kay's involvement. Then he realised that his relationship with Kay might be interpreted in the wrong way, which would in turn – maybe – cause a problem or–

"Well, that's a relief," Holly broke in without questioning his reticence. "I'm sure they'll sort it out for you. But what a pain! I can't believe the nerve of these people."

"You and me both." Moran cocked his head wryly and sipped his wine, enjoying the feeling as the rich liquid stung his throat. His attention was diverted by a small photograph frame on the mantelpiece. The subject was a young man in uniform, a wide smile creasing his sunburned face. The attitude was confident, the beret angle just one or two degrees short of jaunty. He pointed with his glass. "Your boyfriend?"

Holly got up and retrieved the silver frame from the mantel with a graceful movement. She handed it to Moran for inspection. "A long time ago. His name is Andy. He was killed in Afghanistan."

Moran fumbled for appropriate words. "I'm so sorry – I didn't mean to–" *Brilliant, Moran, an absolute winner . . .*

Holly rested her hand lightly on his. "It's okay. It was a *very* long time ago. And you were kind enough to confide in me about your loss yesterday. So, we have something in common."

Moran nodded. "It never really leaves you, does it? The memory, I mean."

The ghost of a smile appeared briefly on Holly's face. "No. But then, I wouldn't want to forget."

"Of course not." Moran took a deep draught of wine. "Not at all."

"It's a lie, isn't it?" Holly said in a quiet voice. "That poem they read out at funerals? You know the one that goes 'I'm just stepping into the back room–'"

"'I'll send you messages almost every day . . .'" Moran finished for her. He pressed the photograph into her hand and let his remain for a moment before withdrawing it self-consciously.

Holly held the photograph at arm's length, breathing deeply, as if something tangible could be drawn from the celluloid, some small reminder of her lost love. She conjured a brave smile. "Well, no messages, no back room. So far."

"Our learned brethren would beg to differ." Moran set his glass down. "They would no doubt point to some deeper purpose. But it's the arbitrariness that gets me." He shook his head. "Makes no sense at all."

"You just pick up the pieces and move on as best you can, don't you?" Holly replaced the frame above the fireplace, allowing her hand to linger for a few seconds before turning to face Moran.

"That's my job, in a nutshell." Moran sat back on the cushions wearily. "Picking up the pieces. Trying to find answers, reasons for the messes human beings create."

"I imagine it's quite cathartic," Holly smiled. "Sorting messes out."

"Cathartic? No, not really," Moran replied. "To pry into men's souls is to uncover their true motivation. Their depravity. But then, it's something I feel impelled to do. Don't ask me why." He looked up. Holly was watching him intently, her hair a golden reflection of candlelight, her expression one of rapt concentration. "God, will you listen to me," he laughed. "DCI Cheerful."

"No, go on, please."

Moran found his wine glass and took another sip. He was feeling a little light-headed. For a moment he imagined that both Holly and the cottage interior flickered, like a damaged film transparency. He rubbed his eyes. Dr Purewal's alcohol-free instructions pricked his conscience for an instant, but what harm could one glass do?

"Why do I do it? Why am I still a policeman? I don't know." He swirled the red liquid in his glass. "Have you ever wanted to rub out your life and start again? Start completely over with a clean sheet?"

Holly laughed. "Frequently. Especially before fifth form Chaucer."

Moran laughed with her, enjoying the way her eyes lit up and her nose twitched like that girl in the Sixties comedy show *Bewitched*. He caught himself with a jolt. Yes, that's what's happening, Moran. You're being *bewitched* . . .

"*Carpe diem,*" Holly shrugged. "That's what we have to do, Brendan."

Moran raised his glass. "*Quam minime credula postero*."

"*Seize the day, trusting as little as possible in the future*," Holly translated. "Gosh. A scholarly policeman."

"Not really," Moran said dismissively. "O level Latin's about my limit."

Holly indicated the crucifix with an elegant gesture "I had a different take on that philosophy once."

"Tell me."

Holly closed her eyes and pursed her lips. "*Carpe diem – quam maxime credula Deo.*" She opened her eyes. "Now I'm not sure which maxim to adopt."

Moran nodded. "Death redefines your outlook, doesn't it? The way I look at it, I can't go back, so by default I go forward. I keep busy. I trust no one. I keep working. Which brings me here. Someone has to find out what's been going in the dark corners of Charnford Abbey, and it may as well be me." Moran self-consciously quaffed his wine to hide his embarrassment. *What gives, Moran? Baring your soul to a total stranger?*

Holly nodded, her forehead creasing in a frown. "Yes. Absolutely. The murder."

"Plus the suspicious deaths of two Charnford pupils. And a member of the kitchen staff."

Holly's face fell. "No! Oh my God! Who? When?"

"I've only just been informed myself. I'm sorry; that wasn't very tactful. You probably know the boys – forgive me." Moran the detective homed in on Holly's reaction, whilst the off-duty Moran cursed himself for his clumsiness and fought the urge to take her in his arms. The detective won by a short margin.

"God, it's the truant pair, isn't it? Mason and Montgomery? You're allowed to tell me their names, surely?" Holly's hands were shaking. She returned the glass clumsily to the table and reached for her cigarettes.

"Not really, no. Not until the next of kin have been informed–"

"Well it's got to be them, hasn't it? I can't believe it . . ."

Moran hadn't anticipated the reaction his news would cause. *Plain insensitive, Moran, that's your problem. Been on your own too long . . .*

He laid a cautious arm on her shoulder. She didn't pull away as he had feared, so he said, "I'm so sorry, Holly. Were they in your group?"

Holly lit her cigarette with trembling fingers. "You don't mind, do you?"

Moran waved his hand dismissively. "Of course not."

She blew a delicate plume of smoke towards the ceiling, her free arm wrapped defensively beneath her breasts. She bit down on her lower lip. "Last year. Yes, they were in the top English set. Always together. Always mucking around, but funny with it, you know? Hard to tell off. Bright as well – both of them. A star material. They'll be taking their A levels next summer. I mean, they *would* have been–"

The cigarette went into the ash tray, the tears came and Holly collapsed into his arms, sobbing like a child. He held her tightly, heart thudding, muttering soothing sounds into her ear as her shoulders heaved. The smell of her perfume and the warmness of her skin made him feel dizzy with desire. After a moment she pulled away, dabbing at her eyes.

"I'm so sorry." She offered a half-smile and blew her nose.

"Don't apologise. It's my fault entirely." Moran blustered like a teenager, furious at his lack of tact. He got to his feet, awkwardly, unsure what to do.

"It's all right, Brendan, really. Sit down, please."

"I should go." He grabbed his coat. "I've upset you. I'd best get on with some work."

"Please stay."

But Moran had already lifted the latch and stepped out into the night. Snow crunched beneath his feet as he made his way across the road to the abbey courtyard, cursing his stupidity with every step.

"Come in, Brendan." Kay's bright welcome did little to alleviate the symptoms of his restless night, but he returned her smile as best he could. The lack of sleep was incidental; what was really bothering him was his tactless idiocy at Holly's cottage. Archie's bark echoed briefly from the garden. He felt a pang of guilt at his neglect.

"How's the patient?" he enquired, afraid of the answer before he had even formed the question. But there was something strangely positive in Kay's disposition that seemed at odds with the dubious pleasure of nursing an ailing alcoholic.

"Absolutely fine." Kay beamed.

"No drink?"

"Not a drop. I've been firm." She grinned. "Come and see for yourself."

Moran frowned. "Really? I should have introduced you years ago." He followed Kay into the lounge, admiring the way her skirt swished about her well-turned ankles.

"Ah!" Patrick looked up as they entered. He was fiddling with a table lamp, a screwdriver and a length of electrical cable. "The man himself."

Moran noted the discoloured bruise on his brother's forehead, and the neat line of stitching. It had been quite a blow by the look of it, but Patrick seemed on top form.

"Hello Pat." Moran tried to inject a note of cheerfulness into his greeting, all too aware how tired his voice sounded. "I hear you had a little altercation."

"Sure. But I'm okay. Top dollar, no more, no less – that's God's honest truth." Patrick dropped the screwdriver and plug onto the coffee table with a decisive clunk and smoothed a hand across his thick pelt of hair. His eyes looked brighter, healthier. Kay joined him on the sofa with a sly smile.

Moran's disquiet spread into horrified realisation as Kay took Patrick's hand and squeezed it affectionately. He gawped, not knowing what to say.

"We've been getting along *very* well." Kay turned and gave Patrick a full eyes-and-all smile.

"I'm not sure this is a good idea, Kay . . . I . . ." Moran struggled to express thoughts of negativity on the one hand, and congratulatory platitudes on the other. In truth, he was profoundly shocked. He had grown used to Kay's single status, and, he realised, the semi-open door of possible re-admission to her affections. Selfish? Undoubtedly. But he was still very fond of her. He had even considered the possibility that one day they might still make a go of it – when he had sorted himself out. Now, in one blow, that had all apparently disappeared, and in the most unlikely and complicated way possible. Maybe Kay was doing this to provoke some reaction, to force his hand, expose his true feelings – whatever they might be . . .

"Well? Why ever not?" Kay countered brightly. "We have a connection, don't we, Patrick?"

"We do that," the patient agreed earnestly. "An affinity, even."

"Oh, big word!" Kay said with admiration. She leaned and kissed Patrick on the lips.

"Well, I don't know what to say." Moran opted for honesty. "It's all a little quick, don't you think? I leave you two alone for a couple of days and–" He gave up, fell into an armchair and rubbed his eyes wearily with the heels of his hands. He didn't need this now.

"I've been busy as well," Kay said. "Sorted your IPO out. Notices are being issued tomorrow morning."

"That's fantastic." Moran felt relief wash through him, Kay's unexpected liaison taking a temporary back seat. He was going to get his house back after all.

"And the hearing will be five days from then."

"Five days?" His elation disappeared. Five more days in the sacristy was five days too long, even with Holly's proximity as a sweetener.

"We have to give the squatters a few days' warning. I'll come with you tomorrow and serve the notice, okay?"

"And I'll be there too, Brendan," Patrick offered. "I feel responsible."

"You won't be there, and you *are* responsible," Moran snapped. "You'll damn well keep out of it."

"All right, boys – that's enough." Kay stood between them, hands raised. "There's no need to fall out over it."

"Fall out? This is my *house* we're talking about, that *he* turned over to the East European mafia." Moran felt his temperature rising. Why did he have to have a brother like Patrick? *He* was the one who needed support right now. But their roles were always reversed so that he was always forced into playing the elder brother, the strong arm to lean on. And what did he get in return? Hassle and grief. For the love of God, his *house* had been taken away . . .

Kay took him by the elbow and steered him into the hall. "Brendan, just take it easy. He's very upset about what happened. He's only trying to help."

"Is he?" Moran shrugged off Kay's supporting arm. "That'll be a first."

"Give him a chance, Brendan." Kay blocked his path into the lounge, her folded arms and angry expression taking him aback. "I wouldn't have expected a jealous reaction from you. I thought you were over that."

"Jealous? Now hang on a minute–"

"No, *you* hang on for a change. I'm the one who's been 'hanging on', waiting for you to make up your mind. For how long? *Years*. And for what? A platonic relationship?"

She was really mad now, Moran could see. A red patch of anger had appeared on her throat, spreading down to the gentle slope of her breasts.

"Oh, so this is about me now, is it?" Moran shot back. "It's all my fault, is it?"

"Yes, frankly, it probably *is*. If you'd been more decisive about us, we'd have been happy. I *know* we would have been."

"You're forgetting something, Kay." Moran thrust his finger out accusingly. "I had a little interruption to my thought processes. I got hit by a truck, remember?"

Kay's hands went to her hips. "Oh, yes, you can fall back on that every time, Brendan Moran, but what about before? What's the excuse for those wasted years?"

"All right, all right. That'll do, both!"

Moran and Kay glared at one another like boxers from opposite sides of the ring. Patrick was standing in the lounge doorway, watching them with an air of faint amusement.

"Let's have no more talk about blame and the past, if you please," he said, addressing them like a pair of bickering schoolchildren. "Coffee, anyone? Caffeine doth sooth the savage breast – or so I'm told, anyway."

Moran wasn't finished. "Just give us a moment, Pat, will you?"

Patrick shrugged, and casting an exaggerated look over his shoulder, he returned to the sofa and his electrical repair work.

There was an awkward silence. "Okay," Moran began, "I'm out of order. I apologise."

Kay bit her lip. "Don't. I shouldn't have said those things either." She sighed and placed the palms of her hands on his lapels, brushing away imaginary specks of dust. It was an uncomfortable intimacy, given the distance that had grown between them. "What can I say? What's happened has happened. Or not, in this case." She shrugged. "Look, Brendan, I haven't been great recently; you know, the dreaded anti-depressants. I'm slowly coming off them . . . but the withdrawal's awful. You know what I mean. My head's above the water – just – but I'm not enjoying the swim very much."

"That's a Patrick expression."

Kay smiled. "So it is. Well, it fits. I haven't been sleeping. It makes me short-tempered and–" she read his expression and forced a smile. "Okay, it makes me an irritable old *cow*."

Moran stretched his face and drummed up a return smile. "It's not just you; my pharmaceutical cocktail doesn't exactly help my mental equilibrium either." He took her hand lightly and squeezed. "It'll get better, Kay."

"I hope so. What a pair." A brief, awkward smile and another silence. "Well." Kay folded her arms. "How's the investigation going?"

Moran blew air and shrugged. "Slowly. The Benedictines redefine the phrase 'closed ranks'. It's unbelievably hard going – especially now the CC has taken Phelps off the case. But I'll get there eventually."

"You always do." She smiled, tight-lipped. "The man who gets results, right?"

"Right . . . Kay . . . ?" Moran struggled to find the right words. "*Is* it my fault? The way you feel?"

Kay took a long, thoughtful, breath. "Partly, I suppose. But don't blame yourself, Brendan. You're you, and that's how it is. I understand."

"Do you? God, I don't know if I do myself." But he knew she was right about one thing: he *did* feel, absurdly, a strong pang of jealousy. Why? He'd had so many chances to cement their relationship, and now, when she was over him, or seemingly so, he wanted her back. But then there was Holly . . .

Kay tucked a lock of hair behind her ear in a familiar gesture. "And besides, I like Patrick. He needs a woman's guidance. I'll sort him out. We get on incredibly well."

"An affinity?"

She nodded and looked down at her shoes.

"Well, I don't doubt it." Moran smiled kindly. "But watch him, Kay. I mean *really* watch him. I know what he's like. I don't want to see you–" he hesitated, realising what he was about to say.

"I can see his potential." Kay brushed his cul-de-sac aside.

"Good. That's good."

"So." Kay drew herself up to her full height. "Coffee, then? To soothe our savage breasts?"

Moran shook his head ruefully. "He's the family poet. You'll get used to it."

While Kay prepared the drinks Moran checked his voicemail. Two messages – one from Neads, one from

Lawson. He deleted the second and listened intently to Neads' clipped tones. Gun at RTA confirmed. Provenance traces back to arms supplied by a gunsmith based in Dundalk. *So, the Irish connection checks out*, Moran thought with a sick feeling in the pit of his stomach. Dalton supplied a handgun to two schoolboys. *So did he pay a visit to Father Horgan as well? And to John Vernon? And if so, why?* He called Neads and asked him to pick him up in fifteen.

"Brendan? Can I ask a favour?" Kay extracted coffee from the frothing machine and poured it into a cafetière.

Moran accepted a cup of steaming cappuccino. "Sure. Fire away." He took a cautious sip – the strong coffee hit the spot immediately. "Wonderful. You haven't lost your touch." He felt a sudden stab of hunger. "Any chance of a quick forage?"

"Of course. Still have a penchant for toasted cheese?"

"Always."

"Coming up." She deftly cut two squares of cheese and slipped two slices of bread under the grill.

"Much appreciated," Moran said, still feeling like the stereotypical green man.

Kay acknowledged the compliment with a toss of her hair. "Well, here's your chance to return the favour. I need to get Patrick to his hospital appointment on Thursday but my car's in for its MOT. I was wondering–"

Moran held out his key ring. "All yours– I can't use it until the doctor passes me fit to drive. The padlock combination is on the key label. Hopefully it'll start. If not, call me and I'll ask my mechanic to take a quick look. No, actually, I'll get him out anyway. You've reminded me – it needs a service."

"Thanks." Kay took the keys with a smile. "I appreciate it."

"No problem." Moran swigged his cooling coffee. "As long as the Romanians haven't nicked it, of course." He drained his cup and placed it on the table with a decisive thump. "In the meantime, joy of joys," he paused to accept Kay's proffered toasted sandwich, "I have a funeral to attend."

Chapter 10

As Moran waited for Neads he turned his thoughts back to Charnford. He shuffled his feet to encourage circulation. Ye gods, but it was cold. The wind whipped along the pavement, funnelling through the bus shelter where a few brave souls were queuing patiently – *as only Brits can*, Moran observed, fighting to get their Christmas shopping in before the weather fulfilled the forecasters' predictions. '*More on the way. Worst since '63?*' the headlines had speculated yesterday. Well, it was bad enough already, Moran thought as he began to trudge back and forth beside the busy intersection. The snow under his feet was hard with a top layer of ice, and he was obliged to affect an undignified shuffling gait in order to keep his balance.

Moran mentally arranged the day's agenda, cursing occasionally as his feet splayed beneath him. After the funeral, chase up Forensics. He wanted to know more about Phelps' buried bones and cornflakes. Something sinister had happened in that chapel many years before Horgan's demise. But to whom did the bones belong, and what was the connection with the dead monk and John Vernon? If, indeed, there was one.

Priority two: nail down the alibis of certain key figures in the monastery. The abbot, Father Oswald, the headmaster. Neads could deal with that. And Vagnoli, the mysterious Vatican visitor. He had been less than forthcoming when Phelps had spoken to him; oily and evasive, Phelps reckoned.

Priority three: peripheral staff. Groundsmen, handymen, the school matron. There was always some titbit of useful information to be gleaned from such sources. His subconscious prompted other candidates: *teachers*. He wasn't sure if he could face Holly yet. Perhaps when the dead pupils' autopsies were complete and the story behind their deaths made public? Not before, he didn't think; no, not before. He'd put his foot in it, and besides, she was too much of a distraction. And this case was difficult enough as it was . . .

His mobile beeped. A text, from the Forensics lab. Moran read:

'*Re. Vernon: metallic fragment, neck wound. Have established that, unusually, the shard contains a high percentage of titanium. Further research identifies only two knife manufacturers employing this method commercially: a. Brian Hanrahan, Dublin, and b. Mike Terrana, USA (Calif.). Have contacted latter and confirmed that he has discontinued this manuf. method. Last knife of this type sold to local police officer previous year. Former still in production. F.*'

Dublin. Dalton's home town. A car skated past, channelling a wash of slush onto his already sodden feet. Moran moved back with an expletive, almost losing his footing. Where was Neads? A horn blared from the parade of shops by the bus stop. Moran slid between the traffic and heaved himself into the car, shaking clumps of snow and ice from his feet.

"All right, guv?" Neads was trying to keep the amusement from his voice. "Nasty out there, isn't it? I'll get the chains on the tyres later, I reckon, especially if we're heading up to the abbey. We'll never get up the hill if it gets any worse."

"Forget the engineering, Neads," Moran told the smirking sergeant. "I haven't got time to waste while you exercise your mechanical skills – and neither have you. The weather's getting cold and the clues even colder."

Neads opened his mouth to object, but Moran filled the pause. "If we get stuck we'll get out and walk. All right?"

They drove on in silence.

Gregory Neads wasn't a bad guy. Just misunderstood. That had always been his personal assessment, and as he steered the car carefully onto the Bath road Neads saw no reason to realign his conclusions. Trouble was, people interpreted his attitude the wrong way. He was confident, sure, but that was a critical strength in the police. No one wanted a wallflower. You had to make your mark. That way you got noticed, got respect. The Chief had noticed him, hadn't he? That's why Neads figured he'd been hand-picked to replace that buffoon Phelps. From what he'd seen of Phelps it was high time he was put out to grass. Anyone over the age of thirty-five was over the hill as far as Neads was concerned. Plodders, the lot of them. All that stress. All that booze. No wonder the unsolved crime stats were up. Neads didn't drink. He wanted his brain the way it was: young, agile and one hundred per cent on the money. He had no time for whisky-swilling no-hopers like Phelps.

Moran was slightly higher up Neads' competence scale – not much, but a little. He cast a sideways glance at Moran's profile. The DCI's eyes were closed and his mouth hung slightly open, the breathing low and regular. Oh great. Asleep again. Neads' lip curled in contempt. *Old man.* It was just as well Greg Neads was on the case.

Left to Moran, they'd be chasing their arses all over Charnford for the next twenty years. The Chief wanted results, and Neads intended to produce them. He'd stitch Moran up, provide the clues and evidence to solve the murder and be on his way up the career ladder faster than he could skid this pile of junk down Charnford Hill. Which was just coming up, as it happened.

Neads peered through the snow-dappled windscreen, signalled right and eased the car off the dual carriageway. Was it this turning? The blank whiteness made everything look the same. Neads frowned. Yes, there was the sign to the abbey. As he eased the clutch out his peripheral vision caught a swaddled figure waiting some way back from the road, as if trying to conceal itself from the glare of the headlights. He blinked and looked again, but the figure had gone. Neads moistened his lips and concentrated on the narrow road ahead.

Moran stood at a respectful distance as the leading monks emerged from the abbey church bearing Father Horgan's coffin to its final resting place. The autopsy had failed to provide further leads, despite Dr Bagri's painstaking attention. Apart from the residue of knife polish, the body had retained its secrets. And now, it was Horgan's finale.

Moran sighed deeply. The Mass had been a sombre affair; with no relatives to call upon for valedictory orations, the ceremony had seemed to encapsulate everything he disliked about Catholicism. Even though the trappings of spirituality had been present in abundance – the swinging of an incense-filled censer, the other-worldly intonation of Latin liturgy – there had also been, to Moran's mind, a woeful dearth of true emotion throughout. Did these men really believe that Horgan's soul could be translated from the spiritual waiting room of Purgatory to Heaven by their ritualistic diligence? Did Moran himself believe it? Had Horgan's spirit been weighed in the heavenly scales and been found wanting? Or was the dead monk's soul enjoying eternal bliss even as they were about to lay his body to rest? Moran didn't have the answers and neither, he suspected, did the monks.

Someone had once said to Moran, 'I'm off for some real fun today'. He had looked blank until the issuer of the remark explained: 'It's an anagram, Brendan – of *funeral . . . real fun – geddit?*' Moran's lip twisted at the memory. He was glad to be out in the fresh air and free of the cloying smell of religion. Neads evidently felt the same, judging by the way he was stamping his feet and rattling the matchbox in his pocket as if seeking confirmation that he wouldn't be breaking any funereal protocol by lighting up on the quiet.

Moran's mobile vibrated insistently in his pocket. It would have to wait. He watched the slow procession to the prepared grave, the coffin followed by the abbot and the remainder of the community, eldest first, novices bringing up the rear. No shortage of young men willing to take the oath, then, Moran mused. The youngest monks looked scarcely out of their teens. What emotions propelled them to step voluntarily out of the world into this environment of abstinence and study, Moran could scarcely imagine.

He shielded his eyes from the low sun. Despite the forecasters' gloomy predictions the clouds had lifted, and the unexpected pin-sharpness of the afternoon seemed to have positively affected Moran's thinking processes. He breathed in deeply, holding onto the moment. It felt liberating. *Normal service almost restored.* As the coffin drew near to the graveside he made a mental note to share the good news with Dr Purewal at their next encounter.

Kay dropped her mobile into the folds of her slim leather handbag. "Left a message," she smiled, and shrugged. "I guess we can go ahead – he said it would be fine."

"Away we go, then." Next to her in the passenger seat, Patrick clicked his seatbelt decisively.

In the rear view mirror of Moran's four-by-four, Kay watched the mechanic close the blue van door and start his engine. He gave her a smile and a friendly wave as he pulled away. Nice chap. From his accent he could have been from the same neck of the woods as the Moran brothers. Quick off the mark, too. Good job he was just finishing when they turned up. Perfect timing.

She smiled at Patrick and felt a deep contentment. Somehow, she just knew this was going to work out. Funny old world. Who'd have thought it? Brendan's brother! *How complicated do you want to make your life, Kay? Oh, as complicated as possible, please . . . no problem, here you go: two Irish brothers: one an emotionally impotent action man with a brain like a computer, the other a brilliant, alcoholic, charming ex-surgeon . . . hmmm, yes, I'll try both please . . .*

"Is it four fifteen or four thirty? The appointment, I mean?" Patrick looked at his watch. "'Tis the rush hour almost upon us, y'know."

"I'll get you there, don't worry." Kay fumbled with the unfamiliar keys. Peering under the steering column she located the ignition and slid the largest key into the lock.

"Damned clinics never run on time anyway," Patrick muttered in a resigned voice.

"And you should know." Kay cast an oblique glance at Patrick's profile.

"Let me tell you, young lady," Patrick replied with an exaggerated accent, "that my clinics ran like clockwork." He wagged a warning finger. "For the most part, anyhow. When I was on the case, you know . . ."

"I'm sure they did," Kay said, patting his knee. "Well, get ready, Patrick Moran, because I'm going to get you *back* on the case. With a *vengeance*." Kay turned the ignition and the instrument panel lit up obediently.

"I'll look forward to that then, my pretty one. I've a soft spot for being taken in hand by a strong-minded woman." Patrick mock-saluted and grinned.

Kay giggled and turned the ignition one further click to the right. The engine gave a coughing lurch. Kay looked to see if the vehicle had been left in gear. No, it was in neutral. Had the mechanic forgotten to do something? She waggled the gear stick experimentally. Patrick moved his hand to confirm her diagnosis and their fingers interlocked. An infinitesimally small sound, like the click of an electronic clock, brought a frown to Patrick's brow, the last conscious action of his troubled life.

The explosion that followed was so intense that the interior of the car was engulfed in a fraction of a second. Kay had no time to shield her face before the roof was blown off both vehicle and garage with a thunderous boom that was heard from the shopping centre a mile and a half down the road. People spilled from Moran's house – foreign-looking folk, one neighbour said later. They fled down the quiet suburban road, leaving the front door wide open like a silent scream.

When the firemen arrived nine minutes and forty-five seconds later the garage was a pile of glowing ash and charred timber, the four-by-four a metal skeleton in its midst. One of the younger fire officers, Peter Steele, known to his mates as Metalhead, was first to the vehicle door. He took in the scene with a single shocked glance and threw up onto the debris-strewn drive as the sound of sirens rose and fell in time with Metalhead's pumping stomach.

"Here we go again," Neads said in Moran's ear as the monks began to sing *Ave Maria.* As if on cue, a group of sixth formers exited the church and took up their positions behind and to the immediate left of the grave. Prefects, Moran surmised. Representing the school. Quite right, too. Moran had been a prefect once, in another life. He eyed the seniors approvingly as they stood to attention, their young faces pale in the weak sunlight. They'd stayed behind for the funeral while the rest of the school had departed for the Christmas holidays.

Yesterday had resounded to the rumbling commotion that was the end of term, the school cloisters transformed into a bedlam of trunk-packing, shouting and high spirits. Moran had deliberated for some time, wondering whether to postpone the holidays and keep the boys on the premises for an extended term while his investigation continued, but in the end had decided to let them go. He had names, addresses, and, more importantly, no suspects amongst the boys.

Today the school was empty and sombre, as if the buildings were mourning the boys' as well as Father

Horgan's departure. Moran wondered at the resilience of young minds; their dead contemporaries already – perhaps deliberately – forgotten, the youngsters had their sights on the immediate future, the prospect of holidays, Christmas celebrations, family . . .

"How long is this going to take, guv?" Neads stage-whispered in his ear.

"Just keep your eyes open, Sergeant." Moran watched the monks line up on either side of the boarded hole in the frozen grass. "You never know – you might notice something useful."

"Sir." Neads monotoned in a peeved voice.

It must have taken some effort to dig a pit that size in the frozen and unyielding soil of the monks' graveyard. Some commitment . . . Moran caught Neads' profile. "And get rid of that cigarette behind your ear – you look like a market trader."

Neads complied, muttering under his breath.

The coffin arrived at the graveside to the gentle sound of plainchant. Then Moran heard a cry of alarm, followed by a ripple of commotion.

Neads stepped forward. "Hello. What have they found?"

Moran was already walking briskly, covering the distance between the headstones with long, loping strides. He shouldered his way between the press of monks and stopped. A pole had been inserted at the head of the grave, surmounted by a yellowed, hair-tufted skull. There was some kind of note attached to the pole, the message scrawled in large capitals. Moran scrutinised the text. It read:

Ex libertas, pax

Neads was at his side. Moran was thinking about another grave, the shallow recess beneath Charnford's chapel. So far, Forensics had only been able to confirm a probable male body, forty years interred. And here was the missing skull.

The monks seemed paralysed with horror, unsure what to do. The abbot was motionless, his arm outstretched as if trying to ward off an evil spirit. Neads opened his mouth to speak but Moran silenced him with a grip on his arm.

The abbot began to sing, a low note that seemed to vibrate the frozen earth beneath them. "Thou art man and thou art dust…" Boniface dunked a brush into a silver receptacle of holy water, sprinkling the drops onto the grinning skull and into the open grave. "And unto dust thou shalt return . . ."

Moran allowed the verses to conclude before interrupting. "I'm afraid we'll have to postpone Father Horgan's internment for a short period. If you'd all like to return to the church and allow DS Neads and myself a few moments to sort things out I'd be grateful . . ."

It was only later that Moran recalled the look in the abbot's eyes, the way the monk's body language had voiced his opposition. And what also stuck in Moran's memory was the look Boniface had given DS Neads as the sergeant hovered beside Moran – a proprietary look Moran could only interpret as longing. Or maybe desire.

Moran despatched the skull to the coroner's office for examination. The cause of death was clear: the skull was fractured, a cracked indentation zig-zagging across the crown like a lightning bolt. Although it looked like a blow from some heavy object, he'd leave it to the path lab to establish likely cause. Still, whoever had moved it from the chapel vault to Horgan's freshly-dug grave must have left traces – at least Moran hoped so. But why the morbid display? Who was the perpetrator trying to scare and why?

And the note: *From liberty, peace.* What was all that about? Moran's take on that one was straightforward enough: someone had known about the body, that it needed a Christian burial, and now, in this rather flamboyant way, they were making a statement that the burial was well overdue. However, the question he most wanted an answer to was just as puzzling: was the display of the skull the work of Horgan's killer, or someone else?

The interrupted funeral service had resumed an hour and a half later. Father Leo Horgan had been left in peace beneath the frozen turf as the light was fading and a fresh batch of snow was blowing in on the chill afternoon wind. The monks had moved away in small groups, black hoods drawn around frowning faces, each nursing private suspicions and anxieties. Moran read their expressions: what was happening amongst them? Who was responsible? What would the abbot do about it? Were they *safe*?

Moran made his way through the empty school cloisters towards the sacristy. After he'd sent Neads off to conclude the interview with Bernadette he remembered his missed call and dug out his mobile. Kay's voice trilled in his ear, asking about the car. Of course. Damn. He'd forgotten to call the mechanic. Hopefully the thing had started. Well, he'd find out later.

Passing through the Court of Arches he caught sight of Father Oswald conversing with a knot of prefects at the end of the main cloister by the school toilets. Duty done, the boys were finally being sent home.

Oswald watched him approach. He was cradling several weighty books, his hands wrapped protectively around them. "Hello Inspector. Good of you to attend Father Horgan's send-off."

Moran nodded. "Good job I did, Father Oswald, wouldn't you say?"

The monk looked unabashed. No telltale signs of agitation. "Yes, indeed. A strange thing, a very strange thing indeed."

"*Well* odd," one of the prefects offered. He was a tall, blond boy with a sharp, intelligent face. "Especially with all the other stuff that's been going on."

There was a chorus of assent from the other prefects. Moran searched their faces and found no subterfuge, no trace of foreknowledge or guilt. Just a bunch of responsible lads concerned for their alma mater and the abbey.

"This is Stephen Catton." Oswald patted the boy lightly on his shoulder. "Our Head Boy."

Moran shook the boy's hand. It was, he noted with satisfaction, a strong and dry handshake. "Pleased to meet you, Stephen. So, off for the holidays, eh? Is that it?" Moran shared a smile with the others.

"Yes sir," Catton replied. He hesitated and bit his bottom lip, then blurted, "Sir? I mean, Chief Inspector?"

"Yes?"

"You *will* find out what happened to Mason and Montgomery, won't you? And to Father Horgan? And this other thing, the skull . . . I mean, who was it? Why was it there?" Catton shook his head, at a loss to make sense of it all.

Catton's concern and sincerity, obviously shared by the other prefects, moved Moran. "I will," he said solemnly. "I will, Stephen. That's why I'm here."

The sacristy was cold and empty. Moran sat on the rickety chair provided by the abbot and placed his mobile on the table. It rang. He picked it up. Phelps.

"Guv?" Phelps spoke softly. Phelps never spoke softly. Moran wet his lips. Something bad had happened.

"Fire away, Phelps."

"Guv. It's your place. There's been an explosion." Phelps' words came out like a reluctant tooth.

"Go on." Although Moran's heart was hammering slowly in his chest, he felt oddly calm.

"The garage. Something happened."

"The garage." Moran repeated Phelps' pronouncement *verbatim* to be absolutely sure, because he had made the connection instantly. Kay. Patrick. The four-by-four. His stomach turned to stone.

"Guv. They don't know exactly what happened yet. It went up like a bomb."

A bomb. Dalton.

"Bodies?"

A long hesitation. "I'm afraid so, sir."

Moran gripped the arms of the flimsy chair. The sacristy temperature felt as though it had dropped to minus ten. "How many?"

"Two." Phelps paused. "Two bodies, I believe."

Phelps couldn't bring himself to elaborate. Moran understood that. He prompted, "One male, early fifties.. One female, mid-forties. That about right?"

Phelps cleared his throat. It sounded as though tough old Sergeant Phelps might be holding back tears. "Yes, sir. That's right. Guv, I–"

"I know, Phelps. It's all right."

"Sir."

"Just let me know when you've got definite IDs, okay?"

"I will, guv. But, I – I don't think there's much doubt–"

"Thank you, Sergeant Phelps. I appreciate your candour."

"Guv, if there's anything I can do? You know. With you being stuck up at Charnford. The weather's treacherous . . . if it wasn't snowing like a bastard, I'd…"

For the second time that afternoon Moran was surprised at how clearly his brain was working. "Any sign of the squatters?"

"No, sir. Witness reckoned they all scarpered when it happened. I've secured the house for you. There's no damage to the actual property. Just the . . . well, just the garage, sir."

"Thank you, Sergeant." Moran absorbed the news. So the house was intact. He had somewhere to live again. "You could check my answerphone messages, Phelps. Let me know if there's anything urgent. Have a sniff around for any missing items. You know, that sort of thing."

"Sure, guv. Listen, how are you getting on with Neads? I can probably twist Lawson's arm under the circumstances – I mean, he'll probably–"

"Everything's fine, Phelps. Thanks. We'll have this sorted in a very short time, I'm quite confident. Perhaps you could pass that along to the Chief?"

"Right, sir. Yes. I will."

"Oh, one more thing, Phelps – there's my dog, Archie. Kay was . . ." He took a deep breath and carried on. "Kay was looking after him. He'll need feeding. And walking. I'd be very grateful."

"Consider it done, sir."

"I appreciate it, Phelps. Thanks for letting me know. And Phelps?"

"Yes, Chief Inspector?"

"Get me chapter and verse from the SOCOs, would you? I'm going to nail this one to the wall."

"You've got a suspect, guv?" There was fresh concern in Phelps' tone.

"I have a suspect."

"Guv–" A brief silence, then: "Guv, I mean to say – that is, there's no tangible evidence that it was deliberate. I'm told there were canisters of Calor Gas . . . the vehicle may have impacted somehow – one of the squad reckoned it was a gear lurch, you know. Maybe it had been left in first? By mistake, I mean."

"It was deliberate, Phelps. And it was meant for me. I'll explain more when I see you. Thanks again."

Moran ended the call to spare Phelps any further distress. On the whitewashed wall of the sacristy there was a lighter mark where a crucifix had been removed and presumably relocated. Cross of salvation, he thought. A picture came into his mind, the agonised saviour pinned to Holly's cottage wall, the expression crafted upon the suffering Messiah's face . . . *this is all for you, Brendan Moran, all for you . . .*

Moran's discipline buckled and he heard himself blurt a throat-hacking sob, a brutal sound that echoed in the small room as if it had been expressed by some suffering animal. All he could think of was Kay's contented smile as she'd clasped Patrick's hand, her last words to him: 'I'm in the right place now, Brendan. I feel it in every fibre of my body.'

Neads opened the door. "Guv? You got a minute? Our maid's done a runner."

Chapter 11

"Visiting? Visiting whom exactly?" Moran asked the bursar, a short, corpulent monk whose job it apparently was to oversee the school and abbey catering.

"A friend. She was very upset, as you can surely understand, Inspector."

Moran understood upset. He had walked along the cloister feeling as though his body belonged to someone else. Some other power was placing one foot in front of the other. When he spoke, words came out. He found that he could still think clearly. *Later. It'll be later when everything shuts down,* his rational mind obligingly informed him. Fascinating how a human brain could deal with news of the magnitude he'd just received and yet still function normally. But shutting down wasn't an option. He wasn't going to let that happen until he had a prime suspect banged up and charged, until the end game had been played out and he could rationalise events into some manageable perspective. He owed that to himself. He owed it to Kay. He owed it to Patrick. He owed it to the Charnford community.

In this context, he gave the monk a withering look. "Father Remus, I gave explicit orders to the community via the abbot that no adults were to leave the premises without very good reason until our investigations are concluded."

"Well, she's not gone far," Remus said, a little huffily. "She's at a friend's house in Gilham. Other side of the woods, you know?" He pointed vaguely in the direction of the abbey church. "One of the maids will give you the address . . . "

"Let's go, Neads." Moran began to move away, but Remus called after them: "I wouldn't drive, not in this. They could hardly get the prefect's coach down the hill earlier. Did you see it? Sliding all over the place. It's an ice rink – getting worse by the minute." Remus pointed to the thick flakes buffeting up against the cloister windows. "The roads into the village are like bobsleigh runs. Unless you have a Land Rover, I don't expect–"

"No," Moran said wearily. "TVP's budget doesn't stretch to Land Rovers. Or snow ploughs."

"But you could get to the village through the woods," Remus suggested, his rotund face beaming with satisfaction that he was able to offer a workable solution. "There's a path – shouldn't be a problem if you're young and fit."

Moran looked Neads up and down. "We do young and fit, don't we, Neads?"

"You'll need some stout footwear, obviously, in this weather," Remus added. "But it's only half a mile. Less risky altogether . . ."

Neads' face betrayed no emotion. It didn't need to; the sergeant's eyes said it all, but Moran wasn't interested.

"Splendid. Well then, Neads." He pointed to the kitchen. "Ask Bernadette's buddies for directions, and then off you go. In the meantime I'll winkle out our Vatican visitor. Come and find me as soon as you get back, would you?"

Neads fumbled in the boot for the police issue wellingtons he hoped were still tucked away in the accessories pocket. The wind blew snowflakes into the open boot, hindering his search. He was furious that Moran had sidelined him so quickly. He wanted to be alongside Moran to capitalise on any slips or missed opportunities. Now he had to tramp through the frozen countryside to interview some Irish bint about her stupid mate who'd got herself killed in that sodding bank job RTA.

Silly cow. Who in their right mind would recruit a couple of schoolboys for a bank job? Bonkers. Absolutely bonkers. He had no sympathy for Bernadette's supposed emotional state. As Neads pulled on the black rubberised boots and wrapped his scarf tightly around the lower part of his face, he determined to pull no punches during the interview. If she was hiding something he'd find it. She probably knew loads about what went on in the school. Maybe even about Horgan and his enemies. Well, he wouldn't be sharing any info with Moran after this little excursion. No way.

Neads blinked through the gusting snow and tried to remember which way the mousey little kitchen maid had told him to go. Ah yes, back of the abbey, across the playing fields, straight through the woods for around five minutes and he'd see the outskirts of the village ahead. Neads prided himself on his sense of direction; he had been a regular in the orienteering top five at school.

The gangly sergeant strode off confidently, banging his gloved hands together for warmth. Just before he reached the school gates he saw Moran emerge from the main entrance and hesitate briefly by the derelict cottages before moving off in the direction of the Abbey Church. The guv's collar was up, hands thrust deep into the pockets of his overcoat. Neads watched Moran disappear into shadow before resuming his own mission with a dismissive shrug. Whatever avenue the guv was exploring, he'd figure it out later. Right now, *he* was the results man. And he intended to prove it. Big time.

"Cardinal Vagnoli?" Moran approached the still, bowed figure cautiously. The abbey church was in semi-darkness, its silence compounded by the fresh snowfall which muffled the lofty space like a soft eiderdown. A candle on a tall golden stand guttered as he moved into the main body of the church, his footfall a slapping echo in the still air.

The figure turned its head, then, as if satisfied as to his identity, turned back to its contemplation. Moran hesitated, his Catholic background insisting he retrace his footsteps and allow the monk to continue his communion with God uninterrupted. Once again he reminded himself why he was here. *A murder, Moran, remember? Two, actually – possibly three. And the dead boys . . . and Kay and Patrick . . .*

He steadied himself with a deep breath before making his way past the organ and the main altar, genuflecting as he did so, coming to a halt beside the monks' stalls where Vagnoli finally sat up and acknowledged Moran's presence.

"I apologise for the interruption," Moran began. "I need to ask you some questions."

"Chief Inspector," Vagnoli smiled. "Please, be seated. I have no issue with your questions." He indicated the empty seat beside him.

"Thanks, I'll stand if that's all right with you." Moran took in the heavy accent, the posture, the confident gesture; signs of a man at ease with himself and his situation. A man with power, he imagined. Used to getting his own way. Persuasive, clever. *Best tread cautiously . . .*

"I am praying for the soul of Father Horgan," Vagnoli said in a solemn voice, head bowed. "I am sorry I did not have the opportunity to speak with him face to face." He looked up. "This afternoon we laid our brother to rest in the cold earth." Vagnoli indicated the door of the abbey church. Moran could hear the wind rattling the hinges and wondered briefly if Neads had found his way through the woods, but Vagnoli had risen to his feet and joined Moran by the altar.

He was tall, the impression of height exaggerated by the scarlet, floor length robes. The Italian monk made an open-handed gesture. "It is so final, yes? We live as though life will go on forever, but it is not so. It is a terrible delusion. Like the *struzzo* – the flightless bird, what is its name in your language? Like the poor bird, we bury our heads." He made a swift ducking motion to illustrate the analogy.

"The ostrich."

"Yes, just so, Inspector. The ostrich. A foolish bird, trying to escape the inevitable."

"No one likes to talk about death, Father Vagnoli. Especially a violent one. It has a way of reminding people of their mortality. And it also makes them very afraid." In his mind's eye, Moran saw Kay turning the ignition key, flame blossoming from the engine. He gave his head a firm shake to dispel the image. *Pull yourself together, Moran.* He gritted his teeth, waiting for Vagnoli's response.

Vagnoli was watching him with interest. "Afraid, of course – of the unknown and the unseen. We all strive to make sense of life, but only in death are the answers we seek revealed. A fascinating paradox, Inspector, is it not?"

"You Catholics have all the answers, don't you?" Moran felt a knot of anger twist in the pit of his stomach. "All neatly sewn up in Mass, confession, good works."

"Do I perceive the animosity of a lapsed Catholic in your words, Inspector?"

Moran shrugged. "Is it that obvious?"

"My impression is that you have yet to conclude your theological considerations." Vagnoli raised his finger. "Because anger in a spiritual context usually means a person is struggling with God. For you, the search for meaning is far from over."

"My search is for the murderer of one of your colleagues, Cardinal Vagnoli. I have little time for personal reflection."

"Is that entirely honest, Inspector?"

Moran exhaled in frustration. Vagnoli seemed to discern the doubt churning in Moran's wounded soul. It was discomfiting. The last thing Moran needed now was spiritual counselling. To deflect the Italian's papal darts he refocused his questioning.

"You're not concerned that there may be a killer at large in the abbey? That an unknown body, perhaps buried decades ago, has been exhumed in the chapel?"

"Concerned?" Vagnoli joined his hands behind his back and moved slowly down the length of the church with long, measured movements. Moran was obliged to walk in step with Vagnoli's lengthier stride, feeling like a destroyer escorting a slow-sailing battleship.

Vagnoli shook his head as he walked. "Your killer will not be here, Inspector. He will have gone – *pouf*!" Vagnoli elevated his arms in a conjurer's exaggerated motion, towering over Moran. "Far away from here and his guilt."

"You don't think one of the brethren–"

"I do not speculate, Inspector. To do this would be to trespass on your territory. But, for what it is worth, no, I hesitate to suspect a member of the community. An outsider, or an opportunist, perhaps? I can only express my regret at arriving at such an inopportune time, but although an outsider, I am no murdering opportunist – if such a thought had entered your mind. And this other body – you say it happened a long time ago, so–" Vagnoli turned down the corners of his mouth and showed Moran the palms of his hands. "It cannot be something I am involved with, Inspector – this is my first visit to Charnford. What happened in the past is outside my knowledge. My advice would be to begin your search for the killer among those associated with the school and community, not the community itself."

"You're aware that the school is in financial difficulty?" Moran probed. Horgan would most likely have mentioned the reason for his willingness to part with Charnford's holy artefact. But had Horgan revealed anything else to the Italian?

Vagnoli pursed his lips. "Of course. Father Horgan outlined his predicament on the telephone. This was his motive for calling me about the sacred *Titulus* in the first place."

"You're aware that the abbot disapproves."

Vagnoli laughed. "Father Boniface has made his intolerance of my presence well known, Inspector. Everybody is aware. The other monks, they are friendlier."

"Does Father Boniface's attitude bother you?"

"I have come to make a – how is it you say? A negotiation. The Holy Father is *most* interested in the *Titulus*, as you may imagine. I would therefore disappoint His Holiness by returning empty-handed. This, you understand, I do not wish."

"You intend to stay until the relic is found?" Moran knew the answer to that already –Vagnoli was clearly not a man in a hurry. His whole demeanour exuded limitless patience. *Well, you'll have to wait until I'm good and ready before you get your hands on it, Cardinal . . .*

Vagnoli halted and raised his arms outwards and upwards, the sleeves of his robes creating an illusion of dark, spreading wings. "For as long as The Most High and His Holiness upon Earth desire, I shall remain at Charnford." He bowed and raised his head with a smile.

Moran nodded, noting the Italian flair for the dramatic. "And the earthbound Inspector Moran also requests that you remain for the time being, if you would oblige me."

Vagnoli raised his hand, forefinger extended. "Of course. But, Inspector, you have said that the school is in difficulty? I have to point out to you that the community itself may not be in the same – boat? Is this the correct . . . vernacular?" He enunciated the word with relish.

Moran frowned. "Meaning?"

"Meaning, Inspector, that there are at least sufficient funds within the abbey for the commissioning of a new library building."

"Oh yes?"

"Some hundreds of thousands of pounds, I believe."

In the distance Moran heard the sound of approaching sandals. The monks were assembling for their evening liturgy.

"It is time for my brothers to attend Vespers." Vagnoli acknowledged the interruption with a brief smile. "I must join them, Inspector. Please do not hesitate to – winkle me out – for further questioning." Vagnoli smiled with pleasure at his recall of another quaint English expression.

Candle flame flickered from the abbey cloister as the monks entered the church two by two, cowls drawn over their faces, arms folded beneath their habits.

"Thank you for your time, Cardinal Vagnoli." Moran left the monks to their prayers. His instincts told him that Vagnoli was innocent of Horgan's blood. There was no apparent motive; in fact, it would have been detrimental to Vagnoli's mission to cause Horgan any harm. Interesting about the library funds, though. Whatever deficit the school was struggling to manage, it seemed that the abbey had no such financial embarrassments. Moran wondered if Horgan had been aware of this anomaly, and how closely the school and abbey worked together regarding such delicate worldly concerns. Perhaps the headmaster could shed some light.

He glanced at his watch. Neads should be returning from the wilds in half an hour or so. The DS had looked furious when Moran sent him off. That pleased Moran. Neads needed a kick up the rear. Somewhere in there was a good copper, even if the cocky so-and-so's current remit was stitching up his acting senior officer. But Moran wasn't going to let that happen, and DS Neads would suss that out soon enough, even if he had to learn the hard way.

Moran found his way to the school entrance. No one was about; teachers and pupils had deserted Charnford Abbey in favour of their homes, and the monks in favour of communion with their God. Moran twisted the wrought iron circlet, pulled the oak doors open and stepped outside.

Under normal circumstance it would have been a magical scene. All around was a landscape of white, the stillness absolute. Moran stood for a long time thinking about his brother, the pointless, wasted years, and the extraordinarily unpredictable renaissance that had cruelly been denied him.

As Neads pushed on through the open field towards the dark maw of the woods he busied himself with vengeful thoughts and wove elaborate fantasy scenes in his mind of a time beyond the investigation. He imagined the pub gathering, the slaps on the back, the shaking heads as he outlined Moran's incompetence and how he, Neads, had grabbed the baton and run with it, leaving the older man trailing. He imagined the Chief's nodding approval and the admiration of the WPC from Fraud who'd given him the eye last week. Fit enough, that one: Redhead, nice figure, come-on-baby expression.

Neads picked up his stride, fired by the image. The going was hard, though. He had to admit he'd never experienced weather like this. His face was buffeted by stinging tendrils of snow, blowing across his bare cheeks like an icy flail. His boots were leaden, each step an effort. Just a few metres to the woods. Neads bent his head and pushed into the wind, willing himself into the cover of the trees. No way Moran could have made it in this. *Old timer*.

Neads trudged on. The whipping wind retreated. He was in the woods. Peering ahead, Neads was heartened to find the lights of the village dimly visible, winking through the persistent curtain of white. His boots crunched the fresh snow, finding a new rhythm now that he had escaped the blinding flurries.

He was thinking about the funeral, annoyed afresh that Moran hadn't let him supervise the removal of the skull. Still, he'd spent time thinking instead. He'd been concentrating on what Bagri had said at the autopsy. About the smell, the knife polish. Thing was, they didn't use knife polish in the Charnford kitchen . . . odd, that. The head cook was dead against it. Neads had been sure the knife had come from the kitchen, but no one had reported any utensils missing either. Remus had every damn thing itemised down to the last teaspoon. Not one piece of cutlery unaccounted for. *That's* what he'd been thinking about: the important stuff, not some irrelevant ancient mystery, however intriguing it might be. What possible bearing could the skull have on Horgan's murder? Just someone messing around. A red herring.

The path dipped sharply, catching him unawares; Neads stumbled and pitched forward awkwardly, his right leg going one way and his left sliding beneath him. His full weight bore down on the trapped limb and he felt his ankle snap like a rotten twig as he made contact with the ground. He screamed and grasped the broken joint to steady it and ease the electrifying pain.

"Damn, damn, damn. Shit!" He howled his frustration to the wind. Unbelievable. *Un-bloody-believable*. He slid forward on his bottom and reached for a nearby sapling in an effort to pull himself upright, but the resultant spasm telegraphed by his unsupported ankle caused him to roll backwards in agony. His coat was now soaking wet, clinging to his freezing skin, driving out any remaining warmth.

Neads told himself to remain calm. This was what training was all about. He was only a comparatively short distance from the safety of either the village or the monastery. All he had to do was keep cool. He grunted a nervous laugh at his unintentional pun. That's the spirit, Gregory. Be positive in negative situations, his training officer had exhorted. *Use available resources* . . . speaking of which, there was his mobile. He felt in his pocket, pulled it out. It was dead. Neads pushed buttons to no avail. He must have fallen on it. It didn't matter; he didn't need it. He took a deep breath and tried to stand. This time the pain wasn't as bad; perhaps the cold was helping. He took a deep breath and hopped forward. His right foot skidded and he fell backwards with a bone-jarring crash that sent fresh waves of pain and nausea through his body.

He lay stunned for a few moments and blinked rapidly as he realised that his face was half-covered in snow. If he'd lost consciousness he could have been buried alive . . . No one would have spotted him, and Neads knew all about hypothermia. The thought galvanised him into action. He slid forward again, this time with slightly more success in that he made a metre or more before the pain made him stop, but then he realised that he had a more serious problem: he had lost all sense of direction. The village lights had disappeared and he had no idea which way he had come. Deep snow covered the footprints he had made before his fall, and it was now snowing harder than when he had set out.

Clamping his chattering teeth together in determination, Neads hauled himself forward in what he prayed was the right direction. The pain from the lower half of his leg had become excruciating – maybe he had a more serious fracture than just a broken ankle. The thought panicked him, and it was a minute or so before he was able to pull himself together. He tried yet again to make meaningful progress but the going was too unpredictable, first sliding him one way, then running him into drifts the other. Eventually he lay back, exhausted. He felt his eyelids flutter; a feeling of lassitude overcame him. It was easier just to relax.

Over the next twenty minutes the falling snow drifted and settled, silently covering Neads' boot tracks, enclosing his body in a white cocoon.

Chapter 12

Phelps pressed the rubberised answerphone button for the third time, frowning and shaking his crew-cut head. It didn't make sense – but then, in a disturbing sort of way, it did. He listened again to the clipped and professional tones of Professor Charles Sturrock, Senior Lecturer in Archaeology at Reading University.

'Hello Brendan. Long time no see. Still, busy men, eh? Now then, this – ah – object you had delivered to me recently. Most extraordinary. I've had a good look at it, conducted a few checks – all quite thoroughly, as you'd expect, so don't worry on that account. I dealt with it myself, as instructed. No third parties and so on.'

Sturrock cleared his throat before continuing. '*Now then, let's be precise. It's hit the time scale at first century, according to the carbon dating. I'm quite confident about that for various reasons that I'll explain when we meet, but one of the most compelling is that the wood has been whitened, or stuccoed, in the same way that the Romans typically used when they manufactured wood panels bearing laws or names. They are usually referred to as 'alba'. The script is exactly what you'd expect from a military Roman governor of that period when processing an execution order. As you know, the remnant is just that – a fragment of an original notice, or to give it its correct term, a titulus. The actual script, the surviving lettering or the causa poenae, I believe, reads like this:*

'This accords with another supposed fragment of Christ's Titulus which is kept in the church of Santa Croce, near Rome. The damaged lettering on that fragment has been proposed to read 'Jesus the Nazarene'. The order of languages is also significant: Hebrew, Greek and Latin. We find the same order on the Charnford fragment, and, as the letters are more or less complete, I can be quite sure as to the correct translation.

'Brendan, I believe this is as genuine a piece as I've ever handled, or am ever likely to handle come to that. And given the significance of its provenance, I must confess to being rather shaken and not a little excited. Still, I respect your request for tact and discretion, so not a word to Bessy, eh? I hope this has been of some help and, as I said, I'm only too happy to meet for a more detailed discussion when you've time. All the best Brendan. Bye for now.'

Click.

Phelps walked to the window, skirting round an overturned armchair. Place was a mess, but then that's what squatters did, wasn't it? Yellow scumbags. They'd run for the hills after the explosion. Hadn't even had the guts to come forward as witnesses. One of the buggers must have seen what was going on in the minutes that led up to the incident, but the Romanians had vanished like a morning mist.

Phelps went to the table and opened the answering machine, ejected the tape and dropped it in his jacket pocket. Had Moran deliberately neglected to mention this? Or was the answer more worrying still – that Moran himself had taken the *Titulus* and then, in some post-traumatic quirk of the mind, forgotten all about it? And if that were the case, what else might the guv be doing – or *not* doing – up at Charnford? Especially after the bad news he'd just received.

Phelps strode briskly to the front door and fished for his keys. He'd been lucky. His neighbours Ray and Helen were away for the week, and he was keeping an eye on things for them. Good neighbours. And, like all good neighbours, they swapped keys. House keys, car keys. Phelps peered into the flurrying snow. Ray's Land Rover was almost covered – and he'd only been in Moran's house ten minutes.

Phelps closed Moran's front door and locked it behind him. Slitting his eyes against the gusting snow he scraped the windscreen with his sleeve and pulled himself into the driver's seat. He had to get to Charnford before something bad happened, and he couldn't help feeling that that was going to be very soon.

Moran's head was throbbing as he made his way towards the kitchens. Something was bugging him, something he couldn't quite put his finger on. To do with the Irish connection. He was sure that Dalton's association with Charnford ranged wider than just supplying the odd firearm on request. The presence of the maids – all Irish, all from the same county. There was an ongoing relationship between Charnford and County Cork. There had to be, and Dalton was the overseer, the provider of labour, favours, and – what else? *Time to do a little research, Moran.*

A narrow wooden staircase between the kitchen and the refectory led up to the kitchen maids' garret. Bernadette had mentioned that she and Maria had been relocated from the maids' lodge on the grounds of Oswald's suspicions of inappropriate behaviour. Moran went up, the steps protesting beneath him.

He knew which room belonged to Maria, the RTA girl. It was next to Bernadette's – the door with the crucifix, she'd told him. Moran went in. The room was small, but tidy. A single bed by the leaded window, a chest of drawers. Couple of nondescript pictures, a Coldplay poster. Maria's scent lingered like a half-forgotten memory. He felt like an intruder – which, to be fair, he was. He wondered about her family, whether they would visit to see where she had lived, or whether they would stay away, the shame of it all outweighing their grief. Funny thing, grief. Unpredictable.

The second drawer in the unit was slightly open. Moran opened it. Underwear, neatly folded. His hands explored amongst the soft fabric and he tried to suppress an almost voyeuristic sense of guilt at this posthumous invasion of privacy. His hands found paper. A letter – no; a bundle of letters. He pulled the bundle free from its covering of brassieres and panties and reclined on the bed, which creaked and sagged as his weight bore down on its exhausted mattress and overstretched springs.

First, a letter from someone named Barry. Some admirer from the old days, nothing of any interest. Next, from her mother. *God keep you, Maria*, it closed. *Don't forget the Holy Mass. Every day, child, and your rosary too. Bless you. Mother.* Next, a sister, Theresa, working in Leeds and asking Maria to visit. Moran tossed it aside.

Somewhere downstairs he heard the movement of culinary equipment and voices raised in laughter. Moran glanced at his watch. Seven o'clock. Where in God's name was Neads? Judging from the smells and sounds drifting up to Maria's eyrie the monks would be assembling for their supper very soon. He turned his attention back to the next letter and scanned the typewritten sheet with growing excitement. Turning the page he looked for the signatory. *Rory D.* Bingo. He reread the opening and drank in the words.

'I just want u to be clear, Maria McCrery, that if yr little job goes badly, u don't say a word about the gun. U don't know anything about it, right? I'm coming over soon to clear up some old business, so u can let me have it back then, right? I might have a use for it. I'll let you know nearer the time. Don't do anything stupid, girl, or u will have me to answer to. I mean it. Don't forget, I'll be listening, girl. As always.'

Moran frowned. *I'll be listening* . . . To Maria? To *what* exactly? Or perhaps *for* what? Moran tried to recall as much as he could about Rory Dalton. What did he know about the ex-terrorist? That he was ruthless, efficient, feared amongst colleagues. Good with incendiary devices, technical stuff. Telecoms. *Phone tapping.* Moran clicked his fingers. That's what the listening comment was about. Dalton was tapping into the Charnford telephone traffic. But why?

Moran examined the room again. A silver-framed photograph on the dresser – a younger, ginger-haired Maria at the beach with, presumably, one of her siblings. Close family, probably, as all Irish Catholic families are, Moran thought wryly – and then, with a jolt, he remembered Patrick and Phelps' telephone bombshell. *A close family. Like mine used to be, once, long ago.*

He sat quietly for a few seconds, clutching the pile of letters. Patrick couldn't be dead, surely? He *couldn't* be. A red mist clouded his mind. Someone was going to pay, and Moran knew who that someone was. His bitter thoughts tailed off as a flashbulb of intuition exploded in his head. *Revenge . . . the patient motive,* his old boss had once said. *It's amazing how long folk will wait for revenge . . .*

The pieces began to take shape. A cornflake in the chamber, Phelps had said. That pointed to a pupil, not a monk. He couldn't imagine Father Horgan – or any other monk, for that matter – indulging in a solo breakfast beneath the altar. So, some kind of midnight feast? A group of boys, maybe? And Vernon, the leader of men, the future Head Boy . . . what had happened? A fight? Some disagreement? Which turned nasty, and therefore needed a cover-up.

But that would require help and guidance of an official sort. A housemaster? Horgan had been a housemaster and had known about the chamber. Dedicated to his charges, Aloysius had said. Dedicated enough to protect them from disgrace . . .

So, if the buried corpse wasn't a schoolboy, then who was he? Someone associated with the school. Connected with Dalton. An employee. An *Irish* employee . . .

Moran dialled Phelps' number. It went to voicemail after five rings. His voice sounded harsh in the quiet room.

"Phelps – can you check out missing persons in County Cork, circa 1965-70? Have a ferret in the local papers. Quick as you can. I'll look up the school records.

Never mind Lawson. If he asks, refer him to me and I'll take the flak." Moran's head was aching; he leaned back on the faded wallpaper, Maria's bedsprings protesting beneath his weight, and shut his eyes. Now he was pretty sure of the mystery corpse's identity . . .

A gust of wind rattled the window. Moran's eyes jerked open. He hadn't drifted off again, surely? He shivered. His hands were cold, sticky – gum from one of the envelopes, probably. He rubbed them together as the wind continued to buffet the thin pane. Moran heaved himself off the bed, found the latch and clipped it back into its frame.

He sniffed his fingers. Something familiar. He remembered Bagri, the little pathologist's nose for an unusual smell. Moran opened the first drawer, moved more clothing aside. In the corner – what looked like a medicine box, on its side. Leaking. He fished it out. The label said: '*Kilkenny's Polish – for all your kitchenware*'. Next to it, a wrapped bundle. He opened it, untying the drawstring like a shoelace. *Cooks' knives*. And one was missing.

Neads became vaguely aware that he was moving, a curious bumping motion as if somebody or something were nudging his bed, trying to wake him. Well, they succeeded, he thought groggily. God, it was freezing. He tried to get up and a spasm of pain shot through his leg.

With a sick bolt of fright he remembered everything. He was lying on his back, looking up into an opaque sky. He tried to move his arms but they appeared to be strapped to his side. He twisted, trying to see who or what might be causing the movement. It was when he tried to speak and realised that his mouth was covered by some kind of elasticated plaster that he felt the first stirrings of fear.

Another jolt. He was moving backwards, quite fast, being dragged on some kind of makeshift sled. He struggled hard, but whoever had tied him had known what they were doing. The sled made contact with some hard object and bounced wildly to one side, almost overturning. Neads heard a voice raised in what he could only describe as a whoop of enjoyment. He strained until the veins in his neck stood out but failed to loosen the tightly-trussed bonds. The crazy, bouncing journey continued.

From what he could see in his peripheral vision – which wasn't much – he was in the open, probably somewhere on the games fields behind the abbey. Where was he being taken? What was his abductor planning to do? Neads toyed with the idea of rolling the sled. He reckoned he could do it with his body weight, but he had to consider his leg; he could cause it further damage by engineering a crash.

On the other hand, he couldn't just lie here and wait to see what happened next. Neads didn't want to dwell on that. He was thinking about Horgan's body in the morgue, that horrendous neck wound. It wasn't going to happen to him . . . Neads had read somewhere recently that there was going to be a lunar eclipse. Didn't the moon affect people? Had he fallen into the hands of a madman? He was gripped with terror, and in spite of the sub-zero temperature he felt sweat trickle down his forehead.

They were moving down a path between two tall hedgerows. If only someone would catch a glimpse of them; surely *someone* would be out and about? But

Neads realised that he had no idea what time of day it was. He had set off for Gilham around, what, five forty-five? He could have been unconscious for an hour, maybe more. And still the snow fell. Sensible people wouldn't be out in this, Neads concluded bitterly.

The sled hit a harder surface, rattling across compressed ice and snow. The car park? Please, God, let Moran be watching. They stopped. A door opened and he felt himself lifted – *hauled* – into a half vertical position. Whoever it was, they were very strong; Neads weighed nearly thirteen stone. Then, a lurching, ascent began. A staircase? Where in God's name was he being taken?

The movement ceased. He was propped against a wall. A door opened with a bang and he was dragged through it and dropped unceremoniously onto the floor. Neads screamed silently as his fractured leg absorbed the vibrations. The door closed with a shudder and he was alone.

All he could see was a high, circular ceiling and a section of wall. Some kind of turret or tower, maybe? Surely his captor didn't intend to abandon him here? If only he could remove the gag . . . Neads started to work on the material with his tongue. After ten minutes he gave up. Hopeless. He tried to roll the sled, but only succeeded in sending fresh bolts of agony through his leg.

Some time later the door swung open with a waft of cold air. Various items were thrown onto the floor with a clatter. Neads swivelled in an effort to see what was happening, but his gaoler was taking care to keep out of his line of sight. Moments later he moaned in terror as the sound of carpentry filled his prison. Whatever fate was planned for him had the inescapable feel of permanence about it. Neads shut his ears against the noise and prayed.

The Bede Library was a pleasantly warm, wood-panelled room located above the senior wing of the school. Moran entered and found it empty; the community were evidently still dining. That suited his purposes.

He made a quick reconnaissance of the bookshelves. A third of the way round the room he found what he was looking for. The Charnford Magazine, Volumes X1 to XV1. He flicked through the first copy that came to hand: 1971. Too late. Another: 1968. Getting there. Next: 1967 Spot on. Moran sat at the nearest table, the scrubbed surface of which was scarred with pupils' initials and sundry graffiti. A clock located above the central mantelpiece told him it was seven forty-five in the evening. A dog barked somewhere, the harshness of the sound muffled by the snow. Moran guiltily remembered Archie. He hoped that the spaniel wouldn't try to escape Phelps' custody; Archie's homing instinct was highly developed.

Moran opened the paperback magazine and scanned the contents page. Teaching Staff, School Officials, Editors' Preface. Various articles, reviews, sports results. Rugby. Under Sixteens. Moran studied the photograph. Earnest young men in striped jerseys, one tenacious-looking lad seated in the middle foreground with a rugby ball balanced on his knee. The ball had been annotated: *1967*.

Moran peered closer. There was something familiar about the captain. Of course. John Vernon, the all-rounder; in years to come, captain of rugby, football, cricket et cetera et cetera. He thought of the white flesh parting under Dr Bagri's implacable knife and shuddered. Moran scanned the other faces. The boy to the immediate right of Vernon looked familiar as well. Moran read the text beneath the photograph. M. Jeffrey, J. Wilds, B. Corcoran, H. Phillips. The names meant nothing.

"Ah, Inspector. Sitting in the gloom?"

Moran looked up as Father Oswald appeared in the doorway.

"Anything I can help with?" The monk fussed with the light switches. "Bit of an anachronism, the Bede, I'm afraid. We're building a new library you know. Quite state of the art."

"You're fond of books then, Father?" Moran said, looking up from the photograph.

"Oh, absolutely. The stuff of learning and so on. We'll be creating an electronic archive as well. It's terribly exciting."

"Is that so? What do they call those devices?" Moran groped in his memory. "Kinders?"

"Kindles." Oswald smiled paternally. "A marvellous invention. Of course, not everyone subscribes to the technology, especially the older monks, but . . . "

"That's progress?"

"Indeed, Inspector."

Moran ushered the monk over. "I wonder, would you mind? In your capacity as librarian, would you know anything about this boy?" He pointed to H. Phillips, the boy next to Vernon.

Oswald leaned forward and ran his finger along the row of seated footballers. "Now then, 1967, gosh. A memory test indeed." He pushed his glasses down the bridge of his nose and squinted. Moran noticed that Oswald's hands were calloused and marked, as if he had spent a number of years in manual labour. Which, to be fair, was what monks tended to do. They had a printing press at Charnford, and a thriving workshop where furniture repairs were apparently undertaken by a team drawn from the community. Oswald was no doubt a member of such a team. Whatever else he felt about the monks, Moran couldn't help but feel admiration for the Benedictines' self-sufficiency.

Oswald straightened up. "No. No, doesn't ring any bells. But 1967 – well, it's a little before my time, Inspector."

"I see. Well, thanks anyway. Anyone else I might ask?"

"Let me think." Oswald stroked his chin. There was a small cut above his eyebrow, Moran noticed, just above the horn rim of his glasses, as if some stray splinter had flown up from his workbench.

"Father Aloysius is sure to know," the monk said. "He'll be just leaving the refectory. Shall I fetch him for you?"

"Don't worry," Moran said. "I'll seek him out. You're a busy man."

"Well, I suppose I do have a finger in many pies, so to speak, Inspector." Oswald hesitated on the threshold. "I was going to ask you if you had any news on the missing–"

Moran stood up. "The *Titulus*? Not yet, I'm afraid."

"And the Cardinal?"

"Patient rather than anxious, I'd say."

Oswald nodded. "I see."

"I thought you were going to ask me how the murder enquiry was progressing, Father, that being my most pressing concern. Yours too, I imagine?"

"Of course. Naturally – and how are things in that respect?"

“Let’s just say I require a little further clarification,” Moran said. “I’ll soon be out of your way.”

“Oh, well, I didn’t mean to suggest–”

“Of course not,” Moran said.

“Well, then, if there’s nothing else?” Oswald opened his palms.

“I’ll track you down if need be,” Moran said. “Rest assured.”

Phelps cursed as the Land Rover lurched into another drift and stalled. He switched the hazards on for the third time and got to work with the spade. The street lights cast orange light over the weirdly surreal landscape. Without their diffused glow it would have been almost impossible to work out where the road finished and the ditch began. Everywhere was a spreading meadow of white. Phelps thought fleetingly that it would feel a bit like this to be standing on the surface of the moon.

He paused and wiped his brow. He was still on the main road; he had yet to tackle the country byways around Charnford Abbey, which would, he realised, be all but impassable. But he had no choice. After he’d broken the news of the explosion to Moran he’d made a few calls. Phelps had many friends in the force, at least one contact in each constabulary – something which had proved invaluable during previous investigations. He’d struck lucky on the third call to Ivan Macintyre, a Leeds-based DS who’d transferred up to Yorkshire after remarrying. Macintyre told him they had one unsolved: a man in his fifties, throat cut. Lecturer at the University. No apparent motive. Phelps checked the victim’s background: Christopher Lowndes, ex-pupil of Charnford

Abbey School. Someone was bumping off old boys like they were going out of fashion.

A little more research turned up something even more interesting: a newspaper article from the late sixties. Just a few lines, nothing special; he'd nearly missed it. A house fire, in Earley. Two fatalities, one severely injured male, aged twenty-four, by the name of Hugh Phillips, believed to be a Theology student at Reading University. Ex-public schoolboy, Charnford Abbey, 1965–1970. A contemporary of Vernon's. Phelps checked the hospital records. Phillips had been discharged three months later. The university then told him, after a short tussle with a records clerk, that according to their archives Hugh Phillips had never returned to his studies. Which was a problem particularly because the police suspected arson, and Phillips had not only evaded questioning, he'd disappeared altogether.

But I know where you went, Mr Phillips. Phelps threw the spade into the Land Rover's boot with a clatter and heaved his bulk into the driver's seat. *Oh yes, I know exactly where you went . . .*

Chapter 13

Neads licked his cracked lips. God, he was thirsty. And cold. He twisted and strained against his bonds, feeling the rope bite into his wrists. His captor had departed thirty minutes earlier, Neads calculated. What that meant, he didn't care to meditate upon. He was alone – which, at the very least, meant a postponement of whatever was in store.

The pain in his lower leg had dulled to a deep, internal throbbing. He didn't think he was bleeding but he knew he needed medical attention urgently; the injury might precipitate a DVT or some other complication. He had to get out. Somehow.

Neads examined the ceiling: it was high, exposed rafters running from cornice to cornice, and tantalisingly far away just off-centre, a hatch or trapdoor of some sort. That meant there was probably a way up. A ladder, maybe? But even if he could stand, he doubted whether he'd have the strength to pull himself up onto some exposed area of the roof. And his mystery rescuer was clearly fit and able. No, he had to use his brain. He had to talk to this person, reason with him. But he couldn't; his mouth was still firmly sealed.

A key scraped in the lock and Neads' stomach did a slow roll. The door was closed and relocked. Footsteps clicked across the bare floor towards him. He heard the sound of some metallic instrument, like a butcher sharpening a knife. Neads' eyes bulged in terror. A wave of nausea passed through his body. It couldn't end like this. He was young. He had his whole life to live. *It wasn't fair . . .*

He felt the rope binding his arms drop away. They flopped uselessly, stiff and numb. Neads felt them lifted, stretched to full extension. From behind came a low hum of contentment, the sound of someone happy in their work. Neads twisted and strained, but it was futile; he couldn't bring his eyes to bear on whatever preparations were being made. However, after a few seconds he understood the purpose and sweat broke out afresh on his forehead, clammy and urgent. He knew what was going on all right: he was being measured.

Moran wished he'd had the foresight to keep a pack of paracetamol in his pocket. His headache was relentless, robbing him of the very thing he needed most: the ability to think. But it was all coming together nevertheless, the way it usually did when he'd given his subconscious time to process the information. Sure, the loose ends would evade placement for a while, like spare patio stones cut to the wrong shape, but eventually, by a process of logical rearrangement, they would fill the gaps perfectly.

Dalton was coming, there could be no doubt; it was just a question of when. Moran wondered how old Rory Dalton had been when his relative had disappeared. A cousin, maybe? Or a brother. More likely a brother, to prompt such intensive surveillance. So, when had the unproven possibility of his brother's murder prompted decisive action? How long had Rory Dalton spent poring over banal recordings, ears sharply tuned for some shred of evidence, some careless word? How many hours devoted to debriefing Charnford workers – workers *he* had been supplying to the abbey? A violent man, yes, but a patient one also.

And his patience had been rewarded. The listener had finally heard something tangible. Moran had no way of knowing exactly what had passed between Horgan and Vernon during their telephone conversation, but he could take an educated guess. Mismanaged school finances, the threat of dissolution – of the school at least – and a well-heeled old boy with a dark secret. But Vernon was a tough character, certainly not one to lie back and cough up. He had rebuffed Horgan's blackmail threats and attempted exactly what Moran would have predicted: removal of the evidence.

And that's where it had all gone wrong for Vernon, because someone else had joined their dangerous game – someone with their own agenda. Vernon's attempt to hide his buried secret had failed. And then the past had caught up with him in the shape of the eavesdropping Dalton's professional hit. Clean, tidy, easy; Vernon, already injured, providing Dalton with an opportunity to finish the job and pin it on the original attacker. But the Irishman had given himself away by using a rare and traceable blade.

Another thought lurched into Moran's mind: *what about the other guilty boys?* What if Horgan had named Vernon's accomplices during the tapped phone conversation? If that were the case, Dalton's hit list would be complete and other lives in danger . . .

The library was silent, the stillness heavy with the burden of his thoughts. Moran rubbed his eyes and let his hands slide down his stubble-spiked cheeks. The rugby photograph lay before him on the desk. 1967. Which of these fresh-looking lads had been with Vernon that fateful night beneath the chapel? Moran contemplated the time-frozen vignette. There was Vernon, and seated next to him the boy with the familiar features. Something clicked into place in Moran's beleaguered brain. *Of course – the homing instinct* . . . Oswald maintained he hadn't recognised the eager, guileless face – but Moran didn't believe him. Even though it had later been horrifically burned the features were discernable – if you looked carefully.

Moran closed the magazine and stood up. It was time to save Abbot Boniface from the nemesis that was Rory Dalton.

Moran was on the steps leading down to the senior wing when the lights went out. He fumbled in his jacket pocket and found his Dunhill cigarette lighter. He'd been sure it would come in handy one day. The flame guttered as a blast of wind battered the school brickwork, finding its way between the gaps and ruffling his hair like a ghostly hand. Moran shivered. Power cable down, probably, he reassured himself.

The senior wing was cloaked in darkness. Moran shuffled along, lighter aloft, feeling like an extra from *Haunted House.* He arrived at the Court of Arches, where the coffee machine stood silent by the prefects' staircase and the gold-embossed achievement boards glinted dully in the localised light provided by the Dunhill. Moran raised his arm a little to view the roll of honour, the surnames and initials of bygone rugby and cricket captains. There he was: *1969: John Vernon.* As he angled the lighter to view the next board, a high-pitched scream echoed along the main cloister, escalating in volume before being choked off by another pane-rattling buffet of wind.

Moran froze, rooted to the spot. Were his ears playing tricks? Just the wind, surely? With his heart beating fat, lazy duplets against his ribs he began a slow advance along the cloister towards Haywood Hall. He passed the junior library, an empty classroom, the staff room . . . and threw up a protective hand as torchlight blinded him.

"Who is it?" A familiar voice. The torch wavered and went out.

"Holly?"

"Is that you, Chief Inspector?"

"The very same." Moran flicked the knurled knob of his Dunhill and Holly's face lit up in the orange circle of light. "I thought you'd left for the holidays. What on earth are you doing in there?"

"Marking. Reports, you know. The work never ends with the term."

"Of course." He hesitated. "Did you hear that cry?"

"Cry?"

Moran felt slightly foolish. Perhaps it *had* been the wind. "I thought I heard a scream – after the power cut."

"The wind." Holly smiled. "I heard it too." She pointed to the window. "Just listen to it."

Moran suddenly remembered Neads with a faint sense of unease. He hoped the DS hadn't got himself lost – in a blizzard of this severity you wouldn't want to be outside for long.

Holly took his arm. "Come in for a sec – I'm working by candlelight."

"Be prepared, eh? I'll bet you've got a copy of the Girl Guide Handbook tucked away somewhere."

Holly laughed. "Not me. This has happened before; the electrics are positively prehistoric."

Moran allowed himself to be led into the dimly-lit staff room. The interior was divided into a series of partitions, each containing a desk and an assortment of personal ephemera. Holly's alcove was tidy and sweet-smelling; two scented candles burned brightly on her window ledge and a vase of fresh flowers, balanced precariously on the edge of her desk, overrode the underlying grassy fragrance of books. Moran waited until she had set the torch down and turned to face him before moving forward and holding her in a tight embrace.

"Wow. I wasn't expecting that," she purred in his ear. "Taking advantage of a woman in the dark. Not what I expect from Her Majesty's finest."

Moran hadn't been expecting it either. He couldn't believe what he'd just done. "I don't usually conform to expectations." He nuzzled her shapely neck. He had not been rejected. It was too good to be true. And actually it was, because he knew that he was about to spoil the moment. "Holly?"

"Mmm?"

"You have to leave the building. It's not safe."

Holly pulled away. "*What*?" She folded her arms and cocked her head to one side. "You know how to treat a girl, that's for sure, Brendan Moran."

"I'm sorry. Not great timing."

"You can say that again. What's wrong?"

"I can't explain. I have to sort something out. I hope it won't take long."

"Is this to do with Father Horgan?"

"Yes." He had to be straight with her. "Look, there's an Irishman, a man named Rory Dalton. He wants revenge. I think he's on his way to Charnford."

She reached out and grasped his wrist. "Is it him? The killer?" Her hand went to her mouth. "Oh God. Please be careful."

"Of course. I have my sergeant–" But he didn't. Best not mention that. "Look, I'll be fine. Just get yourself away out of here for a while. I'll call you later."

"Out of here?" Holly pointed to the window. "In this?"

Moran followed her gesture. He could see very little out of the window; the alcove was covered in snow, and the dark rectangles of glass were shaking with the force of the particles crashing against them. She had a point.

"Okay. Just stay put. Don't move. At least I know where you are."

Holly shivered. "All right. If you're sure."

Moran wasn't. But he didn't tell her that either. Instead he bent forward and kissed her full on the lips. Taking her by the arm, he sat her down at her desk and doused the candles.

"Oh no. Not in the dark, please."

"It'll only be for a while, I promise. And you have the torch," he added, trying to sound positive.

"Great."

"I'll be back soon," he said, and shut the door behind him.

The Land Rover eased its way off the Bath road and onto the hill that led up to Charnford Abbey. Phelps squinted and jammed his nose against the windscreen. The four-by-four's wipers were doing their best, but even their workmanlike sweep was fighting a losing battle against the severity of the blizzard. He felt the tyres slide, shift, and spin ineffectually as the incline became steeper. It was no good. No vehicle was going to make it up here tonight.

As Phelps pondered his best plan of action a flash of headlights in his mirror made him twist in alarm. *Some crazy . . .* He threw himself across the passenger seat as a van (a blue VW, rear wing dented, offside mud flap missing) cannoned into the side of his vehicle, yawed crazily towards the ditch and then, fishtailing wildly, righted itself and was gone in a spectacular flurry of slush.

Phelps groaned, clutching his ribs where the gear stick had all but impaled him, and pushed open the driver's door to inspect the damage. The wind bit into the exposed parts of his body and snow blinded his attempts to free the rear wheel from the confusion of twisted metalwork that had, until recently, been the wheel arch. He soon gave up. The car was not going anywhere. Phelps delivered a hefty kick to the rear bumper and made what he knew to be a futile call for backup. Then he started walking.

It was hard going; when logic prompted him to consider self preservation as a serious alternative it was a single thought that drove him on. The van that had wrecked Ray's four-by-four was the same vehicle a witness had observed speeding away from Moran's house on the afternoon of the explosion. No coincidence – someone was after Moran, and Phelps knew he had to be at the abbey quicker than he was going to be. He dipped his head and pressed on, teeth gritted as much in determination as against the howling blast of the storm.

Chapter 14

The nagging insistence that something had happened to DS Neads would not be subdued, but, Moran rationalised, there was little he could do about it. Neads would have to take care of himself. As he made his way through the empty cloisters Moran mollified his conscience with the thought that Neads had probably got himself lost, or taken shelter in the village until the worst of the storm blew over. But a darker possibility was tugging at this comforting scenario – the possibility that the Charnford murderer had found another victim.

Moran sincerely hoped he was wrong. Granted, he hadn't taken to Neads, but he felt responsible nevertheless; Moran hadn't lost a sergeant in thirty years of policing, and he had no desire to spoil that statistic. He pushed through the swing doors connecting the school to the monks' cloister. Yes, he hoped he was wrong about Neads. He hoped he was wrong about Oswald, too, but he doubted that. Just one piece of the puzzle left and his theory would be proven . . .

"Good evening, Chief Inspector." The voice, coming as it did from the shadows, would have alarmed Moran but for the Italian accent.

"Cardinal Vagnoli." Moran halted and gave a formal nod, wondering at the monk's ability to make him feel like a trainee altar boy. "Can't stop, I'm afraid."

Vagnoli, seated on one of the wooden window seats that ran along the length of the cloister, raised an arm in acknowledgement. "I shan't detain you, Chief Inspector. I am praying for the success of your investigation."

I'll bet you are . . . Moran hurried on in the direction of the abbey church and Abbot Boniface's office, the lilt of distant plainchant telling him that the community had already gathered for Compline, the last official service of daily devotion. The rise and fall of the monks' voices filled the air, the words familiar to Moran's ears:

Convert us God our salvation, and be angry with us no longer.
God come to my assistance, Lord, make haste to help me.
Glory be to the Father, and to the Son, and to the Holy Spirit, as it was in the beginning, is now, and ever shall be, world without end. Amen. Alleluia.

The door to Boniface's office was unlocked, as Moran had expected. His eyes, already accustomed to the dark, confirmed that he was alone. He shut the door gently behind him. Wind gusted briefly in the open fireplace, flapping a sheaf of papers on the desktop like a nervous nest of doves.

Moran sat in the leather chair, flicked his Dunhill and slid open the first drawer. A stab of pain shot across his forehead. He dropped the lighter and clutched his head. Not for the first time he wondered if there was something seriously amiss under his skull. His skin felt clammy as he felt for his pulse, but the beat was reassuringly steady.

The pain cleared and he refocused his attention on the abbot's desk. Letters, orders of service, building plans and parish notices all underwent Moran's brief but thorough scrutiny. And suddenly there it was: innocuous enough at first sight, but its contents had stirred up jealousy, hatred and, eventually, murderous intent.

Moran walked to the window and parted the heavy curtains. The storm was easing. The grounds were virgin white. No sign of Neads tramping wearily from the abbey gates. A sliver of moonlight washed out the Dunhill's weak flame as Moran read the memo for the third time:

To: Oswald OSB
Date: September 10th

Oswald –

Whilst I appreciate your commitment to the library and its archives, along with your undoubted enthusiasm for the upcoming building project, it is with regret that I have to inform you that I have decided to appoint Fr. Horgan as chief librarian and overseer of the building work. I know this will be a disappointment to you, but I trust that you will be able to work with Fr. Horgan – a brother of great experience in all things literary and architectural. I want you to know that I value your contribution to the abbey and its work, and this decision should in no way be seen as a negative reflection on your diverse and enthusiastic work at Charnford.

Every blessing,

Boniface OSB
Abbot

Three months had elapsed since the memo had been written. Three months of bitter, anguished, introverted anger. Moran folded the paper, found the guest's armchair and sank gratefully into it. God, but he was tired. He closed his eyes, and the room receded like a blanket being pulled from under him.

He was beneath the chapel, in the corner of the vault, looking in. Before him a life-sized crucifix had been erected. Father Horgan was standing beside it, pointing at the *Titulus* with a bloodied finger, stretching his arms wide in imitation of a crucified man. The base of the cross was surrounded by grinning skulls, one of which swivelled to stare at him accusingly. The skull belonged unmistakeably to DS Neads. Moran tried to back away, but he was seized from behind in a relentless grip. He turned to see John Vernon's blanched face grinning into his. Moran opened his mouth to scream but nothing would come. The grip tightened and the cross loomed ever closer. Vernon opened his hands to reveal a set of ugly, broad-headed iron nails.

At that precise moment the door opened and Moran jerked awake.

It was not the abbot.

Oswald closed the door behind him and moved silently across the carpeted floor. "Is the abbot expecting you, Inspector? I see you have made yourself comfortable."

"A little too comfortable, it would seem." Moran's heart was racing but his voice was even.

"Falling asleep on the job again? The Chief Constable won't be very happy."

"And you've been in touch, obviously." Of course Oswald knew Lawson. That made sense of Phelps' hurried substitution. "What is it? Bridge club? Confessional favours?"

Oswald chuckled. "Nothing so intellectual, Chief Inspector Moran." The prior moved around the pedestal desk and sat himself comfortably in the abbot's chair. "A common interest in fishing. The Kennet, you know? Early risers catch the best fish. We've passed many a happy dawn together by the lock."

"I'm touched." Moran was overcome by a creeping paralysis. He could move his arms, but his legs were lumps of inanimate meat. His head throbbed a steady four beats to the bar.

"How did you know? You do know, don't you?" Oswald leaned forward and clasped his hands as if conducting a parental interview.

"Know?" It had been an unusually fragmented path to knowledge, Moran reflected. What had been the key, the final combination that had sprung the lock? He couldn't pinpoint it now. All that remained was the knowledge; the certainty. And the crumpled memo in his pocket. The past had threatened to obscure the present, something that Oswald had probably hoped for and no doubt exploited. Did he owe Oswald an explanation? Probably not. Perhaps for the late Father Horgan's sake then, especially after the canny old monk had gone to such lengths to point the finger.

Moran licked his dry lips. "About you, you mean?" He asked this more to test his faculties than to seek clarification. What was wrong with him? Had Oswald poisoned him? Not possible; he'd not had any food or drink since the morning. What, then? *Purewal's prophecy*, his subconscious whispered. *The brain is a very sensitive organ, Chief Inspector . . .*

"You take my meaning correctly, Inspector."

The gentle cadences of the *Ave Maria* filtered into the room, filling Moran's head with images of Blackrock: morning prayers, shoe polish . . .

Oswald tapped his thumbs together. "I need to know – how did you guess?"

"I don't guess," Moran croaked. "Never guess." Was that his voice? The sound came to his ears through a long tunnel, distorted and harsh.

"Can I fetch you a glass of water? You look pale." Oswald studied him through his thick glasses.

"What have you done with Neads?"

"Neads? Your rather self-absorbed sergeant? Nothing – for my part, that is. Of course, I cannot guarantee his safety– but I am overreaching myself, Inspector. Plenty of time for revelations later." Oswald consulted his watch. "Compline isn't due to finish for at least another hour."

"Well then." Moran took a pained breath. "I'll go first, shall I?"

"If you feel able." Oswald flashed a brief, sympathetic smile.

"It's only right to start with Father Horgan." Moran spoke with a huge effort. "A clever man. I understand he was appointed over you as librarian?"

Oswald's face darkened, but his smile prompted Moran to continue.

"Perhaps I could take you up on your offer of a drink?" Moran waited, conserving his strength as Oswald poured water from a decanter and pushed the glass across the desk towards him. It was too far away. If he leaned over to pick it up he would fall. And then his time would be up. No good. Dry lips it was then.

"Thanks." He tried to raise his arm in a casual gesture, but even this small movement was apparently beyond the motor ability of his brain. Odd that his thinking was crystal clear. Moran gunned the mental accelerator. "Horgan was holding two items, you may recall."

"I do." Oswald's face was bright with concentration. "A length of shin bone in one hand and Charnford's famous relic in the other."

"Exactly. And I suppose you thought that was coincidental? After you'd crept up behind him and slashed his throat?"

Oswald inclined his head. "A grasping reflex, the coroner's man said."

Moran nodded. "That's probably what Horgan wanted you to think. Because if you'd worked it out, you'd have confiscated his props pronto."

"I don't understand."

"No. I don't expect you do. Horgan taught languages, didn't he?"

The frown on Oswald's face deepened. "He did."

"French and German being his specialities?"

"Yes." Now Oswald was intrigued. He was leaning across the desk. He seemed to be enjoying himself.

"Good. Well, let's dissect your chosen name, shall we?" Moran paused, the effort of speech draining his strength. In a movie the cavalry would arrive any time now, just as he passed out.

"My name? – Ahhhh…" Understanding broke over Oswald's face.

"Easy, really." Moran forced himself to continue. While he was talking he was still alive. "Think about it: two hands. One word per hand."

"*Os*. The bone *en Français*." Oswald's face shone.

"Spot on. And in the right?"

A rich chuckle escaped from Oswald's lips. "The *Titulus*. Which is made of wood. Or *wald* in German."

Moran nodded. It was about all he could do physically. "Not bad for a man with only seconds to live."

"Indeed. Indeed." Oswald nodded vigorously.

Ave Maria . . . The assembled monks' voices reprised and died away.

"Worthy of a little respect, I'd say." Wrong, Moran. That was a wrong turning. A cul-de-sac. A mood breaker . . .

"Respect?" Oswald hissed. "*Respect*? He might have known his subjunctive from his ablative, but he had *no idea* about technology. About taking the abbey into the twenty-first century. Lord–" Oswald held his head in his hands briefly, and then opened his arms wide in a gesture of hopelessness. "Between the two of them they'd have run the abbey to rock bottom in no time – just like–"

"Just like the school," Moran offered.

"Yes. Just like the school," Oswald spat. "It's draining the abbey's resources. We simply can't go on propping it up with abbey funds."

"I'll come back to that presently," Moran said. "So, anyway, you killed Horgan and tried to spook Boniface, to push him over the edge. The skull, the message – that was you, wasn't it? The abbot doesn't keep too well – mentally – am I right?"

"The skull was a tad theatrical, I admit," Oswald replied. "As for Boniface," he laughed harshly. "He's never been the same since it happened. A clever man, but yes, you're right, he's a card or two short of a full pack."

"And I suppose, unless he does the decent thing and breaks down completely, he's your next potential target? Since he's the only other person who knows of the chamber's existence?"

Oswald nodded.

"So, you were planning to bury them both in the chamber, first Horgan, and then Boniface, seal it up and pray that you could persuade the authorities that they had absconded together? But Vernon came along at the wrong time, and ruined it all." Moran concentrated on his breathing, the look on Oswald's face answering his question. Moran let his breath out slowly. Perhaps what he was experiencing was only a blip in his recovery, not some catastrophic collapse. He'd seen enough stroke victims in his time, spoon fed and helpless, eyes pleading for release. That wasn't for him. Better to go down fighting. "And there was something else, as if Horgan hadn't given me enough."

"Please. Go on."

Moran wet his dry lips. "When you met me in the car park that first morning – you weren't wearing your scapular. What happened to it? Bloodstains, I'm guessing."

"*Very* good, Inspector. You're right. I had to remove it. I was prepared for Horgan's despatch you see, but Mr Vernon caught me unawares. Fortunately for him we were interrupted by Father Benedict. As you know, Mr Vernon got away, but not before he'd made rather a mess of my clothing."

Moran nodded. "Now tell me about you and Maria."

A pained expression passed briefly across Oswald's face. "Ah. Poor Maria."

"She liked you, didn't she? Confided in you? Good old Ozzy, always the sympathetic ear . . ."

"No crime in that, Inspector."

"But that's exactly what she had in mind, wasn't it? A crime. A crazy plot to save the school and keep her job."

"She didn't exactly *tell* me about that," Oswald said with a pained expression, shaking his head.

"But I'll bet that she implied she was up to no good, didn't she? Or at least that she was considering some desperate idea."

Oswald's eyes narrowed behind his glasses.

"You spied on them, didn't you?" Moran said. "You heard them talking. Were you listening at Maria's door? Or through a glass in the toilet next door?"

Oswald snorted, looked down at the papers on the desk.

"My God – you were. That's why you moved them from the lodge, wasn't it? And you knew their crackpot plan was likely to go pear-shaped and reflect badly on the school. So you sat on it. What parent would send their child to a school for bank robbers? When the press get hold of it – and trust me, they will – next year's intake won't give the accommodation staff many sleepless nights."

Oswald shrugged. "The school has been struggling for years. I wouldn't be so presumptuous as to imagine that I could bring it down on my own."

"But anything to help the possibility along, right?" Moran went on. "And there was something else, too." The office lights flickered on briefly, and then went out again. Maybe someone was attending to the fuses somewhere in the labyrinth beneath the cloisters.

"Well, don't keep me guessing, Inspector." Oswald began a casual inspection of the abbot's papers, shuffling them into distinct piles as if preparing for some administrative audit. "Your summary is fascinating."

"Jealousy. You knew about Maria and her boyfriend – Montgomery, was it? And you didn't like the idea of her being interested in anyone else. I'll bet you laid it on really thick about the school's financial difficulties and the threat to their jobs. You *wanted* them to go ahead with their lunatic plan, didn't you? Two over-excited boys, a comely girlfriend, a bank robbery. It couldn't have ended well, could it? And it didn't."

Oswald paused in his task. His hand disappeared beneath the folds of his tunic and reappeared holding a long kitchen knife. He placed it carefully on the desk, folded his arms and sat back attentively.

"You knew all this and didn't raise a hand to stop it. Because it suited your purposes – your ambitions." *Steady, Moran. Don't push it too far . . .*

Oswald was playing with the knife, running his finger up and down the blade.

Moran tried to flex his arm muscles. Pins and needles ran up and down his spine. "And then old Horgan gets the librarian's job. Was that the decider for you? Is that why you slit his throat?"

Oswald shook his head slowly. "You don't understand. *Can't* understand."

"Try me."

The monk drew a long breath. "They were as thick as thieves, those two. Excuse the expression, Chief Inspector."

"Horgan and Boniface?"

Oswald nodded. "Of course I knew the background. We all did. It was never spoken of."

"The abbot's past, you mean? His attempted suicide, his guilt?"

"Exactly. Horgan put him up for abbot, you know? After he'd rescued him from the brink and welcomed him into the brotherhood."

"I thought it had to be something like that."

"Well, I must say, Chief Inspector, I am very impressed by your intuition." Oswald rotated the tip of the knife against the desktop, moving the handle with a wide, circular motion.

"I've been at it a long time." *Too long*, Moran thought. *And maybe not for much longer . . .* "It makes sense that Boniface – or Hugh Phillips, to use his original name – returned to his crime scene. He felt comfortable here in familiar surroundings, and he could repent at leisure under Horgan's watchful eye. Right?"

"Quite so. They ran the abbey and the school between them. Aloysius – well, he's a puppet head, really. Personable and chatty with the parents, that sort of thing. No backbone, though."

Moran issued another instruction to his brain to move his legs. Nothing stirred. "There is a gap you can help with, actually." Moran kept his tone even and low. "How much did you know about the unhappy accident in the chapel vault? 1967, I believe?"

Oswald smiled. "One of the elderly brethren. He knew. He'd seen a boy fetching something from Horgan's room in the middle of the night. He followed him and saw what was going on."

"What? He witnessed an illegal burial and never told a soul?"

"We're a close-knit community, Inspector. We keep ourselves to ourselves. I know that the brother in question offered up prayers regularly for Father Horgan and his guilty secret."

"Is this monk still alive?"

"Sadly not. He passed away last year."

"But not before you found out what had happened?"

"As infirmarian one has certain powers of persuasion at one's disposal."

Moran felt nauseous. He could well imagine what persuasive powers a sick mind like Oswald's might have employed upon an elderly, dying monk. "You know the identity of the victim?"

"His name was Fergus Dalton. A simple lad, but I'm told he would always answer back when provoked. That, apparently, was his downfall."

The elation Moran might have felt at having his suppositions confirmed was quashed, not by any fear for himself, but by fear for Holly, alone and vulnerable and under the same roof as not one, but three potentially homicidal men. "Father Oswald – I have to tell you that you are in grave danger. You and the rest of the community."

For a moment Oswald looked puzzled. Then he threw back his head and laughed. "From Boniface? I don't think so. He's unhinged but harmless."

Moran shook his head. "No, not Boniface. From the same person who finished off John Vernon for you."

For the first time Oswald looked puzzled. "Finished? I assumed that–"

"You assumed that Vernon died of the wounds you inflicted in the chapel?" Moran shook his head. "Very sloppy."

"Then who–?" Oswald had begun to rise from the abbot's chair. He was holding the knife in a loose but workmanlike grip.

There was a click and creak as the abbot's office door swung open. Moran still couldn't move. Only eyes and tongue were functioning. Neither could he turn his head to see who had just entered the room. But he recognised the voice all right. He'd know that brogue anywhere, even though only two words had been uttered.

"Abbot Boniface?" Rory Dalton enquired as he stepped into Moran's line of vision.

"I certainly am not," Oswald replied. "And you are?"

"Rory Dalton's the name. You murdered my brother. You and your buddies."

Moran could see the black muzzle of the silencer in Dalton's fist.

Oswald held up both hands and backed away from the desk, as if trying to disassociate himself from it. "No! You're quite wrong. I'm not the abbot, I'm just–"

"Liar," Dalton said, and shot Oswald through the head.

Chapter 15

At least it had stopped snowing, Phelps reflected grimly as the dark mass of the abbey loomed ahead. But the wind was relentless, slicing through his raincoat and jacket like a rapier. Phelps set his legs to work in a final push up the steepest gradient of Charnford Hill. The full moon broke briefly through the cloud cover, lighting his way so that he was able to discern the outline of the school frontage ahead. What should he do? Ring the bell? Walk to the abbey church entrance? Was it his imagination or could he hear singing over the howl of the wind? What was it Moran had called it? Plainchant, that was it. Not even a blizzard could deter the Charnford monks from their devotions, it seemed.

As he approached the tower he saw the van parked at the roadside. He took a short detour, and, keeping his distance, he circled the vehicle cautiously. Satisfied that it was unoccupied Phelps went for the driver's door and jerked it open. His nose twitched. Perfume. And on the passenger seat, a well-thumbed copy of *Hello!* magazine half obscuring a tube of cheap lipgloss. Phelps rummaged a bit more and uncovered a plastic makeup box, two packets of cigarettes, a wad of £50 notes and a small semi-automatic. He checked the chamber. Full. Phelps put the gun in his pocket. The keys were in the ignition; he removed them and crunched his way across the road.

The front door of the school was ajar. He went in, fumbling on either side for a light switch. He found one, clicked it up and down. The darkness remained. Power cut? Poor housekeeping? Phelps wiped his boots on the rough bristle of the doormat and entered the school building, wondering where on God's earth a woman had learned to drive a van like Michael Schumacher on crack cocaine.

Rory Dalton settled his bulk against Abbot Boniface's desk and examined his pistol in mock surprise. "Well now, if it didn't go off by accident, Brendan. Old age must be making me careless."

Moran had long since given up trying to stir his tendons and muscles into action so he stayed put, expression unchanged, simply because he was incapable of doing anything else. Dalton watched him with interest.

"I've seen somethin' like this before, Brendan. It's not good." He shook his head ruefully, as if mourning the passing of a long-suffering friend. The black shoulder-length hair Moran remembered from the early seventies was now greying at the temples and cut in a more contemporary style. The face had filled out, almost softening Dalton's features, but the eyes were the same: deep, dark pits of evil. "Could be a mini-stroke – at your age very likely, *Chief* Inspector Moran."

Dalton looked him up and down appraisingly. "Gone up in the world since I last saw you, eh Brendan? A high flyer, is that it? Bit like your old girlfriend. She took off up to the heights well enough, didn't she? Reminds me of your two buddies earlier today. Sorry about that, Brendan – my wee surprise for you didn't go quite according to plan."

Moran gripped the chair, his forearms shaking with effort. Had he been able-bodied he would have killed

Dalton with his bare hands. But his vision was blurring, Dalton's voice floating as if on thick water.

"It was just unlucky, Brendan. How was I supposed to know you'd lent them your motor, eh? You always were a generous soul, though."

Moran clung to the chair and consciousness. He could feel himself losing the struggle.

"Still, let bygones be bygones, that's what I say. Forgive and forget. Tell you what, Brendan; if you just hold onto this for me, we'll agree to forget our differences, how's that?"

Moran felt something cold in his hand, his useless fingers being curled around the gun. He made a sound in his throat, an internalised scream of aggression.

"What's that you're sayin', Brendan? Now don't be gettin' agitated. Look what you've done to the poor Father Abbot. Or Mr Phillips, should I say? They'll not be thankin' you for that, come the mornin'. Not a bit."

Dalton's breath was in his nostrils, rank and tinged with cigar smoke. "Nice seein' you again, Brendan. Enjoy your time inside." He stuck his nose against Moran's. "You don't give a toss about what happened here, do you? About my big brother?" Dalton looked into Moran's eyes, searching for some gleam of empathy. "He was an *innocent*, and what did these stuck-up bastards do to him, eh?" He spat the question. "They fookin' killed him, that's what." Dalton had begun to pace up and down, emphasising each question with a stab of his finger. "And *why*? For what *purpose*?"

Moran braced himself for the conclusion.

"For *nothing*!" The broken-veined nose swam into Moran's line of vision. His optic nerves were functioning, albeit in a reduced capacity, but Dalton's voice was a funnelled roar. The veins on the Irishman's forehead stood out like fat worms, sweat erupting from his pores like lava. Moran counted every one, trying to give his brain context and focus. Dalton wasn't going to walk out of here, not while he was still breathing. He clenched at the semi-automatic nestled in his palsied grip. If he could just lift it and squeeze . . .

But Dalton had had enough rhetoric. He was at the door. "I don't expect you to understand," he said in a harsh whisper. "But I do want you to know that I'm not finished here yet. Not by a long way. Goodbye, Brendan."

The door shut with a click that echoed in the dome of Moran's consciousness like an analogue reverb. When the noise had died away he considered his predicament: two metres from the corpse of Father Oswald, in possession of the murder weapon, and unable to move. Not what you'd call an advantageous position. But at least he was alive – if the stroke was going to kill him it would probably have done so by now. He might even recover his faculties if he could just keep a cool head.

Moran concentrated on his breathing, sucking in slow, calming draughts of air. He had to get mobile fast. Dalton's last words were etched into his memory like the bullet holes in the wall behind Oswald's spreadeagled body: *I'm not finished here yet . . .*

The first hammer blow fell and Neads' body spasmed, his face contorting in a rictus of agony. His hand was on fire, the nerve endings blazing electrical signals of panic up to his brain. There they stopped, short-circuited by his body's defence system; shock set in and the pain receded.

There was a pause as his tormentor selected another nail, and then the procedure was repeated with his other hand. At this point Neads' mind disconnected from reality and he passed out. When work began on his feet he felt nothing. He left the present behind for happier childhood days – the sun was shining and his mother, dressed in a light summer dress, held out an ice lolly. As he reached for it his hand sprayed blood in a wide arc, covering the pretty dress from top to bottom.

He woke up, screaming through the gag as loudly as his lungs would produce air. Above the noise he was vaguely conscious that the person crucifying him was humming.

Phelps eased his way along the cloister towards the abbey church. The bad feeling had got worse since he'd entered the blacked-out school. What was he expecting? More signs of life than this, he muttered under his breath. He passed the chapel entrance with a shiver and entered the Court of Arches. Not a soul about. The singing grew louder, and eventually he found his way along the long corridor known as the monks' cloister, which joined the school to the abbey and led to the abbot's quarters.

The abbot's door was ajar. Phelps hovered, listening to the monks' sonorous voices echoing in the high arches of the abbey church. He decided to grab the bull by the horns and interrupt the ceremony. If they didn't like it, tough. They had the rest of the week to sing if they wanted to. No sign of Moran, no sign of DS Neads; that and Moran's insistence that he had a suspect in his sights confirmed Phelps' decision. He squared his shoulders and marched purposefully towards the church entrance.

He had only progressed a short distance before he heard what he interpreted as a strangulated shout. Phelps was a big man, but he could move fast when speed was required. He turned and glued his back to the wall, scanning the cloister for danger. The cry came again. This time he pinpointed the source to the abbot's office.

Phelps shimmied his way along the wall and put his ear to the door. Then he heard something he recognised: Moran, clearly unhappy, berating himself with the sort of language Phelps imagined would meet with disapproval should one of the monks happen to pass by. He gave the door a hefty push, automatically casing the room as it swung open.

"Late again, Phelps," Moran said in a voice that was barely a whisper.

"Sorry, guv. Inclement weather." Phelps took in the prone body and the spreading pool of blood. And Moran, sitting bolt upright in the visitors' leather-upholstered chair, a silenced semi-automatic clasped in his left hand.

Phelps felt for Oswald's pulse. "I take it this wasn't your doing, guv?" He dropped the monk's wrist. Oswald was as dead as a doornail.

Moran was trying to get up and Phelps didn't have to be medically qualified to see that something was very wrong. He gently pressed Moran back into the chair. "Easy, guv."

"Phelps – would you mind *very* much–" Moran's voice was getting stronger. He reached for Phelps' hand.

"Just a sec, guv." Moran hadn't shot Oswald, surely? Phelps fervently hoped he hadn't.

"Phelps, look at the state of me." Moran was reading his mind. "I couldn't hit a lorry at ten paces, let alone place two bullets dead centre in Oswald's forehead."

"Can you move your right hand, guv?"

"Of course I damn well can't – what does it look like to you?"

"Well . . . it's just that the gun's in your left hand, and you're right-handed."

"Good. And–?" Moran broke off in a fit of coughing.

"And you can't move your right arm. So, you couldn't have shot him."

"Bravo, Phelps." Moran cleared his throat with a noise that reminded Phelps of a care home he had once visited. "Now, get me up, would you? Rory Dalton is about to add to his tally, and Holly is in the firing line. So is Neads, for that matter."

Phelps made a sour face. "Holly? Holly who? Slow down a sec, guv."

"No. I bloody well won't slow down."

"Okay." Phelps said, keeping his tone low and reasonable. "So, tell me what happened."

"Help me up and I will. And stop treating me like a suspect."

Phelps relented, watching Moran anxiously as he found his balance. The guv was deathly pale, but his eyes were clear and focused.

"Thank you, Sergeant Phelps. Right. Chapel. Let's go."

Phelps frowned. "What about Oswald?"

"He's not going anywhere. He can wait. Dalton can't."

Chapter 16

"*Rory* Dalton? The guy who–"

"That's right, Phelps." Moran was playing a hunch, that said Dalton would visit the chapel before carrying out whatever else he was planning. Why? Because it was his last chance to pay his respects to Fergus.

"Fergus?" Phelps' face creased in consternation.

Moran stopped and took a deep breath, leaning on a pillar for support. His right arm dangled uselessly but everything else appeared to be working. He felt terrible, but he wasn't dead, and as Dr Purewal had pointed out in her usual caring fashion, that wasn't such a bad thing.

"Guv – you should be on your way to hospital, you–"

"Later." Moran straightened. As he did so the lights flickered again. He spoke tersely. "Fergus is Dalton's brother; the body in the vault. He was accidentally killed in some kind of prank that went wrong." They set off walking again, hurrying through the Court of Arches until they were at the chapel door.

"Sir – I need to tell you about the abbot." Phelps' hand was on Moran's shoulder.

Moran nodded, fumbling in his pocket awkwardly. "I know. His name is Hugh Phillips. He was one of the gang who killed Fergus. Attempted suicide but failed. Horgan got him into the monastery – then mentored him for high office."

Phelps looked impressed. "Okay. Old news, then. Sorry. Here. Let me look." He fished a key ring out of Moran's jacket pocket. "Sure?"

Moran nodded. "Sure as I can be."

Phelps hesitated, his doubts resurfacing. What if Moran was lying? Maybe he *had* killed Oswald. Maybe his mind *had* gone off the rails . . .

He unlocked the chapel, pushed the door gently and stepped back, indicating that Moran should go first. Moran gave him an irritated glance and went in. Phelps followed, and they saw torchlight flickering on the chapel ceiling from the funnel of the vault's entrance. A voice, low and lilting, led them cautiously to the altar. Phelps picked up a brass candle holder and hefted it. Moran blocked the stairwell.

"Hello Rory. Sorry to interrupt."

Dalton spun round. "Brendan? By God, a miracle recovery, is it? Well, I suppose you're in the right place for that sort of thing."

"There's no way out, Dalton. I have backup."

"Have you indeed? Come down and fetch me out, then."

"That's the plan."

Moran felt a nudge. Phelps had produced a small semi-automatic pistol. Moran nodded and accepted the weapon. It sat awkwardly in his left hand, but it was better than nothing. Finger on the trigger, he took the first step. "Put your hands up, Dalton. Where I can see them."

Dalton moved away from the earth of his brother's disturbed grave and leaned against the crypt wall. Moran descended warily. Dalton had both hands in the air. He nudged something with his leg – the next moment the wall had tilted sideways, taking Dalton with it. One moment the Irishman was there, the next, he'd vanished.

Moran threw himself forward and ran his hands quickly up and down the brickwork. Where was the lever? Phelps joined him, stamping the flagstones with his boot heels beside the altar where the *Titulus* had rested in its case. Nothing.

"Come on – he'll be out before we know it." Moran hurried up the vault's staircase, ignoring the throbbing in his temple and the numbness in his arm.

"Wait!" Phelps called him back. His hand was resting on a protruding nail in the wall; it moved vertically, and the wall slid aside. They ducked their heads, and found themselves following a narrow passage that wound in a gentle curve. Phelps shone his torch into the darkness ahead but there was no sign of Dalton.

By the time they saw the dead end ahead Moran had guessed where they would emerge. His feet snagged on something. He bent and picked it up. A bundle of clothing. No: a scapular – bloodstained. Oswald's . . .

Moran left it on the floor. It could wait, too. "Now I know why I thought there was someone watching me in the sacristy. They could come and go as they pleased – to and from the chapel chamber. This was Oswald's escape route the night of the murder. Come *on,* Phelps; there must be an exit lever – *quickly*–"

They fumbled in the torchlight. Moran's heart was beating unevenly now, his breathing becoming more of an effort. And then again it was Phelps who found it: a loose brick at the wall's base. A gap opened, the masonry moving on silent hinges. Phelps clicked his tongue in admiration. "Not bad, guv, eh?"

But Moran had already stepped down into the sacristy, wrenching at the door handle. "He's locked it from the outside."

"Step aside, sir, if you please." Phelps applied his shoulder and the lock splintered, spilling them into the connecting corridor between chapel and sacristy. Seconds later they were racing past the locker room and into the main cloister. As Moran rounded the corner he saw Dalton by the staff room.

Holly . . .

He'd told her she'd be safe in the staff room, but now the commotion would entice her into Dalton's path. However, Dalton had come to a standstill, halted by something coming through the double doors by the study hall.

Phelps made a groaning noise in his throat. "Oh no."

Moran had seen it too. The double doors clattered shut and Abbot Boniface, hauling some kind of wooden construction behind him, came into view. It looked, at first sight, to be a sledge-like bier, but with an elevated section like a sail rising from its centre.

Moran's blood went cold. "I think we've found Neads."

Dalton hesitated, rooted to the spot. He shot a backward glance, almost as if he were checking Moran's reaction, before returning his attention to the abbot.

"I knew you'd come." Boniface said in a loud, confident voice. "I am ready. I have prepared for this moment. Look–"

Moran watched in horror as Boniface swivelled the sled and revealed the extent of his madness. DS Neads was impaled on the cross section of the sail. The policeman's eyes were closed, his mouth slack. Blood ran from wounds in his hands and feet, collecting in pools on the cloister's polished tiles.

Dalton raised a hand as if to ward off the sight. Moran knew the Irishman had instigated countless retributions of his own, but even they hadn't topped the barbarity scale like this.

"Guv–" Phelps grabbed Moran's arm. "The pistol–"

"*Not yet* – stay with me–"

They crept along the cloister like ballet dancers on rice paper, Dalton apparently oblivious to their advance. The abbot threw himself to the floor before Dalton. "A life for a life – you must accept my sacrifice. It is right and fitting."

"Who the hell are *you?*" Dalton had found his voice.

Boniface looked up, his face radiant in confession. "Why, I am Boniface, the abbot of this abbey. I know who you are – you are *his* kin."

Dalton looked confused. The Irishman's eyes flicked between Neads and the prostrate Boniface. Moran's finger rested on the semi-automatic's trigger. He could sense Phelps' impatience as the big man held himself in check.

"What? Are you a madman? Are *you* Hugh Phillips? I thought–" Dalton's voice had a nervy quality to it. He was evidently as baffled by the confusion of identities as he was sickened by the spectacle before him.

"I was," Boniface admitted. "In another life. But I have paid for my sins in part, and he shall pay the balance." Boniface stroked the foot of the cross where Neads' feet had been pinned. "He is *so* like Fergus, is he not? They can rest in the earth together. It is right and fitting."

Dalton's eyes narrowed and his hand went to his pocket. Moran raised his pistol. "Drop it, Dalton."

The Irishman laughed and turned. "And what? This place is history after tonight, Brendan. It's all going to go up. Look what they've done." He pointed to Neads' twitching body and the abbot in turn. "Go on – *look*, will you, and tell me these people deserve to live. Shoot me and you'll never know where the bomb has been planted."

Bomb.

Moran kept his voice steady. "What bomb, Rory? *Listen* to me; we need to help that boy." He swallowed hard. How much blood had Neads lost? How much pain could a body take? Moran knew that seconds counted if they were to save him. His left hand gripped the semi-automatic, his emotions roller-coasting between horror at Neads' predicament and the red rage of revenge that was prompting him to shoot Dalton where he stood.

At that moment Boniface launched himself at Dalton's feet, wrapping his arms about his legs, sobbing like a child. "I beg your forgiveness! Give me your benediction . . ."

Dalton pulled away in disgust and his hand came out of his pocket holding a short, businesslike knife. The knife came down and Moran heard Phelps' intake of breath – a curse or exhortation, Moran couldn't tell, but it was the decider. He fired a single shot and Dalton fell, his body rolling on the floor. The abbot cried out, scrabbling to pull the knife from between his shoulder blades, his face contorted in a mixture of pain and grim satisfaction. He looked Moran in the eye.

"Blessed," he said. "I'm blessed at last." He fell forward, the knife protruding from his back like an accusing finger.

Dalton was writhing, trying to get up. At that moment there was a clatter of feet and a series of shouted commands from the Court of Arches. Three uniformed police officers appeared and hurried towards them, torches flashing.

Moran let out his breath in relief. *The cavalry* . . . He leaned against the staff room door and indicated Neads' inert body. "Phelps, for God's sake get the boy off that thing, will you?" And then he turned his attention to Dalton, who had propped himself against the opposite wall, trying to staunch the flow of blood from his thigh where Moran had sited the bullet.

"You *bastard*, Moran."

Moran put his foot on Dalton's leg and applied pressure. Dalton screamed. The WPC who had led the backup team down the cloister put a horrified hand over her mouth, and then hurried to assist Phelps and the two uniformed officers who had begun to prise the nails gently from Neads' flesh.

"The bomb, Rory, there's a good man."

"Take a hike, Brendan."

Moran applied more pressure and Dalton threw up, spraying the tiles with vomit.

"Come on, Rory. I wouldn't want you to get hurt – again." He ground his teeth in bitter satisfaction, venting his rage. It felt releasing, cathartic. His foot pressed down harder.

"Underneath the church," Dalton gasped. "You can't stop her now. I've told her what to do."

"Who, Rory?"

"Two words, Brendan."

Moran brought his heel up but Phelps grabbed him by the lapels and pulled him away. "*No*, guv. *I'll* deal with him, all right?"

Moran was breathing hard. He wanted to kill Dalton, to maim him, carve him into pieces and scatter the debris to the wind.

"I'll go with you, sir," the blonde WPC said. "To the church, I mean." They had removed Neads from the makeshift cross. He was unconscious, but he was breathing deeply.

Damn good thing too, Moran thought as he gathered himself. His palms were sweaty and his heart was on the second page of Ravel's *Bolero*. He pressed the heels of his hands against his eyes and his vision swam back into focus.

"Thank you, Officer but I need to do this on my own. You'd better stay with Sergeant Phelps."

Moran checked the staff room. Holly had gone. He left the team attending to Neads and set off for the abbey church.

The monks were still singing as he made his way along the gloomy cloisters. Moran briefly wondered if Vagnoli was among them. No time to worry about him now. Somewhere nearby, Moran remembered, there was a service door that led to a cellar, the switch room that governed the distribution of electricity in and around the church and monks' quarters. There it was – an unobtrusive arched rectangle cut into the cloister wall. He pushed gently and met no resistance; the door was unlocked.

Moran already suspected what he would find in the switch room, but he needed to be sure of something else first. He walked to the side entrance of the church, the aisle by which celebrants would enter the abbey to conduct High Mass, preceded by their entourage of altar boys, novices, supporting priests and acolytes. The sheer vastness of the building's vaulted roof space, coupled with the intoxicating smell of incense, assailed Moran's senses.

The community was bent in prayer at their last obligation of the day; Compline was almost over. Moran performed a quick head count. Forty or fifty monks, and, yes, there she was, in the corner by the baptismal font. Holly was kneeling, head bowed in prayer. It was so like her to seek comfort in the safety of the church. He shook his head at his naivety. She was hardly going to wait alone in the dark when she could be in the company of the saints. He made his way back to the switch room, took a deep breath and went in.

Moran retrieved the Dunhill from his pocket and stepped into its circle of light, gingerly negotiating the rough steps. It would be just his luck to survive a seizure, only to break his neck in a cellar. He paused on the third step.

"I'm coming down now, Bernadette. I don't mean you any harm. I just want to make sure you're all right."

He listened for a response. A touch on his shoulder startled him. He turned.

"Holly? What on–?"

Holly placed a finger on his lips. She was wearing jeans and a white blouse. "I'll talk to her, Brendan. I know how to handle this."

He opened his mouth to protest, but Holly silenced him with a light tap of her finger. "I used to be a counsellor, remember?"

She called into the darkness. "Bernadette? My name is Holly. I'm twenty-nine – my birthday was last week. We had a brilliant party. Listen, you're going to be okay. Can we come down?"

A stifled sob came back. Moran nodded grimly, and they continued their descent.

"Don't come any closer." Bernadette's voice was shaky but strident. "I know what I have to do."

Moran paused on the steps, rehearsing an appropriate dialogue. He'd read up on psychological profiling and attended the courses, but he maintained a healthy cynicism regarding formulaic approaches. It was an instinctive game; you couldn't teach anyone the rules, because there weren't any.

Holly shot him an enquiring look. She projected an aura of calm, seemed completely at ease as if she did this sort of thing every day. He had a strong sense that not only did she understand the nature of this particular game, but that she also knew exactly how to play it.

"Don't come in!" Bernadette's voice floated up out of the dark. "I'll do it, just like he told me. I will."

"Do what, Bernadette?" Holly's voice was soft, persuasive. She was going to be Bernadette's best buddy. Moran stood back and gave her space. He felt the roughness of the unplastered brickwork against the back of his hand. His right arm was awakening. His heart was beating regularly. He was alive. For now . . .

"If I don't do it, he'll kill me anyway." Bernadette's voice was barely a whisper.

"Rory Dalton can't hurt you, Bernadette," Holly said reasonably. "He's in police custody."

Bernadette laughed, her voice flat against the dryness of the cellar walls. "He won't be for long – don't think you can hold him. You won't." Her voice was thick with conviction. "You might keep him in gaol for a week or two, but he always comes back. I *know* he does."

Moran spoke up. "Yes, he has done before, Bernadette. Believe me; I understand your concern. I know him, you see. But I promise you, this time he's going to prison for a very, very long time."

"Doesn't matter how long," Bernadette replied miserably. "He'll still kill me when he gets out."

"We won't let him, Bernadette," Holly said smoothly. "He isn't going to hurt anyone again. Ever."

Moran bit down on his tongue, thinking of another day in December – his black December: Janice opening the car door, autumn sunshine picking out the red in her hair, the big wave, the smile . . . he couldn't allow Holly to stay. What was he thinking? But she seemed to be in control. Kay and Patrick's faces slid over Janice's in his mind, competing for his attention.

"Are you all right, Brendan?" Holly's voice in his ear, bringing him back.

"Fine. I'm fine." He cleared his throat, indicated that she should go on.

"I'm going to do this, I am . . ." Bernadette's voice was shaking now, mirroring the tremors running through her body.

"Let me just *see* you, Bernadette, is that all right?" Holly had inched down another step; she gingerly put her head around the corner. "I *really* want to have a chat, okay? We can have a good natter, and then I'll buy you a drink at the local, how does that sound? We'll make a real girly evening of it."

Moran listened with admiration. Holly was good. Damn good.

He became aware that the plainchant had stopped; Compline was over. The final prayer would follow, and then the monks would leave the church, retiring to their cells. They had to keep Bernadette talking . . .

"What do you say, Bernadette? Look, I'm a girl. Just like you." Holly had turned the corner. "Can Inspector Moran come in now? He's made sure that Rory Dalton can't touch you. Believe me, Bernadette. I was there. I saw what happened."

She was there? Moran frowned. It was possible. Maybe Holly had been watching from some vantage point before retreating to the church.

"You're *lying*," Bernadette spat.

"No, she's not lying." Moran inched his way around the wall. Bernadette was crouched by a bank of electricity and gas meters, arms wrapped around her body in a tight hug. But it was what she was hugging that made Moran's throat contract and his saliva congeal. Her torso was a circle of wiring, around which cylindrical packages of explosive had been taped. In her white fist she clutched the detonator, her varnish-chipped thumb poised above the red button.

Bernadette lowered her head in an attitude of resignation and Moran braced himself, took an involuntary step back.

"When's your birthday, Bernadette?" Holly asked chirpily. "What do you usually do? Me, well, I make sure I get rid of the boyfriend. After that I get the girls round. Know what I mean?" She winked. "Girls know how to have fun."

A faint trace of a smile moved across Bernadette's face as she lifted her head. "I used to have fun, sure, a long time ago." She sighed, a heavy, defeated shudder.

"Me and Maria, we came over together. Dalton arranged it for us. Needed the work, you know?"

"I understand." Holly had taken another step. "Money isn't everything, but it helps, right?"

"Sure."

"Tell me about Maria."

Moran assessed whether he had time to get to the detonator before the thumb came down. He didn't need to prompt Holly – she was totally in synch with what was required. Her voice was steady, charming, *normal.* And Bernadette was visibly relaxing.

"Maria was my best friend, you know. Crazy, great fun, do anything for a laugh. That was her." Bernadette smiled sadly. When she looked up it was with a searching expression, appealing to Holly's sense of right and wrong. "Why did she die? I don't understand. She was so . . . *alive.*" A pause. "So, I don't know, *alive.*"

The tears came, racking, shuddering sobs. Moran hovered, judging the distance. The connection had been made – not with him, but with Holly. He was an onlooker, an outsider. He had to be invisible. She had to forget he was here. And Holly was intuitively working with exactly that in mind.

"I know," Holly continued. "I lost someone too, a long time ago. He made me feel special, like there was no one else in the world."

Bernadette nodded, her hands busy with the wiring, patting the coils, reassuring herself. "Yeah. That's it." She gave a bitter little laugh. "Keep the blokes away – we don't need 'em. They're all scum."

The atmosphere was subtly changing, the sense of heaviness lifting. Above them in the cloister Moran could hear the sound of shuffling feet; he hoped the monks would quickly disperse to their rooms, that curiosity at the open switch room door would not get the better of them.

"And *he's* the worst." Bernadette's cheeks creased in sudden anger. "He wouldn't leave her *alone*. And him a *Father*, and all . . ."

"Who, Bernadette?" Holly cocked her head to one side, gently probing, not forcing an answer.

"Who? *Who*? You mean you don't know? Jaysus, everyone *else* knows."

Holly smiled. "I've heard rumours, Bernadette. But go on, fill me in."

Moran listened as Bernadette revealed the extent of Oswald's obsessional attentions. He'd been right: jealousy at Maria's dalliance with the boy Mason had fuelled Oswald's motivation, to the point where his manipulative influence over the dead girl had become intolerable. The zesty, risk-taking Maria had been goaded into a crime of such reckless folly that Moran had to wonder afresh how anyone had ever bought into it at all. And now the perpetrator of this persecution lay dead in Boniface's office, a bullet lodged in his brain.

"I'm so sorry." Holly had squatted next to Bernadette. "We can help you, babe, we really can."

Steady. Moran watched Holly's arm move across Bernadette's shoulder. *Steady* . . .

"No!" Bernadette lashed out with her arm, and Holly, caught off balance, went sprawling. "I *know* what you're doing." She was sobbing now, her voice trembling and shaking. "You can't *fix* this. You can't *help* me. I don't *want* to live any more. I'm as good as dead anyhow." One hand trembled over the detonator; with the other she flicked a greasy lock of hair away from her eyes.

Holly eased herself up with a graceful, gentle motion and brushed her jeans. "Hey, hey; take it easy, Bernadette. Listen to me. You've got *everything* to live for. You're young; you've got your whole life ahead of you. You can start again. We'll help you, I promise." She gave Moran a look. "We promise, don't we, Chief Inspector?"

"We do. I give you my word, Bernadette."

"I can't," Bernadette said flatly. "I can't trust anyone anymore."

Moran shifted uneasily. The heaviness was back, the air pregnant with tension.

"Perhaps you should move away a little, Brendan." Holly's voice was strangely calm. Her eyes locked onto his for a moment before she turned back to Bernadette.

Bernadette grasped the detonator box. "You're like all the rest," the kitchen maid said. "You're like *him*. It's all just *words*. Just *lies*. Oh *God – God forgive me* . . ." Her thumb whitened as she applied a stabbing, downward pressure.

In the fragment of time that followed it seemed to Moran that Holly's features shimmered and shifted, becoming almost transparent as she spread her body over the Irish girl like a candle-snuffer. A warm wind lifted him off his feet, pushed him further back, up the stairwell. He was vaguely aware of an intense pain in his legs, a thunderous roaring in his ears and a blinding white light that coalesced into a simple, wavering line. The line twisted, jerked, and then levelled off until it was completely straight, like a giant ruler stretching to the horizon. To Moran it seemed a fitting end; an infinitely flat line, above and around which nothing moved, where all was stillness and calm.

Epilogue

Phelps closed the car door with a practised flick and drew his overcoat around him. A gust of wind ruffled the bare branches of the two great oaks that presided over this corner of the cemetery like silent guardians of the dead. Phelps shivered and looked at his watch. He was the first to arrive. Others would appear shortly, conversing in hushed tones, perhaps offering a quiet word or comment about the service, remarking that the vicar had handled it well given the tragic circumstances, had set the right tone.

Phelps stuck his hands in his pockets and began a slushy amble towards the recently disturbed earth, a bright, almost orange hue in the late morning sunshine. Set against the overall whiteness of the cemetery it seemed an ugly thing, an unnatural and undesirable blot on an artist's canvas. The snow was virtually undisturbed save for a few furtive tracks made by some small animal, and as his footsteps scored a pathway between the gravestones he began to feel a sense of trespass, as if his presence were an aberration, an insensitive mark of disrespect to the resting souls beneath. He gave his head a brisk shake to dispel the melancholy, and toyed with the notion of a quick cigarette before the mourners arrived.

As he drew nearer Phelps saw that he had been mistaken. Two figures were already at the graveside, hidden from view by a snow-clad camellia bush planted centrally between the intersecting paths that wove between the orderly rows of memorials. Phelps hung back for a moment, and then, suddenly ashamed, strode forward at a brisker pace.

They were an elderly couple, he could see now. The taller of the two glanced at him as he approached, nodded briefly and then turned his attention back to the yawning hole, the two lengths of planking and the frost covered tarpaulin with its four symmetrically-placed bricks.

"Mr Lawson. Mrs Lawson." Phelps nodded a pinched greeting.

"Hello, Sergeant Phelps." Mrs Lawson managed a stiff smile. She was a well-preserved woman in her early seventies, he guessed. The skin was pale and powdered, the lipstick a little too thickly applied. Her hair, gathered into a strangely old-fashioned bun, protruded from beneath her hat like that of a waitress from a bygone era.

Mr Lawson senior extended a gnarled hand, which Phelps shook a little less firmly than usual. "I just want to thank you again, Sergeant, for your kind words concerning the passing of our son. I know you have been working closely with him these last few weeks."

Phelps could only nod in response as Mrs Lawson produced a lace handkerchief and dabbed her eyes.

"I can't believe he's gone," Mrs Lawson said quietly. "It's like a bad dream."

Phelps cleared his throat. "I'm – that is, we are – so sorry for your loss, Mrs Lawson. Your son was an, er, exceptional man in many respects."

"We're very proud of him." Mrs Lawson's voice caught. "I just wish – oh, such a stupid accident. What was that other driver *doing?* In *December*, for goodness' sake? William was always so careful with his driving, wasn't he, Eric?" She turned to her husband for confirmation.

Don't laugh, Phelps told himself. *Don't . . .*

"It could have happened to anyone," Phelps heard himself ramble. "An ice cream van, a patch of ice–" He shrugged. What could you say? "Ah. Here's my guv'nor." Phelps pointed, glad of the distraction.

Car doors slammed softly in the middle distance and Moran came into view, walking stiffly on a pair of gunmetal crutches. Phelps watched the guv'nor hobble towards them with something akin to puzzled admiration. How many lives did Moran have?

"I'll tell you something, Mrs Lawson." Phelps laid a large hand on the woman's shoulder. "There's no one thought more highly of the Chief than DCI Moran."

"I don't understand," Mr Lawson said. "I thought DCI Moran was in intensive care?"

Phelps hesitated. Again, what could he say? That Lawson's ludicrous demise had done more to accelerate Moran's recovery than any surgically applied remedy? Phelps cleared his throat.

"Well, you're right; he *was* in the ICU, until last Monday. The thing is, I don't think hospital suits his temperament." Phelps narrowed his eyes against the glare slanting from the hearse's windscreen. "But he'll have a word for you, I'm sure, Mr Lawson. He likes a chat, does the guv'nor."

"So," Moran said quietly. "You saw the medical report?"

The mourners had departed; only Moran and Phelps remained by the grave.

"Signed and sealed , guv. Top of his in-tray." Phelps found his cigarettes, lit up with relish and inhaled deeply.

"Anyone else see it?" Moran adjusted his crutches, planting them with difficulty in the hard ground. "Or–"

"You know me, guv. Compulsively tidy. Can't have irrelevant papers cluttering up the Chief's office."

Moran smiled. "Thank you, Phelps."

A moment's silence.

"And Holly?" Moran's breath hung like Phelps' smoke in the still air.

Phelps took his time. Eventually he said, "Nothing, guv. Not registered at Charnford. Aloysius has never heard the name. No trace in Cork, either," he added.

"And Bernadette was the only casualty?" Moran coughed, painfully.

"Apart from yourself, guv. Yes. The monks had all left the church. The blast went up, not across, otherwise I probably wouldn't be talking to you now."

"If I'd just–"

"Ifs and buts are no good, guv. That's what you used to tell me." Phelps blew out a funnel of smoke. "Bernadette was always going to hit that button. Whatever you said or did."

"Maybe. Maybe not."

"Look, guv." Phelps looked Moran in the eye. "She was terrified of Dalton. He'd been on her case for years, even before she took a job at the abbey. He's the godfather of the Eire mafia, the big man."

"Not anymore," Moran said with some satisfaction.

"Are you going to the trial?" Phelps buried the stub of his cigarette and covered it over with a wedge of snow.

"Wild horses wouldn't keep me away, Robert."

If Phelps was taken aback by Moran's use of his first name he didn't show it. Both men lapsed into a wordless vigil beside the freshly-dug grave. Hard to believe that the implacable Lawson had just been lowered into that cold and inhospitable trench. Moran felt a sudden pang of remorse. They'd never seen eye to eye. Well, it was too late to make amends now.

Phelps was the first to break the silence. "And the relic?"

Moran looked up. "Delivered safely into Cardinal Vagnoli's hands. I understand that Father Aloysius negotiated a generous donation from his friends at the Vatican."

"So, the school survives?"

"The dead boys would be pleased to know that, don't you think?"

Phelps nodded. "I'm sure they would." Phelps paused. "Guv?"

Moran raised his eyebrows, the tiny action producing a brief sensation of disorientation.

"Was there a reason you didn't mention that you'd half-inched the *Titulus*?" Phelps scratched his head uneasily, uncomfortable at asking, yet needing his curiosity satisfied.

"I only *borrowed* it, Phelps." Moran leaned awkwardly on his crutches and grimaced. "It reappeared in the sacristy one night. The only person who could have done that was Bernadette. My guess is that she knew what Oswald was up to. Dalton was on her case the whole time for information. She knew about the chamber. Maybe she wanted to let Oswald know he was being watched, that he didn't hold all the cards. Or maybe–" He paused.

"Guv?"

"Maybe she just wanted to handle the *Titulus*. To make a connection. She was a good Catholic girl. She might have hoped it would provide some kind of protection against evil."

"Against Dalton," Phelps said quietly.

"Exactly. Anyway, I kept *shtum* for two reasons." Moran freed a hand to tick the points off on his fingers. "Firstly, to gauge the reactions of our Charnford brothers to its disappearance, and secondly, because I wanted to check its provenance." Moran hesitated, wondering whether he should – whether he *could* – confide in his sergeant. He took a deep breath. "You see, Phelps, I wanted to do that . . . for myself, if I'm honest."

"Ah." Phelps considered. "I heard the Prof's report," he said thoughtfully. "Genuine, he reckoned. That's a turn up, eh?"

"Yes. Isn't it? Strange, though–" Moran trailed off, frowning.

"What's that, guv?"

"It was in the cottage, the crucifix on the wall – that's what got me thinking about the *Titulus* and Horgan's posthumous clue. The wood of the cross, the exposed bones . . ." Moran's lips came together in a compressed line. "But the cottage was derelict, and the crucifix never existed." He bowed his head and said quietly, "It seemed so real, Phelps. *She* seemed so real."

"It'll get better, guv."

"Yes." Moran fixed his eyes on the middle distance. A flight of white-fronted geese passed overhead, circling high above the cemetery, riding the winter wind. "I suppose it will."

"God works in mysterious ways, as they say." Phelps' face cracked into a wide grin.

Moran looked up, the sparkle in his eyes rekindled. "Indeed he does, Sergeant Phelps, Indeed he does."

A free collection of DCI Brendan Moran's short stories is available at

www.scott-hunter.net

DCI Brendan Moran's second full-length case is

Creatures of Dust

Read on to sample the prologue and first chapter

The dirty water gurgled its way through the city centre, carrying the odd beer can and other remnants of a more personal nature along with it. Simon Peters paid little heed to the canal's floating detritus. Oblivious to his surroundings he was lost in thought, struggling in vain to make sense of everything that had happened.

As he crossed the bridge the intensity of his feelings stopped him in his tracks. He leaned on the railing and rested his gloved hands lightly on the peeling metal. Physical pain he could learn to live with but emotional pain, he was beginning to realise, was infinitely worse. The latter was exacerbated by the knowledge that his yearning would never be satisfied. She was his deepest need, and he would never have her. Worse still, she loved him too. That was why it was all so wrong. What did it matter that she was a Muslim? To him, that was an irrelevance. To them, it was vital, and as a Westerner he was the ultimate persona non grata. To them, it was unthinkable that Jaseena should associate herself, romantically or otherwise, with an unbeliever. And that was why they'd taken her away.

He stepped off the bridge onto the canal path and stopped. Something wasn't right. He had a sudden conviction that he was being followed. There – by the street lamp at the entrance to the multi-storey. Male, female? He had a fleeting impression of short, blonde hair and a slender athletic build before the figure disappeared into shadow. He walked on. The light was beginning to fade and few people were about; only the occasional car headlight was reflected in the scummy water.

He stopped again. Was that a scuffle of trainers? He spun on his heels. Now he saw his pursuers clearly and his heart lurched. He'd been so caught up in his bitter reverie that he'd forgotten his number one rule: stick with the crowds. Ever since Jaseena's brothers had made a direct threat he'd taken great care not to expose himself to what he believed was a very real danger.

He quickened his pace as best he could, aware of movement in his peripheral vision. Fear tightened his stomach. They'd promised to 'fix him properly' if he ever went near Jaseena again. Ahead, the canal path telescoped into the distance. There were footfalls behind him now, the slap of rubber on the paving. He threw his bag away and tried to run. After thirty seconds he knew it was hopeless; of course they were faster.

They caught him eventually by the rusted struts of the next bridge and waded in – dark faces, fists, a blow to the side of his head. He felt well-aimed kicks find their targets in his rib, his groin. Sickening, agonising pain, and then he was being pushed, rolled, shoved towards the canal. The last thing he felt was the sudden shock of water closing over his head.

It was over.

But he was wrong. He regained consciousness in a blaze of sensation. Bright lights, a needle in his arm, blankets covering him; waves of nausea as the pain intensified. Water and vomit pouring from his mouth. Muted voices, a siren nearby.

"All right, matey, take it easy. You're going to be fine." The paramedic's face loomed over him, wavering and distorted. Before the darkness took him again a burning certainty overrode the sedation just long enough to raise the corners of his mouth in a defiant smile. It was the certainty that, one day, he would have his revenge.

He sipped the lukewarm hospital squash and swallowed with a grimace. After the first three or four days the discomfort of his injuries had lessened to the extent that he was able to focus his mind on his next steps. He had to admit the doctors had been efficient. He had apparently sidestepped the dangerous possibility of pneumonia, and apart from the severe bruising on and around his ribcage he felt almost human again.

"You've taken quite a knock on the head, Mr Peters," the consultant had told him. "Probably banged it on the canal wall. You've really been in the wars recently, haven't you? Jolly bad luck all round." He met Simon's eye and looked away quickly. "Anyway, you mustn't be surprised if you feel a little distracted for a while. It'll get better."

In fact Simon Peters' brain was crystal clear, and very busy. The planning was therapeutic, carrying the added benefit of distracting him from thoughts of Jaseena. There was no point living in the past. He knew what he was going to do. It was time they were taught a lesson. All of them, one by one. His sole regret was that he hadn't thought of it before; he could have saved himself a lot of trouble.

The last week in hospital had dragged interminably. He smiled at the nurses and exchanged pleasantries with the other patients, but inside he was boiling with excitement.

He was impatient to begin.

Chapter One

Detective Chief Inspector Brendan Moran of the Thames Valley Police was concentrating hard. He frowned at the seven irritatingly blank squares glaring up at him from the newspaper like empty accusations. Nine letters. *Also a man's role in medical discipline.* A something D something – Moran threw down his pencil in frustration as the door opened and Detective Sergeant Robert Phelps' head appeared, followed by the rest of his considerable bulk.

"What *is* it, Phelps? Don't people knock any more?"

"Sorry, guv – thought you were on your tea break." Phelps squinted at the newspaper. "Crossword?"

"Got it in one."

Phelps grinned. "Can't get the last clue, eh? Let's have a butcher's – hmm…"

Moran drummed his fingers.

"Andrology."

"What?"

"Andrology, guv. You know, the study of male medical conditions. Waterworks and all that."

Moran eased his chair back and studied his Sergeant. Phelps was a huge man, East End raised, solid as a rock, faultless intuition, but as far as Moran was aware, crosswords were well outside his areas of interest. He regarded Phelps with a new curiosity.

"Have you imbibed a dictionary, Phelps?"

"What's that, guv?" The broad features cracked into a smile. "Oh, right. No, it's not that. Just – well, I'm studying a bit. Part-time, you know." Phelps broke off sheepishly.

"Are you? Are you really?" Moran nodded appreciatively. "Good for you, Phelps. What is it – a degree in obscure medical terminology?"

"No, guv. English Lit. Open University. Bloomin' hard work. I'm enjoying it, though –so far, anyway."

"And who, might I enquire, are you reading?"

Phelps scratched his chin. Even though he shaved twice a day his blue shadow was rarely absent. "Conrad, Chaucer, some bloke called Shakespeare..."

Moran studied Phelps with rekindled fascination. "I'm impressed, Phelps. And not a little envious."

"You could do the same, guv."

Moran shook his head. "You're kidding. I wish I had the time. Come to think of it, when do *you* squeeze in time for study? With a wife and kids to look after?"

Phelps winked. "The midnight oil, guv."

"Ah." Moran nodded. "The insomniac academic."

"Has a certain ring to it, guv." Phelps looked pleased. "Don't you think?"

"I do." Moran shifted his leg with a grimace. Following the explosion at Charnford Abbey and his discharge from hospital he was gradually coming to terms with the fact that he would always walk with a stick. After a car crash that had almost killed him, bouts of narcolepsy, and a mild stroke followed by a near-fatal explosion, Phelps had remarked that with his track record Moran should have been born a cat, not an Irishman.

As if guessing Moran's thoughts Phelps narrowed his eyes. "How are you, guv? I mean, how are you *really*?"

Moran scraped his chair back and stood up. "Surprisingly well, Phelps, thank you." He walked stiffly to the kettle, found two chipped mugs and rummaged in the filing cabinet for coffee. When he looked up Phelps' eyebrows were raised in a disbelieving arc.

"I'm all right, Robert, *really* I am. Thanks for your concern." Moran unscrewed the coffee jar lid and was hunting for a teaspoon amongst the debris when the office shook as if it had been hit by a truck. Both Moran and Phelps spun on their heels, ducking their heads automatically as they zeroed in on the cause of the disturbance.

"Ah." Phelps said, straightening up. "Neads. That's what I came to tell you, guv. He's in to clear his desk. And he's not happy."

Moran looked through his office window at the tall young man, whose face was contorted in hatred, hands pressed onto the clear surface. In the centre of his palms they could clearly see the angry scars of crucifixion.

"Uh huh." Moran went quickly to the door. "It doesn't give him an excuse to behave like an animal, though."

The former Detective Sergeant Gregory Neads was at the other side of the door as Moran opened it. Behind him the inhabitants of the open-plan office were silent, heads craning, mouths gaping.

"Inside." Moran spoke quietly but firmly, squaring up to the taller man.

"I'll leave you two to chat." Phelps squeezed through the gap, giving Neads a warning nod on his way past.

"You apologise?" Neads snarled. "Is that it?"

Moran cleared his throat. Neads had got himself into trouble during the Charnford Abbey episode, falling prey to the unhinged former abbot. The DC had been impaled through hands and feet, strung up as some kind of warped atonement sacrifice for the murder of a former kitchen porter. Months in hospital had followed. Since that time Moran's nights had been tormented by the sickening image of the crucifixion, but he knew that for Neads the fallout would be much, much worse. The boy would need some serious counselling.

"What's left for me now?" Neads' nose was an inch from Moran's. "I'm a *cripple. Pensioned off.* I'm twenty-four. And I'm *finished...*"

"Gregory–"

"Don't bloody patronise me!" Neads hissed. He waved his forefinger in Moran's face, grabbing the desk for support as his balance was compromised. "You were supposed to watch *out* for me. And did you? No! You sent me off on a wild goose chase and left me with that..." he took a harsh, gulping breath, "... that crazy lunatic who ... who–" Neads' facial muscles twitched as he fought to control himself.

Moran put his hand on the young man's shoulder. "Gregory. I'm truly sorry. Listen, have you contacted the Police Rehabilitation Centre? It's in Goring. I think it would be helpful. If there's anything–"

Neads shrugged Moran's hand away and limped to the door. He turned and raised his finger again. "You watch your back, Moran. I'm warning you. You just watch your back..."

The door slammed behind him. Moran slumped in his chair and buried his head in his hands. *Well, that went swimmingly, Brendan. Nicely handled...*

Later Moran eased himself into his car. Since the incident at the abbey he knew he was lucky to be alive. So was Neads – but then, Moran reflected, his own injuries were caused by an explosion, something remote, almost random in its destructive power. Neads' wounds were caused by the premeditation of a very sick mind. There had been ample time for Neads to anticipate his injuries, to listen to the preparatory carpentry work before the first nail was driven into his flesh. Moran felt his skin crawl with the familiar remembered horror of that December night. Neads had an uphill psychological battle ahead of him, that much was certain. What was more uncertain was the effect that his experiences would have on the young DC. *Ex DC*, Moran reminded himself. He sighed. If today's encounter was anything to go by, the signs were not good. Not good at all.

As for you, Moran, he thought, it's all about physical rehab from now on. As if to confirm his self-diagnosis his leg shot him a bolt of pain as he engaged the clutch and steered the car out of the police station car park. *A small price to pay, Brendan, all things considered.* Yes, he was definitely on the mend. His head felt clear; the narcolepsy that had plagued him over the past eighteen months seemed to have vanished without trace. Dr Purewal had been right. A little R and R, plus the odd crossword to keep the grey matter ticking over, had done the trick.

Apart from the Neads episode, his first day back had passed without incident. Mike Airey, the new Superintendent, seemed supportive – unlike his late predecessor. All in all, things were looking up. Moran conceded that he wouldn't be too discontented if, just to ease him in, his return to work turned out to be routine, and – dare he think it? *Dull...*

And for the first month, much to Moran's surprise, it was.

Chapter Two

Simon Peters moved purposefully, every nerve in his body tingling. Rain began to fall – gently at first, but it quickly intensified, hammering the pavement and provoking a mass unfurling of umbrellas. He tilted his face, allowing the water to pound his skin and trickle deliciously down his neck. It felt cleansing and invigorating. He slid his hand into his pocket. The knife was hard against his fingers; he felt the circulating blood surging beneath his skin and his excitement grew.

It was getting dark; rush hour would soon be over and only the stragglers would remain. The town centre was emptying fast as tired workers caught buses or returned to car parks for the drive home to their TV dinners, bawling babies or dysfunctional marriages. *Sad little lives ... pointless, pathetic existences...*

But *he – he* had a purpose. A *mission*. All he needed now was a target...

Moran turned the key in the lock after another uneventful day. He was, he admitted to himself, getting restless. Not that he wished for trouble, but something fresh to stimulate his mind would not go amiss. He thought he might ask Mike Airey for clearance to work on one or two of the cold cases they'd discussed the week before. For the time being, Moran had had his fill of the mundane.

He had no sooner settled into his sofa with a glass of Sangiovese than his phone rang. He toyed with the idea of ignoring it, but he finally admitted defeat. A missed call was always the vital one.

"Moran."

"Hello? Is that Brendan Moran? It's Shona."

Moran frowned, hesitated briefly, and then the penny dropped. Before he could open his mouth, though, the caller beat him to it. "We met at the funeral. Shona Kempster – Kay's sister."

With recognition came the pain of loss and guilt. Kay, his one-time 'special' friend, had died in an explosion in Moran's garage. The blast had also killed his brother, Patrick. Eight months had passed but the wound was still raw, And it didn't take much for it to start bleeding again.

"I – I'm sorry to call. I just needed to talk, I suppose."

Moran tried to remember Shona's face. Shorter than her late sister, thinner. Quite attractive, in an anorexic, waif-like sort of way. He remembered her as a little over-bubbly at the funeral, behaviour that he'd put down to the shock of her sister's sudden death.

"It's quite all right, Shona. Nice to hear from you. Fire away."

"Well, you did say to call, if I – you know–"

"Of course."

"Well–" An awkward pause preceded a nervous laugh. "How are you? How's things?"

"Oh, you know. Getting back into the swing."

"Yep. Right. Me too."

Moran realised that unless he steered this particular conversation it was going to peter out before it had even begun. "Are you all right, Shona? Is there anything troubling you?"

"No, nothing in particular. I think I just need to chew the fat. You know, about what happened. Maybe we could meet up?"

"Sure. When and where?"

"You say. I'm free most of the time."

Moran dredged his memory. He was positive that Shona had been introduced to him as a sports physiotherapist. "Not keeping you busy enough at the clinic?"

"I – I don't work there any more."

"Oh. Sorry to hear that. Anyway, you can tell me all about it when I see you."

"OK. Um, how about next Friday? Cherries wine bar? Eight o'clock?"

"I know the place. Right, well, looking forward to seeing you then, Shona. Bye for now."

"Great. Thanks, Brendan. Bye."

Moran ended the call, shook his head pensively, and returned to his Sangiovese.

Simon Peters found the young man beneath the street lamp, waiting, perhaps for a friend. Arms folded, dark hair plastered across his forehead. A quick check, left and right, but there was no one about – not within clear view of the corner, anyway. Now, let the cleansing begin...

The youth glanced up, unsuspecting. A glimmer of recognition, a stock phrase, almost a sneer: "All right?" He looked away.

This is it. The power Simon felt was a huge adrenaline rush. The youth wore an air of disdain he knew well; it was just like the one he'd worn the last time they'd met.

"Yeah, Anoop. I'm good." The knife came out easily, casually almost, nestling in the cradle of his fingers.

Then, just to be sure, the vital question, which he asked with a smile, knowing the answer already.

"*By the way, are you a Muslim*?"

Moran was dreaming. It was a pleasant dream, a far cry from recent nightmares in which the scene would shift from Charnford Abbey to some dystopian town centre where gangs roamed unchecked, killing and looting at will. The troubled Gregory Neads usually played a starring role in these disturbing scenarios, the ex-detective sergeant's recent mugging and hospitalisation playing on Moran's mind. How unlucky could a guy get?

But this dream was different. It was warm and sunny and he was relaxed – happy, even. Trouble was, someone was ringing a bell, harshly and insistently. He wanted to put distance between himself and the noise so he walked further along the beach, past the ramshackle bar and the smiling barman, past the topless girl with the blonde ponytail ... the bell followed, its jangling undiminished. He turned, tried to push it away, but the barman had left his station and now appeared beside him holding a ludicrously inflated telephone.

"For you, boss. Big news." His smile was ingratiatingly wide, the whiteness of his teeth gleaming in the sun. Moran made a grab for the phone but it moved just out of reach. On the third attempt he woke with a start. His much smaller but equally irritating mobile was vibrating on the bedside table.

"Moran."

"Brendan? It's Shona."

Moran squinted at the bedside clock. "Shona, do you know what time it is?"

"I'm really sorry, Brendan. I just needed to talk to someone."

Moran sighed. "Go on."

"Well, it's about Kay – of course," she added. "I keep thinking – you know, why? Why her?"

"I know. I wish I could give you an answer. It should have been me, but–"

"And your brother. They were getting on so well, weren't they?"

"Yes." Moran thought of the wrecked garage, the shell of his Land Rover squatting in the ruins.

He kept up the sympathetic responses for another ten minutes before Shona's voice slowed to a normal rhythm. Highly strung, that's for sure. Perhaps he shouldn't have been as free and easy with his mobile number. But, he reminded himself, she was Kay's little sister. He owed it to Kay to provide a listening ear. It was the least he could do.

He signed off with a promise to keep the Cherries appointment and fell asleep with the image of Kay's smiling face looping around the spools of his mind.

Seconds later, or so it seemed, the mobile was vibrating again. Moran raised himself on his elbow and smashed the pillow with his fist.

"Moran."

"Guv?" Phelps' barrow-boy growl grated from the phone's speaker. "We have an incident."

"Where?"

"Town centre. Outside Dixon's, Broad Street."

"Details?"

"A murder, guv. Stab wound."

"I'll be there in ten."

Moran ducked under the outer cordon and negotiated the metal stepping stones of the common approach path set up by the crime scene manager.

Phelps waved a welcome. "What do you reckon, guv? Gang killing?"

Moran peered at the corpse. It was a miserable scene: in the crepuscular early morning light, huddled in the shop doorway was a young Asian boy of around twenty-two, twenty-three perhaps, with a dark stain on his jacket and a surprised expression in his widened, lifeless eyes. Moran felt sick at the sheer waste of it.

"Mobile?"

"Negative, guv. Either he wasn't carrying one or the killer took it."

"ID?"

"Nope. Nada."

"CCTV?"

Phelps looked up and down the street and shook his head. "Dead spot."

Moran watched the hooded forensics officer swabbing the bloodstains and committing the results to his tamper-proof evidence bags. A bag of life – or death, according to how you looked at it.

"Ah, Moran. How goes it?" A familiar brogue came from behind them. Sandy Taylor, the police doctor, had arrived to certify the time of death.

"It goes the same as it always goes," Moran said flatly. "Another one for your record book."

"Don't be so morbid," Taylor retorted. "If I kept a record book I'd only get depressed, and I can think of better ways to spend the rest of my life than trying to engage with the world through a haze of sertraline."

Taylor's examination was swift. "Stab wound to the neck. Death probably within seconds. I'd guess that he was half-carried or dragged off the street and dumped in the alcove."

"OK. Strong assailant, then. He's a big lad."

"Indeed."

"Time of death?" Phelps prompted.

"Oh, let's see – I'd say somewhere between one and two in the morning, give or take thirty minutes." Taylor stood up, shaking his head. "Sad, sad, sad. Still, a little more straightforward than your last case, eh?"

Moran grunted. "They're never straightforward, Sandy, trust me."

Taylor clicked his tongue and snapped his briefcase shut. "I do, my dear Brendan. Implicitly."

He paced the flat, adrenaline buzzing through him as if he were a live wire. His hands were filthy with mud, his shoes were soaked through and his jacket was torn. He had made a mistake. Someone had seen him – a girl. To his surprise, she had chased him. He had let her catch up by the canal and she hadn't put up much of a fight in the end. It was all right now. He'd dealt with it, but he was shaking like a man with the ague.

He'd returned the car to the lock-up and walked home in a daze, legs trembling like a pair of rubber stilts. The car was well off limits now. Maybe he should burn it, trash the whole row of garages... *Calm down*, he told himself. *You've sorted it for now. No one knows it's there.* As for the woman, he didn't care who she was. The way she was dressed she could have been any Saturday night girl. Or maybe a professional, with a skirt like that.

Forget it, he told himself. Some collateral damage was inevitable. Stupid cow. What had she been thinking? What had she hoped to achieve? He shuddered; he could still feel her body folding into unconsciousness, pressing against him. He'd hardly touched her; she was probably drunk.

He kicked off his shoes and went into the bathroom. *It didn't matter.* What *did* matter was that he had made a start, and he should mark that somehow, shouldn't he? What he needed was a new name, something to complement his new identity. As the hot water gurgled into the tub he thought of Jaseena's brothers, remembered what they had called him behind his back.

Kafir...

He looked at his reflection in the half-steamed bathroom mirror. He saw a strong face and a look of fierce determination. Yes. *Kafir*. That had a ring to it.

Later, after he had bathed, he went to his laptop and looked the word up.

In Islamic parlance, a kāfir is a word used to describe a person who rejects Islamic faith, i.e. hides or covers [viz. the truth]. The word means 'unbeliever'. First applied to Meccans who refused submission to Islam, the term implies an active rejection of divine revelation.

He said the word slowly, savouring each syllable. Perfect. So be it. If he was a *kafir*, he would be *the* Kafir. Simon Peters popped a breath mint into his mouth and began to think about his next appointment. This time he would be more careful. Best avoid Reading, mix it up a bit. The location was irrelevant to him; there were Allah-worshipping Asians everywhere.

It was almost too easy.

Chapter Three

Cherries wine bar was tucked beneath the old Top Rank building near the railway station in a small parade of shops that included, nostalgically, a greasy spoon called *Rankin' Robin's*. Cherries was not busy. There were a few office workers knocking back a swifty or two before catching the next train home to the wife, one or two singles sitting at high stools by the window, and a dishevelled-looking woman at a corner table nursing a glass of red wine. *What story would you tell me, love*? Moran wondered as she glanced hopefully in his direction. Moran looked away. Everyone had a story, most of them tales of woe or disaster. Best not to know; disasters usually found their own way to Moran's doorstep without much prompting.

Moran drummed his fingers on the imitation brass tabletop and pondered his easy acquiescence to this meeting. He had a bad feeling about it – irrational maybe, but a bad feeling nevertheless.

He was also troubled by the young Asian lad's murde No apparent motive, no sign of a struggle. It bore all t hallmarks of an unprovoked attack. The boy had marks on him except for the knife wound. A norr racist attack would have kicked off with a beating. Mo shook his head slowly. *Normal*. Was he so desensitis There was nothing 'normal' about murder.

His reverie was interrupted by a new custom woman of around thirty-five with a short, blonde

She cast about this way and that, checking each occupant of the bar in turn. With a jolt of recognition Moran realised it was Shona. The last time he'd seen her she'd had shoulder-length auburn hair and, he recollected, an excess of make up – no doubt to mask her distress. On the day of Kay's funeral her face had been drawn, but now she looked completely different. Attractive. *Very* attractive. Moran stood and raised his hand self-consciously. At once she smiled and walked gracefully towards his table, drawing covert admiring glances from the lone male clientele.

"Hi." Her smile was wide and her teeth, as Moran remembered from the first time they had met, were perfectly white.

"Hello. Nice to see you." Moran pulled a chair over and made a gesture of invitation. "What'll it be?"

"Hmm. A glass of Pinot Grigio, if they have it."

"I'm sure they do."

Moran returned with their drinks and settled into his . "Well, cheers." They clinked glasses. Shona took a te sip and placed her glass carefully on the 'Chill at es' logo-embossed coaster. She looked briefly t the table as if unsure how to begin, and then r chin and smiled again, apparently flustered. A appeared at her throat and spread quickly to her l ears. She chewed her bottom lip, a mannerism ered from their first meeting, and sighed.

y, Inspector Moran, you must think it rather 'ed you the way I did."

thinking how like Kay she was. The eyes, ears, the delicate, darker pigmentation of). It's quite all right. I'm glad you did." in the morning?"

[continued in Creatures of Dust...]

Made in the USA
Monee, IL
05 April 2024